"How many times do I have to tell you, Sarah, I made a mistake?"

Her hand plowed through her hair. "Don't you see, Dean? It doesn't matter." Anguish again flooded her features; a cold, sick feeling washed over him that they weren't having the conversation he thought they were having. "It's not just a matter of my forgiving you, if that's what you want. Too much has happened, too much time has passed...."

The look in those honey-brown eyes stabbed him all the way to his soul.

He didn't care what happened now, even if she belted him clear into another zip code. She still cared. A great deal, unless he was way off course.

And, heaven help him, so did he.

Dear Reader,

You've loved Beverly Barton's miniseries THE PROTECTORS since it started, so I know you'll be thrilled to find another installment leading off this month. *Navajo's Woman* features a to-swoon-for Native American hero, a heroine capable of standing up to this tough cop— and enough steam to heat your house. Enjoy!

A YEAR OF LOVING DANGEROUSLY continues with bestselling author Linda Turner's *The Enemy's Daughter.* This story of subterfuge and irresistible passion—not to mention heart-stopping suspense—is set in the Australian outback, and I know you'll want to go along for the ride. Ruth Langan completes her trilogy with *Seducing Celeste,* the last of THE SULLIVAN SISTERS. Don't miss this emotional read. Then check out Karen Templeton's *Runaway Bridesmaid,* a reunion romance with a heroine who's got quite a secret. Elane Osborn's *Which Twin?* offers a new twist on the popular twins plotline, while Linda Winstead Jones rounds out the month with *Madigan's Wife,* a wonderful tale of an ex-couple who truly belong together.

As always, we've got six exciting romances to tempt you—and we'll be back next month with six more. Enjoy!

Leslie J. Wainger
Executive Senior Editor

Please address questions and book requests to:
Silhouette Reader Service
U.S.: 3010 Walden Ave., P.O. Box 1325, Buffalo, NY 14269
Canadian: P.O. Box 609, Fort Erie, Ont. L2A 5X3

Runaway Bridesmaid
KAREN TEMPLETON

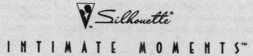

INTIMATE MOMENTS™

Published by Silhouette Books

America's Publisher of Contemporary Romance

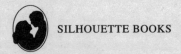 SILHOUETTE BOOKS

ISBN 0-373-27136-0

RUNAWAY BRIDESMAID

This edition published by arrangement with Harlequin Books S.A.

® and TM are trademarks of Harlequin Books S.A., used under license. Trademarks indicated with ® are registered in the United States Patent and Trademark Office, the Canadian Trade Marks Office and in other countries.

Visit Silhouette at www.eHarlequin.com

Printed in U.S.A.

KAREN TEMPLETON's

background in the theater and the arts, and a lifelong affinity for love stories, led inevitably to her writing romances. Growing up, she studied art, ballet and drama, and wanted to someday strut her stuff on Broadway. She was accepted into North Carolina School of the Arts as a drama major but switched to costume design.

Twelve years in New York City provided a variety of work experiences, including assisting costume designers at a large costume house, employment in the bridal department buyer's offices of several department stores, grunt work for a sportswear designer and answering phones for a sports uniform manufacturer. New York also provided her with her husband, Jack, and the first two of her five sons.

The family then moved to New Mexico, where Karen established an in-home mail-order crafts business that she gave up the instant the family bought their first computer. Now writing romances full-time, she says she's finally found an outlet for all that theatrical training—she gets to write, produce, design, cast and play all the parts!

To Gail Chasan, editor and friend,
who refuses to believe me when I say "I can't."

Acknowledgment

To Wendy Wade Morton, DVM, whose veterinary advice—as well as her insight into daily life in the Auburn/Opelika area of Alabama—has hopefully prevented me from looking like a total fool.

Chapter 1

"Hey—what's with the horse out in the waiting room?"

At the familiar sarcastic drawl, Sarah Whitehouse glanced up from the examining table where she held an ill-tempered ginger tomcat in a hammerlock, treating it for ear mites. She allowed a beleaguered grin for her younger sister, Jennifer, who worked at the travel agency just up the street. "Ah. That would be Bojangles."

"Bo-what?"

Sarah grimaced as she wrestled with the pissed-off cat. "Bojangles. Great Dane. Nine months old."

"Nine *months?*" Jennifer rolled her eyes, then shifted in the doorway, crossing her arms so that her engagement ring, modest though it was, twinkled brilliantly. "Hey, listen—"

"Anybody else out there?"

"Uh…oh, I don't know…." Sarah caught the whiff of petulance in her sister's voice. "Two more cats, maybe? At least, two more cat carriers. I can't vouch for what's in 'em. A collie, a Dobie…and some small fuzzy thing I'll have to guess is a canine with indiscreet parents. Sarah—"

"Damn. They must all be drop-ins. The Dane was all I had scheduled, which is why I let Jolene go off to lunch." Sarah ignored the cat's menacing growl as she swabbed his ear. "Anyone seem panicked? Bleeding? In labor?"

Her sister considered for a moment, then shook her head, a half-can's worth of Aqua Net prohibiting any individual movement of her shoulder-length waves. "Nope. Just the usual panting and get-me-outta-here whimpering and butt-smelling routines. Though one owner looks like she misplaced her Prozac—"

"Could you tell everyone to hold on, I'll get to 'em soon as I can?"

With a telling sigh, Jennifer stuck her honey-gold head out the door and delivered Sarah's message, then waltzed on into the examining room and plopped her handbag on a chair in the corner. By now she was pouting.

Sarah got the message.

"I'm sorry, honey…was there something you wanted to tell me?"

Jennifer hesitated, then gave a short, dismissive wave of her hand. "It'll wait. You're busy."

"You sure?"

"No point in talking to you if you're not listening."

"I promise to give you my undivided attention just as soon as I'm finished…." The thing twisted out of Sarah's grasp and spit at her.

Her sister took a circumspect step backward, her nose wrinkled in distaste. "And what is *our* problem?"

Sarah wrapped the cat's leash around her palm, reined him back in. "I think *we* know that ear mites aren't the only things being removed today."

"Oooh," Jennifer said with a comprehending nod in the creature's direction. The cat actually sneered at her as Sarah elbowed the thing into her chest and went after the other ear. "Heck, you ask me, it couldn't happen to a better guy. Except maybe Bruce Miller. Did you know Abby's pregnant *again?*"

Sarah stifled her laugh. "Stop it, will you? I'm having enough trouble doing this."

"Sorry. Couldn't resist." Out of the corner of her eye, Sarah caught Jennifer's glance around the room. "Where's Katey?"

"Little girl's room, I expect." Sarah paused in her torture of the cat and stroked his head. The feline's eyes squeezed shut with each touch, though whether in pleasure or irritated tolerance, she couldn't say. "Begged the living daylights out of me to come, but now that she's here, of course, she's bored to tears."

Jennifer's expression indicated she agreed with her baby sister's assessment of the situation, but she diplomatically refrained from comment. Instead, she said with a bright, lip-glossed smile, "So...how about lunch? Then I can tell you my news."

The sigh just sort of slipped out. "This have anything to do with the wedding?"

"Now, how'd you know that?"

"Thank God—oh, be *still,* you nasty beast—we only have a week more to go through this," Sarah groused good-naturedly. She finished with the cat and pushed him into a carrier. "But lunch ain't gonna happen today, as you may have guessed." Shoving a hand through her cropped hair, she added, "Ed's out on farm duty, and Doc's off, so it's just me. I can't leave. So you'll have to tell me here."

Jennifer squinted at her through smoothly mascara'd eyelashes. "I was trying to."

"Sorry. So...spit it out."

But "spitting it out" had never been part of Jennifer's repertoire. She paused for dramatic effect, which *had* been part of her repertoire since she was two and a half. "We-e-ell...you know how Tim Reynolds couldn't be Lance's best man after all 'cause he's got National Guard training camp that week?"

Sarah leaned one hip against the examining table. "Ye-e-es—"

"But did you know Tim wasn't Lance's first choice, anyway?"

"He wasn't? But they've been best friends since kindergarten—"

"I know," Jennifer said with a slow, conspiratorial nod of her head. "But, see, turns out Lance had someone completely different in mind. He just didn't think he could convince him to do it."

"Jen. Today, please."

"Oh, all right." She struck a pose, hands splayed out to the sides. "Ta-da! Dean said he'd be Lance's best man."

Sarah went catatonic, staring at Jennifer with what must have been an incredibly stupid expression on her face. Her sister however, continued bubbling away like a just-poured glass of warm Dr. Pepper. "Isn't that the *best?* Lance is so excited he's been talking a mile a minute ever since Dean called him and said he'd be in tonight."

That brought Sarah back to the land of the living. Underneath her smock, her sleeveless cotton blouse fused to her back. "He'll be here *tonight?*"

"Uh-huh," Jennifer continued in euphoric oblivion. "And he's gonna be here for a whole week, I guess since he hasn't been here in so long. Anyway, Mama said to tell you dinner's at our house, and for you to get your skinny little butt home on time. You know, hang the little sign on the clinic door that says *Closed?*"

For emphasis, her sister mimed hanging up the sign, flashing long, tapered fuchsia fingernails the same color as the six-inch flowers splashed across her romper. Then she let out a little squeak, as if she'd been pinched.

"Oh! Oh, my God! I just realized..." Jennifer grabbed Sarah's wrist, sending a cloud of flowery perfume wafting up from between a set of breasts that had been making men bump into things since she was fourteen. "Here the two of you were high school sweethearts, and now, after all this time, he's going to be best man and you're going to be maid of honor at my wedding!" Her palm flattened over the magnificent bosomage. "What a *hoot!*"

"Yeah," Sarah said weakly. "Hoot."

"Well, hey, listen, I'll get out of your hair." Jennifer flapped at her sister's boyish 'do. "What's left of it, anyway." She scooped up her handbag and straightened out her perfectly straight collar. "Oh—don't forget. Gown fittings tomorrow morning at Miss Ellis's."

Sarah managed something close to a smile. "How could I forget?"

Jennifer paused by the door, her hand on the frame. "Isn't tonight just going to be *great?*" She crinkled her nose in time-honored cute Southern cheerleader tradition, giggled and disappeared like Tinkerbell. *Poof!* Gone.

Sarah sank onto the desk chair in the examining room, dropping her head onto her arms. She wasn't sure what she felt at that moment, but *great* was not one of the choices. What most shocked her was that the prospect of seeing Dean again should be producing any effect at all. She'd long since gotten over him.

Long since.

"Sarah? You okay?"

She lifted her gaze to a pair of large, worried eyes the same whiskey color as hers set in a face with the same narrow nose, the same wide mouth, the same square jawline ending in an incongruously pointed chin. People always said they'd never seen sisters look as much alike as Katey and Sarah. Like twins born eighteen years apart.

Sarah let out a long, shaky breath and clasped the little girl's slender waist, forcing a smile which God knew she did not feel. "Sure, baby. Just resting my eyes for a moment. Why don't you go tell Mr. Arby to bring Bojangles on in?"

As Katey scampered over to the door, Sarah rubbed her makeup-less eyes with a stubby-nailed forefinger. According to Jennifer's count, she had at least a half-dozen cases to see, and that wasn't counting later appointments or any emergencies that might come in. Of all the times to be the only vet in the clinic. Well, she told herself as she got to her feet and smoothed out the front of her smock, she'd just have to deal with her ambivalent feelings about Dean Parrish later. Preferably before she came face-to-face with him in her living room.

Panic sliced through her.

She heard extra-large-size canine toenails scraping on the linoleum floor as Ben Arby half lugged, half shoved the reluctant Great Dane into the examining room. The black behemoth took one look at Sarah, yelped, and promptly piddled all over the floor.

"Oh, come on, now, sweetie…" She ripped off a half-dozen paper towels from the spindle over the sink and tossed them onto the floor, stepping on them to soak up the puddle as she scratched the dog's ears. "How bad can it be, huh?"

She didn't want to know.

Dean wished he were invisible. At least for a hour or so, anyway, just until he got used to the idea of being back in Sweetbranch before anyone else noticed he was.

That not being an option, he decided to hide out in his pickup for a bit, cruising the back roads, trying to come to terms with that weird sensation when you return someplace after being away for a long time and everything seems so familiar and strange all at once. And here he'd gone and said he'd stay for a whole week. Lord. If he'd been a drinking man, he'd've sworn he'd had one too many when he'd made that promise. He'd figured he'd feel unsettled. What he hadn't figured on was how right it felt to be *home*.

And he didn't quite know what to do with that feeling.

Nine years. Nine years of growing up, of making something of himself in spite of a reading disability that had finally bested him halfway through his junior year of high school. Nine years of forcing himself to stay away from everything good he'd ever known in order to give Sarah Whitehouse the chance to become everything she could. Nine years of wondering if he'd made a dumb-assed mistake.

Well, he thought as he took a swallow of warm Coke from the almost empty can he'd been nursing since Atlanta, nothing to be done for it now. Not a dad-blasted thing.

For a long time, he'd tried to blame his leaving on his Aunt Ethel, his father's older sister, who'd taken him and Lance in after his mother died when he was fifteen, with her constant harping on the differences between him and Sarah. *She's a doctor's daughter, not the offspring of some small-time country carpenter. Lookit how bright she is, gettin' straight A's in school, and that scholarship to Auburn. What's a poor country boy got to offer a girl like that?* she'd say. *Face it—in the long run, you'll end up feeling like half a man. That what you really want? For either one of you...?*

At twenty, he'd discovered, sometimes you're not so all-fired set in your convictions. At twenty, maybe you're not so sure who's right and who's wrong. Or *what's* right or wrong, for that matter. Oh, he didn't doubt his feelings for Sarah at the time, but his aunt's objections slowly ate away at his resolve to make the relationship work, birthing an annoying little gremlin of doubt that eventually became a constant, unwelcome companion. At last, he came to believe that maybe his aunt was right, that maybe he would be an impediment to Sarah's future, that maybe she'd end up resenting him.

So better she hated him then, went the impaired reasoning, than waiting around for their love to die a slow, agonizing death.

He hadn't known his heart would shatter into a million pieces when he realized how well he'd played his part that day. And in the end, he also realized, he had no one to blame but himself.

He steered the Dakota onto the road leading to his aunt's house, the eerie feeling of...displacement, he guessed it was, becoming even stronger. The differences in the scenery stood out like black sheep, simply because there were so few. For instance, he noticed Percy Jenkins had planted a new elm to replace the old one he'd had to take out because of disease. The new tree reached over the roof already, its deep green leaves quivering in the light breeze.

And Myrtle Andersen had painted her house trim a deep blue. He liked it.

And Frank Cuthbertson had finally gotten rid of that old Chevy on the side of his house that his chickens had adopted as a sort of coop-away-from-coop. He chuckled, remembering how, as kids, he and Sarah used to sneak up and pilfer the eggs that sometimes appeared on the back seat, an odoriferous booty the all-too-frequent reward for their clandestine activity.

There were some kids he didn't recognize, of course, as well as the occasional unfamiliar stray dog nonchalantly trotting across the road right in front of his truck. But for the most part, it was all the same. Kudzu-choked pastures sandwiched between the same pecan and peach and apple orchards; the same heady aroma of wild honeysuckle and mimosa; the same Alabama clay that tinged everything in the vicinity a garish orange.

And Sarah's house, too, was just as he remembered it. Still stately and fussy at the same time—the curse of a good Queen Anne—still yellow and white and forest green, although it looked like it could use a new paint job. He drew in a quick breath: Lance had told him Sarah's father had died suddenly about three years ago. Heart attack. The news hadn't really registered until he saw the house, the house Dr. Whitehouse had spent so much time restoring and caring for, ever since Dean could remember. The house he'd grown up in nearly as much as his own. Lance said Sarah's parents had had a midlife baby, too, a little girl just now turned eight. A real shame, a child losing her daddy that young.

Dean leaned over, peering out the passenger's side window. That willow tree in the front yard was even bigger than he remembered, as were the maples tickling the roof from the back of the house. The kennel sign was spiffier, though, more professional. Lance'd said Sarah and her mother had done real well with the kennel, even had a champion or two. Black Labs, wasn't that it? Sarah'd always been partial to Black Labs.

Returning his attention to the road, he reminded himself she wasn't there. Lance had told him she worked most days at a veterinary clinic over in Opelika, assisting old Doc Jefferson....

Lord. The memories were relentless. He sped up, consigning

Sarah's house to his rearview mirror, not ready to deal with any of it yet. Time enough to do that at dinner tonight. When, he assumed, he would see Sarah, for the first time since his Oscar-worthy performance as the slimeball boyfriend.

How the Sam Hill had his brother managed to fall for Sarah's sister? Out of all the girls at Auburn, you'd've thought at least *one* of them might have caught Lance's eye while he was there getting his degree. But no. Lance had to choose someone who'd lived a half mile down the road almost his entire life.

A hiss of air escaped Dean's lips. Wasn't as if he didn't understand. He'd done the same fool thing. Only difference was, he'd turned tail and run, instead of marrying Sarah like he should've done and let the consequences be damned. No, he sure couldn't fault his brother for not finding anyone he liked better. Not when Dean, after all this time in Atlanta, kept seeing Sarah's syrupy eyes and square jaw and long, silky maple-colored hair superimposed on every woman's face he saw, dated, slept with. Not that there'd been all that many of the latter, he admitted to himself, slinging his right arm across the back of the seat and trying to shift his weight off his numb bottom.

They say you can't go home again. Well, he had, but even if all the houses and roads and even most of the damn trees were exactly as he'd left them, he'd be even a bigger fool than he already was if he thought Sarah was. There was nothing left between them but memories. If even that much. He'd hurt her, deliberately and unforgivably. He'd think less of her if she *didn't* hate him.

He'd lost the best thing that'd ever happened to him, a fact he'd regret for the rest of his life. And one which made him wonder how he was going to get through the next week.

Hell. He'd be going some just to get through the next few *hours.*

Sarah actually closed the clinic on time, which gave her maybe a few minutes to sort out her very muddled thoughts about this turn of events. Jennifer had rescued poor Katey right after lunch, to Sarah's immense relief—she didn't think she could've stood an afternoon of bored sighs and moans and groans.

Almost of its own volition, the Bronco steered toward home. Her hands were seized, however, with an almost uncontrollable urge to veer south toward some secluded Mexican beach. Just for, say, the next week or so?

Oh, geez…why on earth was Dean coming for a full week? What was this, some resurgence of family devotion? Or, she thought with a sickening thud just below her sternum, a deliberate move to torture her? Her hands gripped the steering wheel as she passed the little turnoff that would, could, loop her around and send her in the opposite direction.

She watched the loop fade in her rearview mirror. And sighed.

Oh, come on. This was not like her. Sarah Whitehouse did not run from problems. Sarah Whitehouse faced them, dealt with them, solved them. No matter what. So…so…she would go home, change out of these hot jeans, run a comb through what there was of her hair, and simply ignore Dean Parrish.

One hand clamped around the steering wheel, the other found its way to her mouth, where she started to chew on a hangnail. *Wrecked* was the only word to describe how she'd felt after Dean's abrupt departure, the night before her senior prom. After a while, though, she'd forced the unhappiness into a tiny cubicle in the farthest recesses of her brain, like an unwanted Christmas present you don't know what to do with but you can't return, so you stuff it up in the attic, forgotten, until some fool goes up there and unearths the damn thing and then brings it downstairs, setting it on the coffee table like it's some great find.

Thank you, Jennifer, Sarah thought on a sigh as she pulled into her driveway and caught sight of the unfamiliar pickup parked in front of the house. *Thank you so much for reminding me of what I'd worked so hard to forget.*

Not that any of this was Jen's fault. Who knew?

She sat for a long moment, staring out the driver's side window at what was obviously Dean's truck. This was no beat-up number on its last legs. Wheels, whatever. The color was understated enough—a dull silver, like her mother's pewter candlesticks on the living room mantel—but it clearly had enough bells and whistles to make even the fussiest boy happy. Either he'd done very well or he was in hock up to his butt.

A sudden crack of thunder startled her; she peered up at the clouds, which had been playing round-robin with the sun all day, then glanced back at the truck. Then her house.

Not yet. She just couldn't. She'd…just go check on the new pups first. Yeah. Good plan. She pushed open the door to the Bronco and hopped down.

The door crashed shut behind her; she held her breath. After a few seconds, when no crowd appeared, she let out her breath in a little huff, then headed across her front yard toward the kennels, the wind whistling in her ears.

The idea of seeing Dean again was wreaking more havoc with her gastrointestinal tract by the second. Right now, the last thing she wanted was to be anywhere *near* Jennifer's wedding, let alone be *in* Jennifer's wedding. An event she'd been looking forward to, despite her grumblings, until about six hours ago. Now, she'd rather eat Aunt Ida's okra-and-hamhocks casserole three times a day for the rest of her life—

"Sarah?"

The voice was deeper, the edge harder. But it was his. Still gentle. Still featherbed warm. And ingenuously seductive. And the instant she heard it, she knew she was in seriously deep do-do.

Cursing fate, she turned, her arms tucked tightly against her chest. She couldn't get a real good look at him; the light was fading quickly as the storm approached, and he stood on the porch at least thirty feet away. One hand, she thought, was braced against a white trellis laden with blueberry-hued morning glories, now tightly closed and flinching in the ruthless wind.

Apparently, however, he could see her just fine. "Good

Lord!'' he shouted over the wind. "What the hell happened to your hair?''

That these should be the first words out of his mouth, after all this time, came as no surprise. What was startling, though, was that it was as if no time had passed at all. There he stood, like he had hundreds of times before when he'd been waiting for her to get back from school or shopping or whatever.

But it was very different, even so.

Instinctively, almost protectively, her hand cupped her head. "What's wrong with it?'' she called, simultaneously annoyed and pleased at his reaction. "It turn green or something since I last looked in the mirror?''

He shook his head in slow motion. "Not green. *Gone.*''

"Oh, right.'' She shrugged. "It got to be a pain. So I chopped it off.''

Dean now descended the porch steps, one hand anchored on the banister, each step deliberate, careful, as if he knew she was a breath away from bolting. The wind whipped dust and leaves in Sarah's face, so she still couldn't clearly see him, even as he came closer. When he'd narrowed the gap to five feet or so, he stopped, blatantly staring at her. The debris finally ceased its assault long enough for her to stare back.

"You've changed, too,'' she said, crossing her arms again to support her roiling stomach.

He smiled, but it wasn't real steady, she didn't think. "Yeah. Guess you're not the only one with shorter hair.''

He fidgeted with his hands, like a little boy giving a speech in front of his class, then slipped them into the pockets of pleated-front chinos. That was something, right there: a new pair of jeans was about as dressed up as Sarah had ever seen Dean get. The pants were topped by a conservative knit shirt in a remarkably unconservative shade of aqua, stretched across shoulders and a chest that had broadened nicely over the years. Another blast of wind made her squint.

"You…look good.'' She had to say something. And it was true.

Dammit.

tucking away all those thoughts of touching and feeling and tasting.

"At least you didn't claw my eyes out," he said softly.

She held up her hands. "No nails. Sorry." Then, realizing her hands were shaking, tucked them behind her back. "Maybe some other time."

He blew out a puff of air that might have passed for a laugh. "Do you think…would you mind if we talked for a few minutes, alone? Before we have to face everyone else?"

For some reason, probably to avoid his eyes, she found herself staring at his mouth and remembered with startling clarity just how his lips had felt on hers. With that, all the thoughts she'd so carefully tucked away came tumbling free.

She snapped her gaze away from his mouth, from his face entirely, dragging her attention to a rhododendron bush a few feet away. But the image wouldn't fade. She fisted her hands— maybe digging her nails into her palms would serve as a reverse aphrodisiac. If she'd had any nails. Rats.

This was *not* the way it was supposed to happen. She had expected to see the Dean who had broken her heart. Not the one who had stolen it to begin with.

And that screwed up everything. Big time.

So she forced to the surface the one memory she would cling to with every fiber of her being, the one that would keep her heart from ever getting torn apart ever again. Not by Dean Parrish, anyway.

"Hey, remember?" she said at last in a level voice, daring to look up at him again. "I'm just a hick from boring Sweet-branch, Alabama? What on earth could we possibly have to talk about?"

Then she reeled smartly, nearly twisting her ankle in the process, and stalked away, huddled tightly against the wind as the clouds swirled overhead like oil spills in water.

Chapter 2

Following her would be pointless. Besides, he'd only come back to stand as best man to his brother, maybe help out his aunt with some chores around the house, run some errands. Not to let Sarah Whitehouse get to him.

The thunder became more insistent as he watched her retreat, her arms tucked against her ribs. He hoped she'd get back to the house before all hell broke loose, although that didn't look likely, judging from the churning gunmetal clouds overhead. But, he reminded himself, she was a big girl. She wasn't going to melt in a little rainstorm.

Oh, boy, was she a big girl.

Even as a youngster, Sarah's long legs and quick, energetic movements had always reminded him of a beautiful colt, sleek and sassy and filled with the promise of what she would become.

A promise that had been more than fulfilled.

Dean blinked in the wind, realizing Sarah had disappeared from sight some time ago. He turned back to the house, got as far as the porch steps and sank onto the next to bottom one as if deflated.

He wished—oh, how he wished!—he'd found her short hair repulsive or odd or just plain ugly. Instead, those bourbon-colored eyes looked even more enormous framed by the soft fringes of the simple cut, which also accentuated her proud jawline, her full mouth, that adorable little chin his fingertips could still feel when he'd tilt her face to his for a kiss.

With a sigh that rivaled the moan of the wind, Dean leaned his head against the banister. This sure wasn't the little girl who'd been his best friend. Or even the adolescent who'd tripped up his hormones, at fourteen or so. This was a *woman,* regal and sexy and gorgeous and brilliant and completely unaware that she was any of those things. Except maybe the brilliant part, he amended with a rueful grin.

And just think. She could have been his.

The tears came almost immediately.

Sarah assumed Dean had gone back into the house; she didn't look back and she didn't care whether he had or not. But if she thought storming off in a snit would bring her peace, her brain needed some major retooling. As if she could walk away from the truth! Not that she hadn't tried—and thought she'd succeeded, actually—more than once since Dean had left. Hell, a body'll believe anything, if you tell it the same lie long enough.

Here she'd thought she'd worked through the pain of his abandonment, his betrayal. That she'd convinced herself that whatever they'd had, no matter how intense, was still nothing more than a teenage romance. Puppy love. The inevitable flaring of a mutual hormonal surge.

Now the truth nagged at her like an obnoxious telemarketer, insisting part of her would always love Dean Parrish, no matter that she'd denied her feelings for nearly a decade.

Ever since Jennifer dropped her little bomb this afternoon, Sarah had been trying to hold back the memories, the good ones even more than the bad, intuitively realizing how tenuous her control really was. It'd been like trying to keep out a flood with a piece of plywood, but until a few minutes ago, she'd managed. Now they hammered at her brain, brutally, relentlessly, bringing with them a crying jag that bordered on hysteria.

She realized she was gasping for air as if she were literally drowning, her hands clamped to her ears—a futile gesture to staunch the barrage, and the pain that came with it. Like a drunk, she weaved toward the kennels, the wind whipping grit in her face, which would turn into hideous clay-colored tracks on her cheeks, as the memories crashed in, wave after wave, surging and flooding and briefly receding only to crest again. For a moment, she thought she might die.

For a moment, she wanted to.

What she *didn't* want was to remember the laughter in Dean's eyes, or his teasing smile. She didn't want to remember how he'd listen to her tirades about school or her mother making her do dishes *again* or how Priscilla Long had made fun of her in front of the entire student council, how he'd listen and hug her and tell her it would be okay but never, ever say she was being silly. She didn't want to remember long walks with their arms wrapped around each other's waists, when they'd talk for hours about whatever came into their heads, about their hopes and dreams and plans. But most of all, she couldn't bear to remember the one sweet, perfect time they'd been as intimate as two people can be.

Except his presence had smacked her in the face with the hard, now undeniable fact that, of course, she'd never really forgotten any of it.

A gust of wind knocked her off balance, making her trip over a tree root; she stumbled, regained her footing, wiped her cheek with her shirt sleeve. Had she really been that naive? To think if she refused to acknowledge the truth, it would somehow slink away like a guilty dog with its tail between its legs, never to be seen again? Or thought about again? Or admitted again?

That no one would ever find out?

Out of breath, unable to see, she fell against the trunk of the old magnolia tree at the gate to the vegetable garden, knowing she was courting disaster—she'd already seen lightning fork the slate sky ahead of her. But tears of sorrow and anger and confusion had rendered her immobile, her fomenting emotions parodying the charged atmosphere of the imminent storm.

He'd told her he'd never loved her.

"Dammit!" she cried, the word lost in a roar of thunder. She pounded the solid trunk with her fists, the bark scraping her skin. "Oh, you loved me, Dean! You did! I know that as well as I know my own name." She clumsily wiped the tears off her cheeks with the back of her hand and said on a whimper, "I know it as well as I know you'll never, ever get to me again, you…you *doodyhead!*"

Time ground to a halt while she leaned back against the huge trunk, letting its steadfastness support her, as she cried, and cried, and cried some more, until her sobs settled into shaky sighs. She rummaged in her jeans pocket with a hand stinging from self-inflicted abuse, found a mashed tissue, blew her nose. If nothing else, she had to take it as a sign that, as the tree had not been struck by lightning, she was probably meant to live. At least until after this dang wedding.

She took several deep breaths of the rain-fragrant air until she felt some semblance of normalcy return, then stuck out her chin. She'd made it this far; she'd be fine. All she had to do was stay out of Dean's path.

And get the truth tucked safely away again where no one could find it.

After God knew how long, Dean finally forced himself off the porch steps and back into the house before he started an epidemic of eyebrow-raising. Not that it would have mattered, as it turned out: his brother and future sister-in-law were far too busy oohing and aahing over the newest batch of wedding presents, as well as each other, to have noticed his absence, and Sarah's mother was in the kitchen, judging from the sounds of pans clanging and the familiar contralto voice belting out a dimly remembered hymn.

Only Katey was unoccupied, perched cross-legged on a window seat, her chin resting in one hand while the other hand automatically stroked a large, smug-faced Siamese cat lolled across her lap. Situated as far from the lovebirds as possible, the child stared out at the approaching storm with that long-suffering expression kids get when they're forced to make the best of a bad situation.

Dean felt a smile tug at his lips; he'd seen that expression before, many times, on another face, an expression that usually presaged some prank or other that like as not had gotten both Sarah *and* him in trouble. The cat shifted, cantilevering one splayed paw out over Katey's knee, and Dean frowned slightly, trying to remember the beast's name. Something weird Sarah'd thought up when she got the kitten for her twelfth birthday. Which meant—good Lord!—the animal had a good fifteen years under its belt. Maybe it wasn't the same cat.

Hands in pockets, Dean drifted over to Katey and nodded toward the empty half of the window seat. "Mind if I join you?"

The child flashed him a holey grin that would have suckered him into buying ice in January. Then she eyed the couple as if they'd suddenly developed oozing sores over most of their bodies. "Kinda makes you sick, don't it?"

"*Doesn't* it," Dean gently corrected her as he eased himself onto the seat, then stretched out his long legs, crossing them at the ankles. He could still hear his mother declaring there was no excuse for shoddy grammar. Ever. Just pure laziness, if not contrariness, far as she was concerned, stringing words together every which way the way people did. There were times he still expected his mother's hand to descend from heaven and whomp him one on the backside for some linguistic infraction or other.

Dean slanted Katey a smile, remembering he was in the middle of a conversation. "Yeah, I guess watching your sister and Lance drool over each other's a little hard to take. But you

know…'' He reached over and scratched the cat's chin, eliciting a blissful rumble. ''They *are* in love, you know.''

''It's *disgustin'*.''

Dean chuckled. ''When you come right down to it, though,
that's what most people want.'' While Katey seemed to con-
template how on earth she'd managed to be born into the human race, it suddenly came to him. ''Balthasar!''

''Huh?'' Katey said, her nose wrinkled under wide eyes. Her
resemblance to her big sister made his heart stumble.

''Isn't that the cat's name?''

The little girl looked from him to the cat and back to him.
''How'd you know that?''

In an instant, he realized she'd been told nothing. That she
had no idea he'd known her sister before. Eventually, she'd
figure it out, but right now she probably thought he'd just
sprung up like a mushroom after a rainstorm. Nor was it his
place to tell her any differently.

His shoulders hitched in a nonchalant shrug. ''Oh…I
think…Lance must've told me. I'd just forgotten for a moment,
sugar.''

Enormous eyes shot to his, brimming with tears. ''Why'd
you call me that?''

The child's sudden mood change threw him. ''I…don't
know. It just kind of popped out. Does it bother you?''

One tear slipped down a soft cheek. ''My daddy used to call
me that.''

''Oh…'' Dean hesitated, then leaned forward, his hands
loosely clasped together. ''You really miss him, don't you?''

Katey nodded, then wiped her nose with the back of her
hand, jutting out her chin. *Sarah's* chin. ''Sarah says I'll always remember him, but—'' she shook her head, straight
maple-colored hair swishing softly against delicate shoulders
''—but I think she's just trying to make me feel better.'' She
swallowed and looked out the window again. ''Every night, I
imagine him sittin' beside me on my bed and sayin' my prayers
with me, just like he used to. But I can't hear his voice no
more.'' Dean saw her lip quiver, then the effort exerted to

control it, and decided to let the grammatical slip pass. Then the child leaned her head to one side, considering. "Are you lonely, Dean?"

He choked on his own startled laugh. "What makes you ask that?"

"Lance said you don't have a wife or girlfriend or nothin'. I just thought most grown-ups had somebody, 'less they were widows like Mama."

He slowly shook his head. "Nope. Not me, honey," he said, then stiffened, wondering if that endearment, too, would provoke a reaction. Apparently not. The child continued the conversation without missing a beat.

"You know," she said in a low voice, "Sarah's all alone, too."

His heart lurched like a fish out of water. "She is, huh?"

"Uh-huh. Well, sometimes she goes to the movies with Dr. Stillman from the clinic, but they're just friends."

"Oh? And how do you know that?"

Katey shrugged, scowling at her sister and her fiancé. "Because they don't look at each other like *that*—"

"Katharine Suzanne!" rang out from the kitchen. "What about this corn?"

Then, just like Sarah would've done, Katharine Suzanne shoved the disgruntled cat off her lap and took off out the front door, her waist-length hair flapping against her narrow back.

A mixing bowl in a choke-hold between one arm and her bosom, her other hand clamped around a wooden spoon, Vivian Whitehouse pushed through the swinging door and glanced around the room. Not seeing her quarry, her questioning eyes lit on Dean. He cleared his throat and nodded toward the front door, still ajar.

A sound that was half sigh, half chuckle, rumbled from Vivian's throat. "Figures." Then she added, "Sarah's not here, either?"

"Uh…no, ma'am." Why did he suddenly feel so self-conscious? Wiping the palms of his hands on his thighs, Dean said, "Last I saw her, she was headed toward the kennels."

A pair of shrewd gray eyes bore into his. "You talked to her?"

"For a moment."

Vivian nodded, then banged back the swinging door again, jabbed the spoon into the center of the bowl and clunked both down on a counter just inside the door. Wiping her hands on the front of her untucked shirt, she passed Dean on her way toward the front door. "I'll be back," she said, then thrust a no-nonsense index finger in his direction. "Then you and I are gonna talk. So don't you dare move your backside out of this room, you hear me?"

As the front door closed behind Sarah's mother, Dean became aware of affianced couple's attention riveted to his face. He gave a nervous laugh in their direction, then raised his hands guiltily, staring at the space where the imposing specimen of motherhood had just been standing.

"Wouldn't dream of it, ma'am," he murmured.

The dogs had smelled Sarah before she got within fifty feet. Rich, baritone barking and excited puppy yips mingled with another roll of thunder as she approached. Five minutes, she promised herself. Just five minutes.

"Hey, y'all!" Sarah scooted into the kennel, upwards of two dozen noses nudging her calves and knees as she tried to greet them all at once. A laugh bubbled out of her tight throat as one puppy immediately latched onto her sneaker lace and gave it what-for, complete with a fierce growl designed to bring the shoe into immediate submission.

Pointing at the lowering sky, she warned, "Y'all better get inside, now. It's fixin' to rain any minute." In confirmation, a bolt of lightning split the clouds, accompanied by a crack of thunder that made her jump and several of the puppies scurry toward the open door of the converted barn.

Sarah shooed the rest of the gang inside, shutting the half-door behind them, then swung open the chain link gate to one of the overlarge pens, staring into assorted sets of tiny golden brown eyes.

"I know you don't want to, but you gotta. Come on, now."

Like children forced to come in when they still wanted to play, the dogs reluctantly obeyed, some of them gazing back outside with what seemed to be genuine regret, as if they knew wonderful wet stuff was going to fall out of the sky any minute. Labs and water went together like biscuits and gravy. Sarah allowed a sympathetic smile.

"Sorry. I'm in no mood to clean up mud today, okay? So whaddya think? Should I go check the babies— Oh, *Lordy!*"

Katey jumped as much as she did.

"Shoot, baby, don't sneak up on people like that!" Sarah lay her arm across Katey's shoulders, as much to steady herself as out of affection. "What on earth are you doing here? Looks like the sky's about to burst wide open."

Katey hunched her thin shoulders in a gesture Sarah took to mean there really was no reason other than it seemed like a good idea. Or that Mama had asked her to do something, was more like it. "I just figured you were here. And…I didn't have nothin' to do."

"*Anything* to do." Sarah pretended sympathy. "And Mama couldn't even find something for you to do in the kitchen…?"

"What's wrong?" Katey asked, squinting. "Why are your eyes all red?"

Rats. Sarah cleared her throat, forced a smile. "Just got a bunch of dirt in 'em, is all. You know, from the wind?"

Which got a tell-me-another-one look from the little girl. But then the newborns eeked again, and Katey clasped both hands to her chest in supplication.

"Just for a minute," Sarah said. Wouldn't take much longer than that before her mother sniffed her out, anyway.

Katey skipped over to the pen where mama and pups were quarantined from the rest of the dogs, Sarah following. It was chowtime; the tiny black lumps looked more like oversize fat bugs than dogs as they jostled for position at their mother's teats.

"This is the cutest batch we've ever had," the eight-year-old solemnly declared, her fingers entwined around the chain link. Sarah hid her smile. Katey said that about every litter. Without fail. "C'n I hold one?"

"Let's just see how Mariah feels about it, okay?" Sarah slowly opened the gate so as not to startle the mother dog, then entered the pen, settling onto the floor beside the bitch and her six pups whose birth she had witnessed just two days before. Squirming as much as the pups, Katey squatted at her right knee. "Think it'd be okay if I held one of your precious babies for a minute?" Sarah asked, then carefully picked up one of the pups and cuddled it against her chest while the mother dog rooted at her offspring's rump, just to be sure.

Katey sighed, stroking the little furrowed head with one finger.

"Wish I'd've been here when the pups were born."

"It was two in the morning, baby. And Mama dog did it all by herself. I was just here for decoration." Sarah traded pups. "Now, *sheep,* on the other hand, don't even know which end the lamb's supposed to come out of." She thought of last March when she and Doc helped George Plunkett and his pubescent son Joshua usher two dozen new lambs into the world, and yawned automatically. "Except they always decide to do it when it's raining and dark."

"Well," Katey announced, unperturbed, "when *I'm* a vet, those dumb sheep will just have to have their babies when I'm on duty."

Sarah regarded the little girl with a wry smile. Knowing Katey, she probably *would* get the dumb sheep to birth during office hours.

"So…still wanna be a vet?" She touched her forehead to Katey's. "You didn't seem real interested this morning at the clinic."

Katey squirmed, her dark brows dipping. "Well…" Sarah could almost hear the child's brain fast-forwarding through several dozen possible answers. Then the little face relaxed into a grin as she let a puppy sniff her fingers. "I'm just a kid. I've got a short attention span."

Sarah let out a laugh, then hugged the little girl to her. No matter what, this precocious little girl never failed to make her smile. Even more than the pups. ''You've never been 'just' a kid, you know that? Even when you were a baby, you always wore this funny, grown-up expression.''

''I did?''

''Uh-huh.'' Sarah pretended to shudder and Katey giggled. ''It was freak-y, too, having this little tiny baby look at you with this serious face all the time—''

''Sarah Louise?'' The lights flickered in the kennel as her mother's low voice, easily overriding the next wave of thunder, filled the old barn.

''In with Mariah, Mama.''

''Katey with you?''

''Yes, Mama,'' Katey piped up.

Clad in her usual attire of oversize man-tailored shirt and jeans, the full-figured woman now blocked most of the light coming into the stall. Vivian never had lost the weight from the last pregnancy. Not that she seemed to care.

Vivian settled what was supposed to be a stern gaze on the little girl. ''I believe there's something you're supposed to be doing, young lady?''

The child looked from one woman to the other, then let out an affronted sigh. ''Yes, Mama,'' she muttered, getting to her feet. Wiping her hands on the already filthy seat of raspberry-colored shorts, Katey unlatched the gate and let herself out of the pen, stoically allowing Vivian to plant a kiss on the top of her glimmering chestnut head as she passed. Size two sneakers ground emphatic squeaks into the smooth cement floor as the child retreated.

Vivian joined Sarah in the cage, huffing a little as she lowered her ample form to the floor, then patted Sarah's knee. ''You okay?''

Sarah cuddled the tiny dog to her chest. ''The pups needed to be checked.''

That got a snort as Vivian tucked a stray hank of silver-streaked, ash-brown hair back up into a loose bun at the back of her head. ''Chicken.''

"Damn straight," Sarah shot back with an attempt at a grin, then averted her face when her mother tried to look her in the eye.

"You've been crying."

"What gave you your first clue?"

"Puffy eyes, blotchy face, swollen lips—take your pick."

With a huge sigh, Sarah said, "I saw him."

"Yeah. I know."

Sarah leaned her head back against the whitewashed partition of the pen with a soft thud. "Could you just tell everyone I tripped and drowned in a mud puddle or something?"

Vivian grunted in what Sarah assumed was sympathy. "Now, baby, you knew he'd come back some day." A beat. "And you knew what that meant."

Sarah pulled her head forward, concentrating on the writhing mass of pups in front of them. "I just thought for some reason I'd have a little more time to prepare myself."

"Hah! Bad news never seems to be terribly interested in giving much warning." Vivian shifted her weight with a soft wince. "What're you going to do?"

With a sigh, Sarah leaned her head back again and shut her eyes, the puppy snuffling the hollow of her throat with whiskers soft as the inside of a daisy. "Kinda liked the mud puddle idea, myself."

"You could tell him."

Sarah opened one eye and tilted her head just far enough to see the side of her mother's face, sternly refusing to allow one more emotion into her already overcrowded brain. That didn't stop her face from flushing, however. "Tell him what, exactly?"

The puppies' mewling filled the silence as Vivian seemed to consider her answer. "You still being sweet on him might be a good place to start."

The two women regarded each other for a moment, then Sarah looked away. "And what makes you think that?"

"I'm psychic."

Sarah swallowed past the knot of anger in her throat, then

said quietly, "Dean Parrish chewed up my heart and spit it out in little pieces all over Lee County." Frowning, she shut her eyes and rocked her head from side to side against the wall. "I don't deserve that."

"That's right."

Sarah's mouth pulled into a straight line as her voice dropped an octave. "And he sure as hell doesn't deserve *me*." She let out a long sigh. "You were right, you know. Back then. About our not being suited for the long haul."

Vivian picked something off her jeans. "Maybe…he's changed."

"Yeah, and maybe Auburn'll get a major league football franchise next year." Sarah shook her head, finally opening her eyes, regarding nothing in particular. "You didn't see the look on his face, the night he broke up with me." She carefully placed the pup back with its siblings.

They sat in silence again for a full minute, Sarah fully aware if her mother touched her she'd start bawling all over again. Except what she did was far worse. "The question is, what did you see in his face *today*?"

Sarah turned away, determined to hold it together, determined not to be the pawn in whatever game her mother now seemed so determined to play.

"Honey, all you can do is take this one step at a time—"

"What's done is done, Mama," she said sharply. "There's no going back."

After a long moment, Vivian gently bumped shoulders with her daughter. A conciliatory gesture, Sarah figured. "How you handle this is up to you," she said softly. "And it's just one week. Dinner tonight, the rehearsal dinner, the wedding. That's all. Think you can manage that?"

Just one week. Right. With a toss of her head, Sarah said on an exhaled breath, "Doesn't look like I've got a whole lot of choice in the matter, does it?" She stood, then held out a hand to help up her mother, the one person who, no matter what, had been there for her, had helped her through the most painful period of her life. And who, Sarah knew, felt more than bad about her part in creating the situation now facing all of them.

"There are always choices," Vivian said with a grunt as she struggled to her feet. No longer taller than her daughter, her eyes met Sarah's dead on. "Always." She shrugged and draped an arm around Sarah's shoulder as a teeth-rattling thunderclap ripped open the clouds at last, letting loose a barrage of stone-hard raindrops onto the tin roof overhead.

"Like now," her mother shouted as they stood at the barn door watching the deluge quickly turn the yard into a river of slimy orange mud. "Do we stay and wait it out, or make a run for it?"

"Oh, come on, Mama," Sarah challenged with a wicked grin. "I've never known you to wait anything out." She dashed into the driving rain, calling over her shoulder, "Last one to the house cleans dog poop for a week!"

Not surprisingly, Sarah lost the bet. It always astounded her how quickly her mother could move, despite her generous proportions. In any case, they were both drenched by the time they made it to the house and up the steps. Flushed with exertion and laughing too hard to breathe, they wriggled out of sneakers that looked dipped in pumpkin pie filling, dumping them by the back door before stumbling over each other to see who got to the kitchen first.

"Oh, yuck!" Jennifer waved a half-peeled cucumber in front of her as if to ward off evil spirits. "You two are *gross!*"

Dripping all over the kitchen floor, Sarah grabbed a kitchen towel to wipe off her face. Still laughing, she threw a broad wink at Katey, giggling and half hidden behind a mountain of corn at the kitchen table, then directed her attention to the flinching Jennifer. "Would somebody *please* tell me how Vivian and Eli Whitehouse managed to produce such a *priss?* It's just water, Jen—see?" She shook her head like a dog, sending a spray halfway across the room, cackling in glee as her sister squealed and nearly tripped over herself trying to back away.

"Mama! Make her stop!"

Vivian, her own hair hanging like tangled vines around her face, shifted her eyes to her oldest daughter, her mouth twitching. "Sarah Louise, stop torturing your sister."

"Yes, Mama," Sarah said, tucking her hands behind her back and shuffling one bare foot back and forth over the puddled floor. Then she went after Jennifer with a war whoop and the wet towel, sending her shrieking out the kitchen door.

And sending Sarah straight into Dean's chest, which, along with the rest of him, happened to pick that moment to come out to the kitchen.

She felt strong, rough hands close firmly around her upper arms, her chest and hips meld into his as he steadied her to keep from being knocked over. For more seconds than she wanted to know, his breath, sweet and warm, fanned over her still damp face, making her shiver. Her nipples pebbled, instantly and just this side of painfully. She froze, not sure whether it was her heartbeat or his she felt pounding against her skin.

"Well, now…" One side of his mouth hitched up around a low drawl that was affected and deliberately irritating and made her bare toes curl against the cool lacquered floor. "I see you're just as clumsy as you always were. Nice to see not *everything's* changed about you, Sarah Louise."

She wasn't sure, but she thought he drew her just a little closer, close enough that she knew with certain dread that two layers of limp, thin, wet fabric were no barrier to his being able to feel her taut nipples against his chest. The half-grin grew downright insouciant. Lightning flickered eerily across his taut features as he said in a voice too soft for anyone else to hear, "But then again, it would appear that *some* things have improved considerably."

It would *appear* the man had a death wish.

Panicked eyes locked with his, a little cry of alarm escaped parted lips…and, exquisitely timed with the next roar of thunder, two surprisingly strong fists crashed down with unerring aim on either side of his collarbone.

The cups in the glass-fronted cupboard rattled like maracas as Dean let go of Sarah with a grunt, then watched as she streaked past him and out the kitchen door. Rubbing one wounded shoulder, he heard her footsteps pound down the hall, up the stairs and down the upstairs hallway to her room, ending with a door slam that rattled the cups in the cupboard all over again.

Whoo-*ee*—she sure as hell was *stronger* than she used to be.

Still coddling his shoulder, he leaned against the open swinging door, half in, half out of the kitchen, and shut his eyes for a moment. She'd left more than a set of bruises behind. Her scent, damp and natural, lingered in his nostrils. And the effects of her body pressed against his still lingered below his waist. Although, *lingering* wasn't perhaps the most accurate description....

"Well, just don't stand there like a lump, boy. Get your butt in here."

With a slight start, Dean shifted his attention to Sarah's mother, who was toweling off her hair, having already changed into dry jeans and another loose shirt. Dean couldn't remember ever seeing the statuesque woman in anything fitted, even when he was a kid.

But when would she have changed clothes? His brow wrinkled as he obeyed, letting the door swing to a close behind him. Vivian apparently picked up on his confusion, answering with a loud laugh.

"Laundry day. Seemed to make more sense to pull dry things out of the basket right here than tramp all the way upstairs. Besides, gives me two less things to put away, right?" She tossed the damp towel out into the laundry room, then haphazardly braided her long hair in a single plait at the nape of her neck as tangential strands curled around her broad face. "So tell me..." Yanking open a small drawer next to the sink, she poked around in the jumbled contents until she found a rubber band, with which she tidily finished off the braid. "How's life in Atlanta?" She settled back on a stool, crossed

Another smile, this one perhaps a little more relaxed. ''You, too.'' Now he added a brief chuckle. ''Crew cut and all.''

''It's not *that* short—'' She clamped her mouth shut, her face tingling from his knowing smile, the gentle teasing she'd forgotten how to handle. She used to encourage it, though. And give it right back.

Why couldn't she take her eyes off his face?

Which was older, of course. But…more mature, too, which was not the same thing. Age, perhaps, had sharpened features that might've seemed severe save for the smile she knew came so easily and often to his lips. Well, used to, anyway. His hair seemed lighter, but she couldn't tell if the streaks were sun-bleached or premature gray, blended as they were into the moderate style that hooded the tops of his ears, curled over the top of his collar. Age, again—and an overdose of sun from summers of lifeguard duty—had bestowed the beginnings of crow's feet at the corners of his eyes, a faint bracketing around his mouth.

Time and gravity had wrought the physical changes. What had brought about the maturity, she had no way of knowing. But it was there, settled into his eyes. Even their color seemed more intense, like everything else about him, the gold-green she remembered now deepened to the color of damp moss.

She saw wisdom, she thought. Understanding. Maybe a little regret, but that might be wishful thinking. But what she didn't see—happiness or contentment or even satisfaction—she found threatening in some vague, unexplainable way. Not vague at all, though, was an almost irrepressible urge to skim her fingertips down his cheek. To see if he smelled the same. Felt the same.

Tasted the same.

Her heart now fairly thundered in her chest.

His smile had faded in the wake of her extended silence. He glanced away for a second, then let out a short, nervous laugh. ''Damn, this is awkward.''

''You could say that,'' she allowed with a curt nod, mentally her arms. ''Must make this place look dull as Luke Hanover's old bloodhound.''

''Sometimes, dull is good,'' Dean admitted, not missing the merest hint of a hitched eyebrow. He decided to let Sarah's mother come to her own conclusions, which she undoubtedly would.

Vivian simply studied him for a long moment, a half smile lifting her full, round cheeks, those gray eyes searing right into his brain. Other than that, she had no reaction. Whatsoever.

Dean leaned back against the counter, his hands gripping the edge. Woman was making him nervous as a cat watching a frog. This prodigal son business was not what he'd expected. Sarah's mother could just as well run him out of her house with a shotgun at his backside for leaving her daughter like that. Considering Sarah's devastated expression when she'd fled his room that day, it was a miracle he was still in one piece. That Vivian Whitehouse was actually being *friendly* was an even bigger miracle.

If not downright weird.

After a few seconds, the smile blossomed. ''Still know your way around a bag of briquettes, boy?''

''Excuse me?''

''That no-count brother of yours can't barbecue worth beans. But I seem to recall your daddy and you used to cook up a storm.''

The knot in his stomach began to ease a little. ''Yes, ma'am, I guess so. But…well, I don't mean to be rude, but…speaking of storms?''

''Shoot…this'll be over before Katey's finished shucking the corn. Grab a Coke out of the fridge and take a load off. I'll be right back.''

Katey sat at the kitchen table in front of a pile of corn large enough to feed the whole county, shucking it so slowly there was no doubt Vivian was right. The child offered him a doleful expression and a put-upon sigh and tugged off another handful of husk.

Dean nodded toward the corn, his brow creased in sympathy. "Think your Mama would mind if I helped?"

"Yes, I would" came the stentorian voice from the pantry. "That's her job. You just let her be."

Katey screwed up one side of her mouth. "Thanks, anyway."

"Sorry, honey," he said, briefly touching her shoulder. "I tried."

He pulled a Coke out of the refrigerator and popped the top, surveying the enormous kitchen appreciatively, a room that had always represented love and warmth and security when he was growing up. Even as the angry storm slashed against the windows, this room was bright, inviting, safe. He sagged against the counter and took a swig of the soda, only half listening as Vivian chattered to him from the other side of the door.

The all-white room hadn't changed much since he'd last seen it. The same handpainted porcelain plates marched across the soffit over the light oak cabinets his father had put in—as well as the butcherblock countertops—when the Whitehouses had first bought the old place almost twenty-five years ago. He'd only been five at the time, but he still remembered coming over and "helping," and how Vivian had fussed and clucked over him and fed him enormous chunks of hot cornbread dripping with butter or still-warm peanut butter cookies or that last piece of chocolate cake that "was just going to go stale if someone didn't eat it real soon," all of which were courtesy of the enormous converted cast-iron stove, which still took up a good chunk of one wall like a giant sleeping bull.

His focus shifted toward the sink, where he could almost see a teenaged Sarah, like a hologram or something, standing with her hand on her slim waist and a teasing smile on her lips, her long hair rippling like a waterfall over her shoulders as she'd throw him a towel to dry so they could go riding their bikes up to the lake before it got dark.

He swallowed hard, then his eyes wandered back to the pine table where Katey sat at her task, her tongue stuck out in concentration. The table had also been his daddy's handiwork, and he noted underneath the growing pile of husks it was still adorned with familiar handmade rag placemats and a pot of fresh flowers in the center. He thought of all the dinners and all the jokes and all the laughter he'd shared at that table. And how much he'd missed all that.

And how, if he hadn't panicked, believing other people knew more than he did, maybe he wouldn't've had to.

He realized his eyes were moist, about the same time he caught Vivian standing in the pantry door, a bag of briquettes in her arms. Conspiracy lighting up her dove-colored eyes, she walked heavily across the old wood floor and shoved the bag into his arms.

"You have one week," she said in a low voice. So the child wouldn't hear, he presumed.

"I don't…" He frowned. "Huh?"

Vivian sighed, then leveled him with a piercing look that could have converted rocks into diamonds. "To win her back, you fool."

This time he did jump, just as if the frog had sprung into his face. But her earnest expression stilled him immediately. Worried him, too.

"Look, mistakes get made," she said in a low voice. "And you can either learn from them and try to fix them, or you can give up and be miserable for the rest of your life. So…there's your choice. Don't screw it up."

Before Dean could protest that he seriously doubted whether winning back Sarah's affections—even if he'd wanted to—was either reasonable, possible, or the best choice for anyone concerned, the kitchen door swung open and the lady herself appeared. She'd showcased those long legs in a pair of white shorts, topped by a blousy white cotton shirt with the top two buttons left intriguingly undone. Whiskey eyes flashed from her mother to Dean and back again as she stood with one hand on the side of the door, the other on her hip.

Leading Dean to wonder exactly how long she'd been standing on the other side of the door.

Chapter 3

Judging from Dean's furtive expression, she'd been the topic of conversation. Judging from her mother's, by Vivian's, choice.

No way was she going *there*.

So she went instead to the refrigerator—acutely aware of Dean's appreciative scrutiny of her legs as she passed—pulled out a Coke, then returned to the living room to check out the wedding gifts, leaving her mother and Dean to think whatever they liked.

Played it pretty cool the rest of the evening, too, if she said so herself. Whenever she caught Dean watching her at supper, she rearranged her features into what she hoped was an expression of aloof nonchalance.

Not that the rest of her would cooperate. She forced herself to eat—otherwise four people would have jumped on her case—but the corn and burgers and salad and watermelon and apple pie felt like wet sand in her stomach.

Dean's own peculiar expression didn't help matters, a look which she caught far more often than she liked simply because the man would not take his eyes off of her. They didn't exchange as much as a dozen words during the meal, which nobody noticed what with Jennifer and Katey and her mother all holding forth about the wedding, but she felt as if he was trying to absorb her through his eyes. Just as she was fixing to tell him to perform some physiologically impossible feat, Jennifer came to the rescue.

"So, c'mon, Dean," her sister wheedled as only she could. "You've just gotta tell me what this wedding present is."

Dean finally tore his eyes away from Sarah and contemplated her sister with an oblique smile. "Oh, I've *gotta* tell you, huh?" he said, winking at Katey. "And why is that?"

"Oh, boy," Lance interjected with raised hands and a laugh. "You do not want to know what this woman is capable of once she sets her mind to something. Might as well give it up now, while you still have all your toenails."

"Lance!" Jennifer slapped him with her paper napkin. "You make me sound like Attila the Hun or something. I'm not that bad—"

"Yeah. You are." Lance caught his fiancée in his arms, eliciting a tiny squeal. "That's why I love you so much." He sealed his left-handed endearment with a smacking kiss on her lips.

Jennifer tenderly grazed his cheek with two fingers, then faced Dean again. "So? You gonna tell me or sacrifice your toenails?"

Chuckling, Dean wiped his mouth and hands on his napkin and stood up. "It's in the truck."

"The *truck!*" Jennifer's eyes grew wide as the watermelon rounds stacked on the plate in front of her. "You left my wedding present out in the *rain?*"

"Trust me," Dean said, backing toward the driveway, "when I pack furniture, nothing short of a nuclear disaster is going to harm it."

"Furniture?" By now Jennifer had jumped up from the table and zipped past Dean on the way to the Dakota, followed one by one by the rest of the family. "Lance said you had enough

orders to keep your shop busy through Christmas…'' She'd
reached the truck and now danced with impatience. ''But you
found the time to make something for us?''

''Sure did.'' Dean swung down the tailgate and hopped up
into the bed where a lumpy, canvas-wrapped object nestled
near the cab. After several minutes of peeling away layer after
layer of protective covering, he picked up the object—which
still wore its last layer, like a chaste slip—and jumped down
off the truck with it. Now everyone followed Dean and the
object up onto the porch, where he set it down and stepped
away, nodding toward Jennifer.

''Be my guest.''

Jennifer hesitated, then slowly drew off the last layer of
canvas. ''Oh!''

The fine handrubbed finish of the mahogany rocker glowed
in the last rays of the setting sun like the embers of a dying
fire. A Windsor design, with delicate, smooth spindles splayed
upward from the seat, the arms were gracefully curved, the
rockers perfectly balanced. But everyone there knew just how
difficult such a deceptively simple-looking object can be to
make, because there was no room for the slightest imperfec-
tion.

Sarah blinked, then swallowed. She'd always known Dean
was talented, remembering the beautiful pieces he'd build in
his father's workshop. But the care and attention to detail in
the chair said it all. She'd always said he'd make something
of himself. Never doubted it for a single second.

And would he have gotten as far as he had if he'd stayed?
If he hadn't gone to Atlanta, his talent would have withered
like a seedling not given the proper light or food or water. As
would have their love, eventually.

It all made sense. Now.

''That is the loveliest rocker I have ever seen,'' Vivian,
never one to flatter, allowed, and the smile that lit up Dean's
face was nearly Sarah's undoing.

''Thank you,'' he said softly, then addressed his brother and
Jennifer, who stood with their arms around each other's waist.

"I just hope the two of you enjoy using it half as much as I enjoyed making it for you."

"Oh, Dean…" Jennifer slipped away from Lance and took Dean's hand, stretching up to kiss him on the cheek. "It's absolutely gorgeous. Thank you." She giggled and gestured toward the chair. "Can I?"

"Well, ma'am, chairs aren't meant to be looked at, now are they?"

With another giggle, Jennifer slid into the chair, sighing in contentment. "It really is perfect." Sarah saw Dean lean over and whisper something that brought a flush to Jen's cheeks and a hand to Dean's wrist as she nodded and smiled. Then Dean skipped down the porch steps and back out into the yard, where he was accosted by a vociferous little girl who just had to show him around the property before it got any darker. Vivian then dragged Lance off to help her with some chore or other, leaving the two sisters on the porch.

"So." Sarah leaned against the railing, arms crossed. "What did he say?"

Her sister went crimson.

"Good Lord, Jennifer—what *did* he say?"

"Promise you won't say a word to anyone? Not even Mama?"

"What on earth…?"

Jennifer cleared her throat, stroking the satiny arms of the chair with her fingertips. "He said that…he hoped I'd get to rock our babies in this chair."

Sarah let out a whoosh of air. "Is that all? Perfectly understandable, considering the nature of the present—"

"Sarah. You don't understand." Jennifer leaned over and pulled her sister closer. "I'm *late*."

"For what?"

"Sa-rah…" Jennifer waited. Expectantly, as it were.

Sarah's mouth fell open. "You're *preg—?*"

"Shh!" Jennifer madly flapped her hands. "Nobody knows. Not even Lance. It's only three days. It may be a false alarm."

Sarah squatted in front of her sister, grabbing her hands.

"You little minx!" With a throaty chuckle, she added, "You ever been late before?"

"Not even ten minutes."

They both dissolved into giggles.

"What's going on?" Lance asked behind Sarah, making them jump.

"Oh, nothing. Just girl stuff." Sarah got to her feet with her back to Lance, winked at Jennifer. *"You going to tell him?"* she mouthed to her sister, who gave a twitch of a head shake in response.

"Saturday," she said, and Sarah understood.

What a wedding present, she thought as she made her way back to the picnic table. She rifled through the leftovers as if checking out the goods at a yard sale, finally plopping down on the bench with the last piece of apple pie. A pair of thin arms threaded around her neck. "C'n I show Dean the kennels?"

Her mouth full of pie, Sarah twisted around to Katey. And Dean.

"Ob cos," she mumbled around mashed apples and piecrust, then swallowed and thought probably a smile was in order. For Katey, at any rate. "Of course," she repeated. "Just don't bother Mariah if she's nursing, okay?"

"I know," Katey said with a tolerant sigh, then took Dean by the hand.

Sarah's heart wrenched when she saw Dean's strong, callused fingers close so carefully around the little ones trustingly placed in his. Unthinking, she looked up, and found her eyes caught in his much the same way his hand held Katey's—with a tenderness that spoke of trust and loyalty. And unbroken ties.

It had been a long, long time since she'd seen that look in his eyes.

She didn't want to see it now.

"Come on, Dean." Katey tugged at his hand, leaning all of her sixty-five pounds away from him. "It's getting dark. Let's *go.*"

"Okay, honey, I'm coming," he drawled, turning to her

with a wide smile. "Let's go see those beautiful dogs your Mama's raising."

Dean shared the smile with Sarah as he swung Katey up on his back for a piggyback ride, then loped off toward the kennels, the little girl dissolving into uncontrollable giggles when he broke into a gallop. Sarah simply sat and watched, her chin sunk in her hands, as the glue holding together her broken heart disintegrated a little more.

Lance straddled the seat beside her and followed her gaze. "They sure hit it off," he said.

With a little start, Sarah straightened up, nodded. "Yeah." She swung her legs to the outside of the table and rested her elbows on the top, staring back at the house. Away from the kennels. As if cued, hundreds of fireflies began looping in and out of the bushes and long grass, reminding Sarah how she used to pretend they were actually tiny flashlights carried by a band of invisible little people who lived under the porch. When had she stopped believing in magic?

Stupid question.

"Where's Jen?" she asked Lance.

"I don't know, exactly. She disappeared inside to look for your mother. Had the oddest look on her face, too." He turned worried brown eyes to her. "You think everything's okay?"

Sarah fought to keep a straight face. "She probably thought of something she had to tell Mama that couldn't wait one second longer. You know Jennifer."

"All too well," he said with a half laugh, then immediately frowned. "But what's up with you and my brother? Is *somebody* going to fill me in as to what exactly's going on here?"

Sarah peered from underneath her lashes at Lance, whose only resemblance to Dean was the same slanted smile. Dean favored his father; Lance had clearly inherited his mother's delicate features and dark hair. "That depends," she hedged, "on how much you already know."

"Shoot, Sarah…I don't know enough to fill a postage stamp. Other than remembering you two hanging out a lot when you were kids. I mean, I didn't pay a whole lot of attention, but I thought you were close. What happened?''

Sarah sighed, plucking an acorn the wind had deposited in her lap and pitching it back at the tree whence it came. She liked Dean's brother a lot. At twenty-three, he'd gotten his accounting degree and even started his own fledgling practice, mainly trying to help the outlying farmers understand the concept of cash flow and credit so they didn't keep getting screwed in the middle of planting or lambing or harvest season. No way to get rich, but he wouldn't starve. Besides, he was acquiring enough clients with actual money here and there that in a few years he'd probably do pretty well.

And he was crazy about her sister. Jennifer could have done far worse than Lance Parrish, that was for sure. The young man doted on her but never let her take herself too seriously. And Jennifer kept him from getting buried in his facts and figures, kept his sense of humor fine-tuned so he never took himself too seriously, either. They were a good match. And they'd make great parents.

A hand waved in front of her face. "Hello?"

"What? Oh...sorry." She shifted slightly on the bench to restore circulation to her posterior, looking just past Lance toward the back pasture, quickly being swallowed up in darkness. "Yeah, your brother and I go way back. And we went together for a while. But we broke up. He went to Atlanta. I stayed here." She rolled her shoulders. "End of story."

"Uh-huh. And that's why he kept staring at you all through supper with that stupid expression on his face."

Sarah felt her own face tingle. "It's the hair," she parried, ruffling it. "He just can't get over the fact it's not there anymore."

"And if you believe that..." Lance shrugged and let the sentence hang like smoke in the air.

With a brisk shake of her head, Sarah said, "Look, I'll be completely honest, okay? Just so no one starts imagining things that aren't there." She hooked one heel up onto the bench, laced her hands around her knee. "Your brother hasn't set foot in Sweetbranch since he left, has he?"

"Well, no..."

"Doesn't that tell you something? Honey, Dean obviously wants the big-city life, the big-city glitz and glamour and excitement. He made that more than clear to me the day he told me it was over between us. There was nothing here to hold him then, and nothing has changed on that score." She stood up, stretched out her legs. "He's made his life. I've made mine." One shoulder hitched. "We live on different planets, Lance. What I guess I hadn't realized was that we always had—"

"Sarah! Josh Plunkett's on the phone!"

She swiveled toward the house. "What's he want?" she called back to her mother.

"Says one of the lambs got out during the thunderstorm. Dang mule somehow stepped on it, broke its leg. The boy's next door to hysterical."

"Tell him I'll be right out, to keep the lamb still and himself calm."

Sarah started for the house to get her shoulder bag and car keys when Lance called after her. Eyebrows raised, she looked back over her shoulder.

"What you said about you and Dean being from two different planets? They're making remarkable strides in space travel these days, you know."

Sarah allowed a half smile for the young man, not having the heart to point out that Dean's planet was probably in another galaxy. Billions and billions of light years away. And she drove a Bronco, not the USS *Enterprise*.

A couple minutes later, as she steered the car out onto the road and headed north toward the Plunkett farm, she saw Katey and Dean come out of the kennel, easily visible thanks to the sensor light over the kennel door. As Sarah acknowledged Katey's exuberant goodbyes with a wave of her hand, she couldn't help but see Dean still wore that whipped-dog expression. Frowning, she concentrated on the twin beams of light in front of her.

And ignored the panic threatening to choke her.

Even though Dean had left the Whitehouses' hours ago, he still couldn't get the image of a pair of endless legs out of his head.

No. It was more than that, he thought, scrunching his pillow under his head. There were plenty of long legs in Atlanta. None of them, however, belonged to Sarah Whitehouse.

And there were other images, like specters, determined to plague him that night: Sarah's brilliant smile and quick laugh and gentle, loving teasing; Sarah sitting with one long finger tucked under her chin as she concentrated on some convoluted explanation of Katey's; Sarah head to head with Jennifer as they shared sisterly secrets; Sarah joking with her mother, their laughs blending in the sweetest harmony heard this side of the Robert Shaw Chorale.

The way that laughter died whenever she caught him looking at her.

Finally, tired of flopping around in bed like water on a hot skillet, he sat up and perched on its edge, raking both hands through his hair. Too many Cokes, he thought.

Too many memories.

He fumbled for his Timex on top of the nightstand, waiting a moment until the tiny phosphorescent green numerals came into focus. Twelve forty-five. He'd been in bed for nearly two hours and hadn't been to sleep yet. Didn't look as though the sandman was going to pay him a visit anytime soon, either.

The old floorboards protested when he stood and crossed to the open window. He leaned against the sill, curtains of some diaphanous material—his aunt had redone his old bedroom immediately after he'd left, Lance had told him—brushing against his bare shoulders, making him shiver. The moon was full; stark, deep shadows carved the front yard and road beyond, between patches of silvery light bright enough to read by.

He needed a walk.

Thirty seconds of blind rummaging through his soft-sided suitcase yielded a pair of clean jeans and T-shirt. He stumbled a bit in the dark as he pulled them on, the harsh grating of the zipper magnified in the deep middle-of-the-night country silence. Seconds later, he was out the back door.

The only sounds he heard as he ambled down the road in the general direction of Sarah's house were the occasional chirping of an insomniac cricket and the murmurings of leaves as the night breeze disturbed their repose. The navy blue sky, punctuated with too many stars to take them all in, showed no signs of the earlier storm, but the air was cool and clean and fresh, the hems of his jeans soon soaked from the dampness leeching from the ground.

He passed the row of cypresses bordering the west edge of the Whitehouse property and stopped, staring at the house, wondering what the general reaction would be if he just walked up and knocked on the door. Took all of two, maybe three seconds to decide there were easier ways to commit suicide.

Then he noticed her car wasn't in the driveway. Concerned, he checked out the back…nope. She'd left on her call at nine-thirty. Where the hell could she still be at 1:00 a.m.?

He stood, hands on hips, mouth drawn. Okay, so whatever he and Sarah had once had was shot to hell. He knew that. He also knew—for the sake of family harmony, if nothing else—he owed it to both of them, to everyone, to at least try to salvage something of the present.

Otherwise, he might never be able to sleep again.

He settled himself into an Adirondack chair on the front lawn, and waited.

Nothing was ever simple. The lamb's leg had refused to respond to her normal manipulative techniques, so she had to load the eighty-pound animal into the Bronco and take him into the clinic where she could do a radiograph and see exactly what was going on. Turned out the joint had been sheared in half right at the growing cartilage, with the farthest piece displaced sideways. That meant sedation—at one point, Sarah wondered if the thirteen-year-old Josh would need it more than the lamb—and some careful pulling and twisting until everything was lined up and she heard that reassuring "click" that indicated the joint had slipped back into place. If the animal managed to keep on the splints, with some careful tending he'd be just fine.

She hoped her own prognosis was as good.

As she pulled into the driveway, she muttered a prayer of gratitude that the Bronco wasn't a real horse that needed stabling. Cut the engine, go to bed…the day was over at last—

"What took you so long?"

With a little scream, she banged into the open car door, scraping her arm.

"Lord Almighty, Dean! You scared the hell out of me—"

"What took you so long?" he repeated.

"The call was more complicated than I expected, what do you think?" she lobbed back, rubbing her whacked arm. "That happens, far more often than I usually admit. And what on earth are you doing here at—what time *is* it…?" she tilted her watch up to the moonlight, squinted at it "—one-fourteen in the freakin' morning?"

She could make out broad shoulders lifting and falling, delineated by a thin outline of moonlight. "I couldn't sleep. So I took a walk, ended up here, saw you weren't and got worried."

"Well, here I am, nothing ate me on my way home, and I'm about to drop in my tracks." She slammed shut her car door. "I'm going to bed, if you don't mind." She started up the driveway toward the house, spinning around in shock when Dean grabbed her arm.

"We need to talk."

Oooh, no, she thought, smelling danger like a wolf. She was exhausted, and vulnerable, and the damp night hair had heightened Dean's scent far more than she knew she could safely handle.

"Look—if I don't want to talk to you when I'm awake, it's a sure bet I don't now." She jerked away from him and continued toward the house, awake enough to notice even that brief contact had sent a wave of shivers skittering over her arm. "Good night, Dean," she tossed over her shoulder.

She should have known it wouldn't be that easy.

"Sarah, I'm sorry—" she heard behind her "—I know it's way overdue, but I feel terrible about what happened between us."

Ignoring the little voice that said keep walking, don't respond, don't get into it, she whipped around. "And that's supposed to mean something to me? Please don't tell me you're that naive."

"I'm just trying to apologize here, if you'll give me half a chance—"

"You *are* that naive!" she countered, incredulous. She crossed her arms across her ribs so tightly it hurt. "Here's a flash for you, Parrish—apologies are what people do when there's some chance of making things better again. You could apologize for, maybe, being late for a date, or dialing a wrong number, or forgetting a birthday, even. There's no apology for what you did to me—"

"Give me a break, would you?" he shot back, his voice tight with restraint. "I was twenty years old and confused and stupid, all right?"

Her hands flew into the air as she backed away, shaking her head. "I don't want to hear this, Dean—"

She stumbled over something, which slowed her down enough for Dean to snag her wrist. "Well, too bad, because you're going to. You don't think I saw the hurt in your eyes tonight, every time I looked at you? You don't think I know why you took off before dinner? For God's sake, Sarah—this is *me*. Maybe it's been nine years since we saw each other, but I can still see inside your head better than anyone else."

He dropped her wrist; she stayed put, pinned by the electricity in his gaze.

"Running away isn't going to change anything, and you know it," he said, more softly. "And I don't think either one of us wants this crap hanging over our heads on Saturday. So let's have this out, right now, right here, so we can get on with our lives.''

She hesitated another few seconds, realized he'd just pester her to death until he had his say. "Okay." She let out on a short breath. "Talk."

A ragged sigh of relief floated over her head, but remorse flooded his features. "My aunt kept hammering away about how different we were, how you had all these goals, and I didn't. And your folks…I knew they liked me and all, but when things started to get serious between us, you don't think I knew what they were thinking, too?"

Before she could even think of what to say to that, he went on.

"And eventually, I thought, yeah, they were right…if I stayed around, if we got married, you probably wouldn't finish college, we'd end up having a couple of kids, and a few years down the road you'd realize you'd thrown your life away for some worthless high-school dropout with no future. I couldn't let that happen to you. So…I decided the best thing was to leave, to get away so you could do what you needed to do and I wouldn't get in your way. Especially…" He pinned her with tortured eyes. "Especially after we made love," he said, his voice low, the words arcing dangerously between them.

She went very, very still.

"No comment?"

All she could do was shake her head.

"Don't you see, honey? We'd gotten in way too deep. Even as a twenty-year-old airhead, I knew that much." He paused, still apparently expecting a reply. When there wasn't one, he added, "I loved you so much…and I didn't know what else to do, how to fix things." He lifted his hands, let them fall to his sides again. "It seemed to make sense at the time."

She stared at him for several seconds, the words not fitting together in any sort of logical order at first. Then, suddenly, they did, and her skin went cold.

"You *lied* to me?"

A breeze stirred the leaves overhead; something skittered

underneath the rhododendrons. ''Yes,'' he finally said. ''I lied. And what really sucks is that I can't even say I never meant to hurt you, because I did. I had to make you hate me, or I never would've been able to leave at all.''

She regarded him for another moment, her hands braced on the back of her hips. Her shoulder bag slipped, the strap banging into her forearm; she let it slide down to the ground, walked away a few steps, then strode back. ''All…all that business about hating Sweetbranch was an *act?*''

Dean ran his hand over his face, then through his hair. ''I never hated my home, Sarah. I didn't want to leave. But I thought I had no choice.''

''And this is somehow supposed to make me feel *better?*'' As the implications began to sink in, she felt bitterness choke her heart like bindweed—invasive, profuse and virtually impossible to get rid of. ''Let me get this straight—you lied to me, told me you'd never loved me, that you found everything about me and this town so boring you couldn't stand the thought of being here one minute longer, not even long enough to take me to my prom. And you did this because you *loved* me?''

He looked away, a muscle popping in his jaw.

''You *jerk!*'' she shrieked, taking a wild swing at him which he easily dodged. Tears of fury pricked at her eyes, but she would not let them come. She would *not*. What she did was walk away.

Twenty paces later, she found herself standing next to the forty-foot willow in the middle of the yard, one knee on the wrought-iron seat circling its base, her head and right hand resting on the trunk.

So. He *had* loved her, just as she thought. No—not as *she* thought. As *he* thought, in some convoluted manner unfathomable to her. She would never have just run from a problem, especially not a problem with Dean.

The suffocated laugh didn't even make it past her lips. Yeah, right. Who was she kidding? Hell, if running from problems was on Olympic event, she'd be a gold medalist.

Suddenly, she knew nothing about anything, except she was so very, very tired.

The grass rustled softly as Dean came closer; she didn't move. Despite the fury raging inside her, she realized how few males in her admittedly limited experience would have come clean the way Dean just had. Man had guts, she had to admit. Still, his confession wasn't going to eradicate the past, just like that.

"I cannot believe," she began, rocking her forehead on the top of her hand, "the only solution you saw to this so-called problem of our differences was to make me think everything we'd shared was a complete sham."

"You had all these plans," he said quietly, his voice as much of a caress as it had always been, "these dreams…and I let myself be convinced I couldn't be a part of all that." Her eyes actually hurt when she looked at him. He shrugged. "I told you…it was stupid."

Now she turned, collapsing like a rag doll on the bench, her back against the tree. She could only see his silhouette. Just as well.

"Oh, what you did goes way beyond stupid, Dean. You didn't care enough to even attempt to talk about what was bothering you. To see if we could work this out together. That concept completely eluded you. Instead, you made me feel like some cheap throwaway who wasn't worth even losing a little sleep over. Do you have any idea what that summer was like for me, Dean? After you left? Do you?"

After a long pause, he said, "They told me you got sick. Mono, right?"

She hadn't expected he'd known that. Momentarily thrown, she scrambled for her next sentence. "Before that. Of course I missed the prom, which, like any normal teenage girl, I'd been looking forward to since the first day of high school. But then, I was supposed to give the valedictorian speech at graduation, remember? I didn't want to read from cards, 'cause I always thought that looked tacky, so I memorized the speech.

Except, I blanked.'' Her laugh was harsh. ''Couldn't remember one single word. I was completely humiliated.''

Even in the dark, she could see his posture turn defensive. ''You blame me for that?''

''It's a known fact that sleep deprivation causes severe loss of memory function. And I couldn't sleep…*at all*…for three weeks after you left.''

He swore.

''My sentiments exactly.'' Several beats passed. ''I'd never planned on saying any of this to you, you know, considering I didn't think I'd lay eyes on you again. But since we're playing True Confessions tonight and I'm so tired I don't give a flying fig what comes out of my mouth, you might as well know exactly how much you hurt me. And trust me, telling me nine years later that none of it was true doesn't do a damn thing to erase what I felt *during* those nine years.''

''I didn't think it would,'' he shot back. She saw his hand snake around to the back of his neck. ''But it didn't seem to make any sense to let you continue to think it, either.'' He hesitated, then sat down beside her in such a way she had no choice but to meet his gaze. She did chose, however, to ignore the pain she saw there. If she acknowledged it, she would lose her advantage. That was not an option. ''I know I screwed up, Sarah. I also know, no matter what I do, I can't turn back the clock. I'm not trying to fix something that can't be fixed.''

Again, she had nothing to say to that.

His head fell back against the trunk. ''Does it still hurt?'' he asked gently. Too gently. Like the old Dean. Like *her* Dean, the one who'd always protected her, supported her. Loved her.

''No,'' she lied. ''I got on with my life. Which as you can see is going pretty well. Now, if you don't mind…'' She slapped her thighs with the palms of her hands, then pushed herself off the bench. ''I really need to get some sleep—''

He'd risen when she did and spun her around so his face was inches from hers. His heat was everywhere—in his touch, in his breath on her face, in the feral glint in his eyes. Just like it had been the night they'd become lovers. She gasped, softly, from arousal, from the lingering betrayal, from a determination not to react to any of it.

"Maybe it doesn't hurt you anymore," Dean said in a fierce whisper, "but I can't say the same for myself. I had no idea the pain would bounce back on me like a back draft, consuming my every waking thought. And there are a lot of waking thoughts, because you're not the only one who lost a great deal of sleep after we broke up."

"That's too bad," Sarah said, attempting to pull away. But his grip strengthened.

"Sarah, listen to me! Whether you ever forgive me or not, you *will* understand how much I regret hurting you the way I did. How much I regret what I lost."

Every muscle in her body tensed, her fingers curling into fists as she resisted the urge to slug him. "And exactly how long have you felt like this?"

"Since the moment you ran out of my room, nine years ago."

For a stunned moment or two, jubilation and fury warred in her head, only to be swiftly eclipsed by as a sense of bitter hopelessness, as it hit her, hard, just how much his confession upped the stakes. Oh, dear Lord...how different things might have been, if she'd only known, if he'd bothered to say something sooner...

"All this time..." She shook her head. "You know, Atlanta's only two hours away. And we've always had a phone, even way out here in the boonies. We get regular mail deliveries, too—"

"I get the point," he said with a sad smile. "But I figured you probably hated my guts. And..." He sighed, looking up for a moment. "I still thought I'd done the right thing, for a long time. By the time I realized I hadn't, I figured it was too late—"

"Yes, it is," she said, grasping at anything that would stop this, right now. She knew he was genuinely sorry, knew he meant every word he'd said. But she didn't dare let his contrition get to her. She was only safe as long as he was still the bad guy.

"It *is* too late, Dean. So you know what I think? I think, if that cozy scene in the kitchen a few hours ago is any indication, what you want is another roll in the pine needles. You've got a first-class case of the hots, is all that's going on here.'' She planted both palms on his chest and pushed away from him. ''In your dreams, buddy boy. Go on back to Atlanta and find yourself some big-city sweetie to scratch your itch. This hick ain't puttin' out, you hear?''

She picked up her bag from where she'd dropped it on the lawn earlier and hoofed it toward the house.

''Dammit, Sarah!'' he roared, probably waking up everyone within a five-mile radius. ''You haven't heard a single word I've said!''

''Go home, Dean,'' she called over her shoulder, praying Katey, at least, was sleeping through this. ''Nothing's changed.''

''*I've* changed, Sarah,'' she heard behind her. ''Hey— I can even read without moving my lips now, did you know that?''

His words slashed through her. But she didn't stop.

''We're going to be family, Sarah Louise,'' he said, more softly but no less importunately. ''For Jen's and Lance's sake, at least, we need to get past this.''

She'd gotten as far as the porch steps; now she turned, one hand gripping the newel post, and saw he'd followed her across the yard. He stood with his hands clenched at his sides, solid and determined and dangerous. His eyes glistened in the moonlight, and she thought once again how impossible, how easy it would be to let herself succumb to his entreaties.

And how wrong she'd been. *Everything* had changed between them. More than he even knew.

Dean stepped closer, his mouth drawn. ''Look, I told you— I don't expect things to get back the way they were between us, especially not after all this time. All I'm asking is for you to see me as I am *now*.''

She waited until the first, then the second, wave of pain passed, before she said, quietly, ''I'm not sure I can do that.''

The man she once loved with everything she had in her glared at her for several seconds, then turned and strode off into the darkness.

Chapter 4

"*Idiot!*"

Dean kicked the mailbox post at the end of the Whitehouses' driveway, then slammed his palm against the sturdy metal box. "Stupid, stupid, stupid..." He repeated the word like a bizarre mantra for several seconds, then rasped his smarting hand across a stubbled cheek.

Gee, Parrish. You handled that real *well.*

She'd said she didn't want to talk. He could have waited until morning, maybe found some time when she was at least a little more receptive. But no-o-o—he had to blurt out some sorry-assed confession that made him sound even more callous than he'd been originally.

Dean was beginning to wonder if making stupid moves was part of his genetic makeup, or his destiny, or karma, or whatever the term was these days for repeating your mistakes.

He stared at the dark house for a moment longer, then finally hauled his butt back down the road, not wanting to go back to his aunt's house, not knowing what to do, as razor-sharp fragments of emotions churned inside him.

Okay. She was right. He *had* lied. And she had every right to be furious.

But he hadn't lied just then, and he didn't know how to make her understand he never would again.

Ten minutes later, he halted in front of Percy Jenkins's pasture, bordered with a haphazard post-and-rail fence he remembered the cows always seemed to take on faith was meant to keep them off the road.

His chuckle sounded bitter in his own ears. Lord. A lousy pasture, a few rotting timbers, and down reminiscence road he went. Oh, what the hell, Dean thought on a sigh, ominous in the heavy silence. Might as well get 'em all thought out and used up and done with. Maybe then he'd get some peace.

He leaned against the rickety fence and surveyed the moon-washed pasture, its emptiness bringing him an odd sort of comfort as he thought about cows and Sarah and old fences. They'd be out walking, passing this way, and the easygoing beasts would amble up to the so-called barrier, sticking their massive heads over the top with soft snorts and snuffles, knowing Sarah would always stop and rub their noses and shoot the breeze with them, just as if they were people.

She always did have a way with cows, you know?

For several seconds longer he stared into the silver-laced darkness, fighting. Then, at last, he lowered his head onto his arms and let the tears come.

The sun had been up for some time when he finished his hour-long jog. Which had had little positive effect, except perhaps to sweat a couple of quarts of poisons from his body. He'd meant to shower as soon as he got back, change out of his sleeveless sweatshirt and running shorts, but the scent of coffee lured him into the kitchen—where his aunt's trenchant gaze slammed into him as she sat with her own cup of coffee at the chrome-and-Formica table in the center of the room. Only a desperate need for caffeine kept him from doing an about-face.

It was nearly eight-thirty; he was surprised to see her still in her pastel-flowered housecoat and slippers. But her thinning gray-blond hair was pulled back into its customary bun, not a single wisp allowed free of its confines, putting the world on notice that she was ready to face the challenges of the day, hardheaded nephews included. His head throbbed in spite of the exercise, his eyes were gritty, and his brain felt sand-bagged: this he did not need.

Ethel Parrish had fifteen years on Dean's father, had been married once, briefly, before he was born, but that was all he knew. He also knew she'd never resented taking on her nephews, including an eight-year-old, and she'd treated them well. That didn't mean she was particularly easy to get along with.

She didn't start in right away, which meant she was mulling over her plan of attack. Damn—it was much worse when she'd had time to think about what she wanted to say. Keeping a wary eye out in case she pounced, Dean found a bag of English muffins in the bread box, slipped one into the toaster.

The night, or what had been left of it, had been hell. Knowing sleep wasn't in the cards, he hadn't even bothered undressing. In fact, the only part of him that *had* fallen asleep was his backside, gone dead from sitting in the glider on his aunt's porch for three hours while his thoughts tumbled around in his aching head like laundry in a dryer. But at least he could say the time hadn't been wasted. Not by a long shot. Because, by the time somebody's rooster a farm or two away started its raucous crowing at 5:00 a.m., he'd come to a number of conclusions, not the least of which was that Sarah Whitehouse had become an unreasonable, pigheaded, oversensitive pain in the neck and he was better off without her.

Oh, sure, his ego had taken it on the chin when she'd refused to listen to him, when she insisted his intentions toward her were less than circumspect. It had hurt. But now, in the day-light, he supposed he'd been the victim of some sort of nos-talgic fantasy. That seeing her, after all this time…well, it wouldn't be the first time his imagination had taken off without him.

Despite a physical attraction so intense it scared him, it was perfectly obvious now that nothing but guilt had driven him over there last night.

The muffin leapt out of the toaster, making him jump. He snatched it, wincing as the heat seared through his calluses, and dropped it onto a plate.

So, hey—if she wasn't interested in what he had to say, he sure wasn't going to bust his butt over it. Besides, there were other women who'd listen to him just fine. Lots of 'em. Especially in Atlanta.

Which had led him to debunking Nostalgic Fantasy Number Two, which was that Sweetbranch was no more a part of his life these days than Sarah was. After all, he had a thriving business in Atlanta which was just about to expand; he had even already looked at a couple of possible factory sites. Upward of a dozen people worked for him, depended on him; with the expansion, that number could easily grow to fifty. More.

That he hated living in a big city, he thought as he finally pulled himself together enough to butter the muffin, couldn't be allowed to factor into the equation. He'd made his economic bed in Atlanta, so that's where he'd have to lie for the foreseeable future. Even if it killed him.

Carrying the muffin with him, he found his way to the coffeemaker and filled the cup nearest to his shaking hand, refusing to look again at his aunt until he'd taken at least three large swallows of the brew. The instant he clunked the cup onto the counter, though, she said, "Heard you go out last night."

He pivoted his torso only as much as necessary to face her, managing to form a tiny, contrite smile. Anything larger hurt too much. "Sorry. I wake you?"

"No." She scrutinized him from between slitted, bald eyelids. "What were you doing?"

"Just went for a walk." Another swallow of coffee.

"Where?"

He was beginning to remember why leaving hadn't been as difficult as it might have been. He finally turned all the way to her, leaning against the front of the sink. "Nowhere in particular. Just couldn't sleep.'' Inside his skull, a marching band began drill practice.

"Heard Sarah Whitehouse's truck go by about one. You go to meet her?''

Dean clamped a hand to his head to stop the pounding. "No.'' Which was the truth, after all.

"No sense digging up old bones.''

"Yes, I know.'' He lowered his hand, then blinked, carefully. "I wouldn't worry myself, if I were you.'' He finished off the coffee, rinsed out the cup and set it upside down on the dish towel on the counter. "After my shower, I'm going up to the house. See what condition it's in.''

The blue eyes brightened. "You fixin' to sell it, finally?''

The headache made him contrary. "Haven't made up my mind yet.''

You had to hand it to Miss Clarissa Ellis, Sarah mused as she gingerly sat on a velvet wing chair in the lady's living room, nursing her second cup of coffee. The woman sure knew her way around a Singer. For more than forty years, the tiny brunette had been considered the town's high priestess of fashion. Of course, in her heyday, women still wore elegant clothes, at least some of the time, at least in Alabama, enough, anyway, that Miss Ellis could easily keep five or six seamstresses busy. Nowadays, though, there wasn't much call for custom-made clothing, except for the occasional wedding party.

Which was why Sarah was currently being held hostage by a dozen yards of baby-pig-pink polyester organza and a gazillion pins, in a room with five twenty-two-year-old women with perky breasts and perky fannies and even perkier high-pitched voices, four of whom were swathed in bilious lavender clones of Sarah's dress.

Sarah had flatly refused to wear lavender. If she had to spend an afternoon looking like a butch Little Bo-Peep, so be it. But filial devotion only went so far. So Jennifer agreed, reluctantly, that Sarah could wear pink, her sister's *second* favorite color. All Sarah could say was, at least it wasn't lavender.

Now, if she could just talk Jen out of the *hat*.

"Sarah Louise?"

Oh, joy. That would be Melanie, Jennifer's best friend. Blond curls, violet eyes, pink cheeks. Shirley Temple with boobs. On her, lavender made sense.

Sarah tried to smile. "Yes?"

"Jennifer says Lance's brother's back. And that he's *real* cute."

Just the person she wanted to talk about. She shrugged. "He's okay, I guess. If you like that type."

Melanie giggled, curls and bosoms bouncing in sync. The girl was nothing if not talented. "He's gorgeous, he's got a good business going, and he's male. With a capital *M,* if even half of what I hear is true. What's not to like?"

"Don't get your drawers in a twist, Melanie. He's only here for a week."

"A week, huh?" Two of the cutest dimples you ever did see popped out as Melanie flashed a smile. "Honey, that's *more* than enough time." The lips pouted. "Unless…you have some sort of claim on him? I mean, you're not going with him to the Jenkinses' pot luck tomorrow or anything, are you?"

Girls like this should come with warning labels. Sarah stretched her lips into what she hoped looked like a smile but which probably more nearly resembled an iguana's smirk. "Me? Heavens, no." She waved at the young woman with the back of her hand. "Have at him, honey. With my blessings."

The girls all tittered—loudly—and Sarah cringed. She loved her sister dearly, but one of her was quite enough, thank you. *Five* Jennifers was cause for Alka-Seltzer.

She'd have to make do with coffee. That, at least, was something to be grateful for. Black, hot, there. All the criteria neatly met in one steaming cup. Sarah sipped, sighed, and tried to lean back in the chair without doing herself major damage. Miss Ellis, her mouth full of pins, was holding forth about how she had gone to this huge wedding in Atlanta and the bridal

gown came from this really fancy salon named Fairchild's—
and would you lift your arm, darlin'?—and the owner now
manufactured her own line of bridal gowns but had still custom
designed this absolutely stunning dress for the bride and do
you know Thelma Rose Entwhistle told her it cost nearly ten
thousand dollars?

They all gasped, right on cue, then proceeded to assure the
dressmaker that *her* dresses were every bit as pretty, they were
sure, and how clever of her to be able to make them for such
reasonable prices.

Sarah rested her head on the back of the chair and shut her
eyes. This was proving to be the longest morning in the history
of mankind. She hadn't slept at all, she had to go into the clinic
in the afternoon, her head hurt and the dress itched. And
through it all needled the intense desire to throttle the living
daylights out of Dean Parrish.

Somewhere around 3:00 a.m., after she'd gone over his
"confession" for at least the hundredth time, she'd finally
heard what he was saying.

So what was with this inferiority business, anyway? How
could he have possibly thought he would have ever gotten in
her way, as if loving him would have ever interfered with her
career goal? And how the hell did he figure he was worthless
just because he hadn't finished high school? Good Lord—it
wasn't as if she hadn't been aware of his problem, considering
how many tests she'd tried to help him pass. But if there was
one thing Dean Parrish wasn't, it was stupid.

The more she thought about it, the madder she got, because
the more she thought about it, the more it sure sounded as if
he was saying *she* hadn't been smart enough to know he wasn't
good enough for her, so he played the big macho man and
made the decision for her.

The toad.

Someone told an off-color joke, sending Melanie into par-
oxysms of shrill laughter. Itchy and bitchy, Sarah decided Melanie Kincaid was just about what Dean deserved. She couldn't
wait to see him squirm out of those L'Oréal-polished claws.

Which he would, right? I mean, Melanie wasn't even his type…right?

She flicked a glance at Bubbles and started to chew on a hangnail.

Hey—whatever happened, there wasn't anything she could say, was there? She was the one who'd made it clear they had nothing to say to each other, right?

Right?

She switched fingers and started in on another hangnail.

She wished she could figure out what was really going on in Dean's head. His eyes—remorseful, haunted—slipped into her thought just as the anger slipped out of it. Again.

Oh, no, you don't, she thought, snatching it back, cramming it down by her heart.

They're just eyes, girl. And he's just a man. Remember that.
Like she could forget.

Her nipples heaved against her bra the same time this little tingling sensation jolted through a part of her body she basically had no use for. She squirmed.

And swore.

Six sets of eyes turned to her, six mouths open in midsentence. She smiled, pointed to her ribs, prayed her skin was a normal color. "Pin."

The eyes turned away and the mouths resumed their conversations.

Remember what happened the last time you let those little tingling sensations have their way?

She wiggled in the chair again as if she could get away from her treacherous body, winced, then sank her chin into her hand and stared out the window. Oh, crud…she knew him too well, knew he wasn't going to give up on this fence-mending business, just because she'd told him, more or less, to go to hell. Which meant he was only going to keep getting in her way. Which meant…

Melanie giggled again, and Sarah dredged up a little smile.

Throwing him off the scent, she believed this was called.

* * *

There were more memories than cobwebs in the old farm-house, invading Dean's psyche as insistently as the musty, closed-up smell invaded his nostrils.

As farmhouses go, it was fairly modest—large kitchen, dining room, living room downstairs; three bedrooms and a bath upstairs. But it had been pretty, once. Before his father died. Granted, his mother would never have won an award for her housekeeping, caring much more about her crafts than whether or not anyone could eat off her kitchen floor, which, as she pointed out, was rather silly, if you thought about it. Otherwise, why have dishes?

But the house had always been in good shape, even if he and Lance and his father had had to constantly shift piles of books and magazines and assorted crafts supplies from chair to table to floor, even if the house always smelled of hot glue and varnish and dried flowers. His father had kept it in excellent repair and both inside and out got fresh coats of paint religiously every three years.

However, Dean's father had died when Dean was fourteen, his mother falling ill almost immediately afterward. It had been impossible for Dean to take care of her, his brother, and the house all at the same time. And houses are like spoiled women: they need constant cosseting in order to look their best. By the time Marion Parrish died, the house was already showing signs of neglect; now, years later, it made a perfect setting for a Stephen King movie.

As if protesting being disturbed after all this time, the tilted floors screaked mournfully as Dean walked through the virtually empty house. Most of the furniture had either been sold or given away after his mother's death, Ethel insisting there was no reason to keep it. But, here and there, a few pieces remained, having had no takers for whatever reason. Not because of their worthlessness, however, since his father's skill had long been admired.

The ample living room with its oak-manteled fireplace was bare except for a corner hutch his father had made, a simple pine piece, not too big. His mother had displayed some of her handmade dolls on the top shelf, kept sewing supplies behind the doors on the bottom.

Then there was that buffet in the dining room that had belonged, he believed, to his mother's grandmother. Ash, he discovered as he wiped away a thick layer of dust from a small section of the massive piece. The stain had darkened over the years to an oppressive umber color which pretty much matched his mood. He made a mental note to strip and restain it. Maybe Jennifer and Lance might like it. Or he could take it back to Atlanta, sell it there.

He pushed open the obligatory swinging door to the kitchen, which was retro before retro was "in," with its black-and-white linoleum tile and glass-paned cabinets. Great gaping holes coated with stringy, fuzzy webs indicated where the stove and refrigerator had been; the walls had aged to a putrid mustard color. Sarah had always hated that color, even when it was new—

He sucked in his breath. Why on earth should he care what Sarah thought? He was selling the house, he was going back to Atlanta, that part of his life was over.

Period.

Wiping thoughts of Sarah out of his mind as easily as he wiped dust off his hands, he left the kitchen and went upstairs, made an expeditious tour of the equally barren rooms on the top story, then came back down, just in time to hear the muffled clatter of a bicycle being hastily abandoned out by the front porch. He peered out the front window, saw the child's bike. Frowning, he opened the front door, started, then felt his lips curve into a smile of genuine pleasure.

"Katey? What are you doing here, honey?"

She offered him a shrug and a gap-toothed grin in that order, then climbed up the front steps onto the porch, long braids bouncing against the front of her canary-yellow T-shirt as she ascended. "Thought I saw your truck go by a little while ago and wondered if this was where you were going." She craned her neck, looking past him into the house. "I've never seen inside."

Taking his cue, Dean stepped aside and let Katey in, re-minding himself not to hold the little girl's resemblance to her oldest sister against her. "You've been here before?"

Katey meandered over to the hutch and tugged at a bottom door until it popped open with a loud scraping sound, the force bouncing her into the wall. "Lots," she said, absently rubbing the seat of her matching yellow shorts with one hand as she straightened up. She yanked open the other door and looked inside, but since it was empty she withdrew her head, then shut both doors at once.

Dean stood with his hands on his hips as he watched the child explore the house with the ingenuousness of a kitten. "How come?"

Another shrug, then: "I don't know. I was out riding my bike one day and just sort of found it, I guess. It's pretty and quiet and cool under those pine trees out back. You know there're ducks in the pond?"

"Still?" He hadn't been out to the pine grove yet. Couldn't bear it, he didn't think.

"Oh, yeah. Like a zillion of 'em. Anyway—" Katey crossed the hall into the dining room, immediately investigating the buffet with the same detached thoroughness as she had the hutch "—I was telling everyone about it at dinner one night and Lance said it sounded like the house the two of you lived in with your parents and would I take him to see it and I said, sure. So I did, and it is. Was, I mean. Your house." She skimmed one finger over the top of the buffet. "It's neat. You gonna live here again?"

"Actually, I'm thinking about selling it."

Katey twitched her head up to him, her brows arched over deep amber eyes. "Why would you do that?"

"I live in Atlanta, Katey. I sure don't need a house here."

The little girl regarded him as if trying to read his mind, swishing the end of one braid against the palm of her hand, then headed for the stairs. "You goin' to that big potluck at the Jenkinses' tomorrow?" She threw the question over her shoulder as she walked up, deliberately grinding her sneakers against the bare treads.

Dean was beginning to acclimate to the constant subject-switching. As he followed Katey, he asked, "Is that the one your sisters were talking about last night? A wedding anniversary or something?"

"Uh-huh." Her high, soft voice echoed in the stairwell. "Their fiftieth. Since they don't have kids, everybody thought'd be neat if the neighbors gave 'em a party instead." She peered into each bedroom, which were all empty except for Dean's parents' room, which had an old thirties wardrobe on one wall. Naturally, Katey headed for it like a bee to a flower and yanked open one mirrored door.

"It's a surprise party," she said, bending her head back to see if anything lurked on the top shelf. "Mama's…taking them—" she backed up farther and stood on tiptoe "—to the movies in Opelika in the afternoon while everyone gets the party ready." Then she pulled open one of the cedar-lined drawers. And uttered a little cry of discovery. "Ooh…how pretty!"

Amazed the child had actually unearthed something, he crossed to her. "What is it?"

"A quilt or somethin'."

It was a quilt. Dean swallowed hard. The quilt that had been on his parents' bed. With a great deal of sideline encouragement from his new friend, he lifted it out of the drawer that had kept it safe and intact for so long and reverently unfolded it. His great-grandmother had made it, his mother had said. As a child, he'd always been fascinated by the whirling colors that somehow all fitted together into the beautiful pattern. It had a name, the pattern did, but he couldn't remember it. What he did remember was creeping into his parents' room of a Sunday morning and seeing them cuddled underneath the kaleidoscope of colors, his father's face usually buried in his mother's abundant dark hair, holding her close against his chest as they slept. To Dean, this was far more than a pretty covering for a bed. The quilt meant love. Security.

Happiness. As much as anyone's allowed in this lifetime.

A bittersweet pang of longing and regret constricted his heart for a moment. While it was a shame his parents only had fifteen years together, maybe, what time they did have was full and rich and real.

He'd never felt so alone.

"Dean? You okay?"

The quilt still clutched in his hands, he turned his attention to the beautiful child at his side, her familiar eyes full of concern. "I'm sorry, honey. This…" He lifted up the quilt. "This just brought back a lot of memories." Quickly, he refolded it and replaced it in the drawer.

"Aren't you gonna take it?"

"Not just yet. Right now, it still belongs here."

Katey nodded as if that made sense to her, then took the lead and headed out of the room and down the stairs, Dean once again tagging behind. Seconds later, they were sitting on the porch steps.

"You gotta come, Dean. Everyone's goin' to be there."

He'd clearly dropped a thread somewhere between the upstairs and the porch. "Come to what?"

She gave a tolerant sigh. "To the Jenkinses' party. Remember?"

"Oh. Yes." He frowned. "I don't know, honey…"

"Please?" She lifted cow eyes to him and Dean wondered how many young men down the road would commit foolish deeds in honor of those eyes. "Jennifer's going to be there with Lance, and Mama's going to be busy with all the food, and I think Sarah's bringing Ed, so I'm going to be all by myself."

"Ed?"

"I told you about Ed. He's the other vet at the clinic."

"Oh…right." Suddenly, this party looked more interesting. And he thought of the quilt and his parents and the strange longing the quilt had caused in his belly. And he thought, again, how lonely he was. Successful, yes. Busy, yes. But lonely just the same. And God, he was tired of being lonely.

"Sure, Katey," he said with a decisive nod, wondering if he'd always been this masochistic, or was only just now noticing it. "Sure, I'll go. But..." He gave her a broad wink. "Only if you'll be my date."

"Really?" she said, her eyes even bigger.

"You bet, honey."

The child's grin exploded into brilliance as she stuck out her hand to clinch the deal. "You can pick me up at four."

It was one of those days hot enough to weld Sarah's feet to her sandals, the midday sun eking through a scrim of yellow-gray clouds promising nothing but mugginess. As planned, Vivian carted the Jenkinses away to a two o'clock movie in Opelika, leaving Sarah "in charge" of the party that was to be in place when her mother brought the couple back.

Sarah now stood on the Jenkinses' front porch, tugging at the sodden front of her T-shirt and watching helplessly as two dozen women armed with mountains of Tupperware and foil-covered pans and plates and bowls descended on the old couple's house like a hailstorm. Half of them landed in the kitchen, yakking and getting in each other's way as they went about doing all those last-minute chores that women always seem to have to do at these things, never mind that all the food was supposed to be ready when they got there. The other half milled around in the backyard, yakking and getting in each other's way as they set up card tables and snapped out permanent-press tablecloths to cover them and set the pans and plates and bowls on top of that, every woman coming behind every other woman and shifting her dish to a more advantageous position.

There were husbands, and children, too, who'd come with the women. The first group had serious business to tend to, namely scrutinizing Tom Rogers's new Ford pickup; while the kids took off for the pasture or the barn to play until their mothers called them to eat.

Anything to keep out of the way of the women.

Realizing she was superfluous, keeping out of their way soon became Sarah's goal as well. Not that Sarah was without a project, however—before she'd left, her mother had handed her two naked cake layers and a bowl of fudge frosting and said, just be sure most of this actually gets on the cake, young lady. Sarah was in the process of frosting said cake in the most out-of-the-way corner of the kitchen she could find—and repeatedly sampling the contents of the bowl—when she heard a familiar honk in the driveway.

She stuck the spatula in the frosting, wriggled through assorted womenfolk, then ran through the house, banging back the screen door and consequently letting in at least a dozen flies. "You bring the Cokes?" she shouted in the direction of the white Jeep Cherokee parked almost out to the road.

"Hello to you, too, and of course I brought the Cokes," Ed Stillman yelled back, leaning one long arm and a broadly grinning face out of the car window. "The real stuff, too. None of this caffeine-free junk."

She laughed. "Man after my own heart. Bring 'em on in," she said with a wave. "We'll put them in a cooler."

"You sure you're ready for this?" she asked a minute later with a waggle of her eyebrows as he threaded his way through the horde of cackling women, each of whom tossed him a curious glance without missing a beat in her conversation.

Thick black brows dipped over eyes nearly the same color as the frosting. "Now you're making me nervous. What, exactly, should I be ready for?" He thunked the Cokes up on the counter.

"Speculation, for one thing," Sarah said, jerking her head backward to indicate who would be doing the speculating. She licked her fingers. It was such a messy job.

Ed deliberately leaned closer. "They looking yet?" he whispered, teasing.

Sarah peeked over her shoulder; a dozen sets of eyes all darted elsewhere.

"Yep." Attempting to swirl the icing like her mother did, she made a little hole in the cake which she had to patch. A ceiling fan groaned lethargically overhead, making more noise than breeze. "Told you."

"Well…" He stuck a finger in the bowl and scooped out a generous dollop of frosting, for which he got his knuckle rapped with the spatula. "You'll just have to tell 'em the truth." He stuck the gooey finger in his mouth, then frowned, eyeing the lopsided cake. "Your mother's actually letting you do this?"

"She's *making* me do this." Sarah sighed, then looked askance at him. "And what, exactly, is the truth?"

"That you had your chance." Bony shoulders lifted in a shrug. "But you blew it. After all—" he swiped another fingerful of icing "—*I* thought we'd make a great team. Look how well we worked together getting those twin calves out of old man Kramer's cow last month."

"Uh-huh," Sarah said, moving the bowl out of Ed's reach. "And a cow is just what your mother would have if you and I got hitched. And I refuse to have your mother's demise on my head."

Ed's eyes became slits. "Now, *there's* an odd picture." Then he sighed, reached around Sarah for more frosting. "But you're right. And, not being one to sit around and pine over unrealized fantasies, I'll have you know I have a date later this evening."

"A date? As in, you go pick up some woman at her house and take her out to dinner and movies?"

"You've been on one?"

She smacked him again with the spatula, then noticed his huge grin. "Let me guess. This girl, you mother would like."

"This girl, my mother would *marry*…" He stared at the cake while absently tugging at his earlobe. "Uh…Sarah?"

"Yeah?"

"It's dead, honey. Let it go."

Sarah rubbed the side of her nose with her knuckle, then sighed. "It is rather free-form, isn't it? Oh, well…" Unaffected, she pushed the cake away and leaned back against the counter, picking up the bowl and handing him a spoon. "So…tell me about this girl."

"Mmm…" Ed mumbled around a mouthful of frosting.

"No girl. *Woman.* Rebecca Goldberg. Thirty-two, five-seven, red hair, blue eyes, with a drool-inducing figure and a brain to match. She's a visiting prof over the summer at Auburn in architectural engineering. Heads a small but very prestigious firm in Atlanta, so she's back and forth a lot. Daddy's a doctor, Mama's a lawyer, and they give very generously to their temple." Ed paused, considering, then said, "Yep. That about covers it."

Sarah's mouth hiked into a half smile. "You bozo...this isn't your first date with her, is it?"

"Uh, no," he admitted, scraping the side of the bowl with the spoon. "We've been seeing each other for a couple of months."

Sarah let out a guffaw as she waved her spoon for emphasis. "Have you told her yet that your idea of a good time is spending an afternoon in a stinky barn dodging kicks from crazed equines? How on earth did you even meet her?"

"She's been into the clinic a couple of times." At Sarah's raised brows, he explained. "Becca also has six cats and two dogs. Marrying a vet would be extremely cost-effective for her."

"Marrying?"

"I know. I didn't believe it, either."

Sarah shook her head in amazement, then drew her brows together. "So how come you didn't bring her today?"

"She's in Atlanta. Won't get back until about eight." He paused. "She's, um, preparing her parents."

"Oh, brother." Sarah scanned the Ichabod Crane double leaning against the counter next to her, all bones and furry skin and spongy hair, attired in a pair of faded cutoffs that were more fringe than fabric and a woebegone Yankees T-shirt her mother wouldn't even have used as a rag. "And what, exactly, is she preparing them for?"

"Hey, I clean up good."

"I sure hope so, for your sake. As well as hers." Then she held out her arms. "I'm real happy for you, you big doofus. Congratulations." She put her hands on his shoulders and pulled him into a hug, breaking into giggles at the instant hush that fell over the room.

"Where do you want the paper plates?"

She broke the hug at the sound of Katey's voice, looking down into the little girl's face. "Hey, baby—when did you get here? Did Jennifer bring you?"

"No," rumbled a deep voice. "I did."

Glittering green eyes collided with hers, just as two disparate thoughts collided in her brain. The first was that the nettled expression on Dean's face was more than worth whatever other indignities the week might bring. The other was that she suddenly remembered how much she and Dean used to joke and tease and banter, just like she was doing with Ed. And how, more than anything else, she missed their friendship.

Blinking back the sting of unexpected tears, she smiled at Katey and pointed to the backyard. "Put the plates out there with the cups and stuff. You'll see which table."

"Okay," the little girl replied, taking Dean's hand. "Dean's my *date*," she announced, looking up at Sarah from underneath silky eyelashes.

"Oh, I see," Sarah replied, trying to sound pleased, not daring to look at Dean. "Well, just make sure he gets you home by midnight."

With a fluttering giggle, Katey pulled Dean through the back door and out into the shady backyard. Sarah watched them through the screen door, her arms folded across her middle, praying for something she had no right to pray for.

"Care to tell me what that was all about?"

She'd forgotten Ed was there. "Hmm?"

Ed finally relinquished the frosting bowl, shoving it to the back of the counter, then slid one arm around her shoulder. "Come on—let's go find someplace where no one'll bother us, and you can tell Father Confessorstein all about it."

But not all confessions are created equal, she mused, allowing a half smile. "Give 'em more food for thought, huh?"

He gave her shoulder a nice, brotherly squeeze. "It's what I live for, sweetheart."

Chapter 5

So that was Ed, Dean mused as, through the screen door, he watched them leave the kitchen.

He suspected Katey was right about the relationship. No chemistry, he was sure. Sarah's hugging him didn't mean anything, either, he told himself; she'd always been demonstrative.

He sucked in a deep breath, corralling his thoughts. So…if he knew there was nothing between Sarah and Ed, and more important, there was also nothing between Sarah and *Dean*, what were all these jealous thoughts pinging around in his brain?

"Dean Parrish!" Vivian called. "Get your carcass over here. Someone wants to see you!"

He glanced over in the direction of the summons to see Vivian escorting one very stunned—and tickled pink—elderly couple toward him, swarmed as they were by a horde of well-wishers, through which he caught Amanda Jenkins's broad, partially toothless grin.

"Wouldja lookit there, Percy! Ha-*ha!* Come 'ere, boy!"

Smiling, Dean worked his way through the crowd. "I

thought that was you ridin' around in that fancy truck!'' The old woman wrapped Dean's cheeks in her work-worn hands and drew his face down to hers, planting a noisy kiss on his forehead. "Vivian told us you was comin' back for the wedding." She let him go and chuckled, her hands on prodigious hips. "If I was forty years younger and didn't have this old coot around—" her thumb jerked in the direction of her husband, a thin man with strings of black hair combed over a bald spot, a long-suffering smile plastered to his craggy face "— I'd be all over you like honey on a biscuit. Whoo-*ee,* if you're not the best-lookin' thing I've seen in a dog's age. Ain't that right, Katey?'' she said with a hug for the little girl. "Don't you think your sister's gonna have the handsomest brother-in-law in all of Lee County?''

While Katey said her "yes, ma'ams,'' Dean wished he could drop into a hole somewhere. Amanda Jenkins had a voice that could be heard clear to Montgomery, and not all the females at this shindig were old and married. In fact, one particular blonde had put the bead on him before the engine had cooled in his truck. A few years ago, he might've sidled up to the pretty young thing and played along, seen just how far he could get.

But that was a few years ago.

So, today, when those violet eyes riveted to his, the small white teeth flashed their brightest, he just returned the smile out of politeness. Then he took Katey's hand in his and moved to another part of the Jenkinses' backyard, hoping Miss Congeniality would take the hint.

Still, from the moment he'd arrived, the feeling of community, he reckoned it was, nearly knocked him for a loop. Maybe everybody knew everybody else's business, sure, but everybody cared about everybody else, too. He'd missed that sense of belonging, more than he'd realized.

Over his thwomping heartbeat, he turned his attention to the food. And my oh my, this was one impressive spread, even for this part of the world. The Jenkinses' picnic table boasted the main courses—mountains of fried chicken, hams, barbecued ribs, tender shreds of pork barbecue, chicken and stuffing casserole—while a herd of wobbly card tables groaned under the weight of salads set in bowls of ice, more casseroles, breads, desserts. Something that passed for a breeze stirred the leaves overhead, the tablecloth hems, but there was no getting away from the heat. Not that anyone's appetite seemed the least affected.

Especially Ed Stillman's.

Towering over everyone in the food line, the vet grinned and nodded in reply as this or that person addressed him while he helped himself to a little of everything in sight. Dean quickly surveyed the crowd; Sarah was nowhere around. Guiding Katey by the shoulders, he sidled in beside the man. Ed looked up, saw them, smiled.

"Sorry…we didn't get introduced back there in the kitchen." He stuck out his hand, somehow balancing his precariously loaded plate. "Ed Stillman."

Dean carefully shifted his own plate to one hand and extended the other. "Yeah, I kinda figured. The other vet, right?"

"That's me." He gave Dean's hand a quick, firm shake, then took hold of his plate again before disaster struck. "And you're…Dean, right?"

He allowed a short nod, then said, "My brother's marrying Sarah's and Katey's sister."

"So I've heard." Ed balanced a chicken leg on the top of an already enormous pile of food, then looked around, presumably for some place to sit.

Dean nodded toward the house. "Porch steps," he said, then, to Katey, "You going to sit with us?"

"You kidding?" she said, scrunching up her nose. "I'll be over there…" Her tiny hands busy balancing an amazingly full plate for such a bit of a thing, she tossed her head in the direction of a clump of assorted giggling little girls seated in the shade of a huge oak away from the house.

"Okay, honey," he replied before she glided toward her friends, the long braids swishing like pendulums against her back. "Well, there goes my date."

"Hey, at least yours went through the food line with you." The two of them gravitated toward the front porch. "I lost mine long before that."

"You here with Sarah?" Dean asked, gingerly settling on the top step. He hoped the question had sounded nonchalant.

"Supposedly."

There was a pause. Curious, Dean glanced over, noticed Ed staring at his plate. "Something moving?"

"What? Oh! No, no, no…" Ed sighed, then waved his plastic fork over the plate as if performing a magic rite. "Where do you start?"

"Ah…the ancient Riddle of the Potluck," Dean said, realizing he liked this kinda crazy-looking guy with the hairdo that reminded him of a combed-out poodle. "From the top, is what I usually find works best."

Ed laughed, bit half the meat off the drumstick, then said through a full mouth, seeming neither concerned nor annoyed, "Anyway, Sarah invited me, told me to bring drinks, got me here, then vanished."

Relief sluiced over Dean's nerves like a spring shower, comforting and startling all at once. "Probably in the kitchen," he mumbled.

"Sarah?" Ed chortled. "You *have* been away a long time."

"What do you mean?"

"She's a great vet, but she can't cook worth diddly. She had me to dinner one night, right after I got here. Man, I thought I'd been poisoned. Now I make it a point only to accept dinner invitations when I know her mother's cooking. Whoever marries that lady had either be a great cook or be wealthy enough to hire one."

Dean laughed and stuffed half a roll in his mouth.

"So. Sarah tells me you make furniture?"

"Uh…yeah," he allowed, wondering how much weight he should give to the fact that he'd been the topic of at least one conversation. "I've got my own shop in Atlanta."

"She said. You do all new stuff, restorations, what?"

"If it's out of wood, I make it. My specialty is period re-

production work, though.'' He speared a piece of ham with the
flimsy plastic fork and waved it around as he spoke. ''People
sometimes bring in pieces that are either unsalvageable or that
they just want duplicated, and I can usually match the original
so closely you'd think it was an antique.'' The ham went into
his mouth.

''Modest, too.''

He shrugged. ''What can I tell you? My daddy taught me
well.''

''Mmm.'' Ed's dark eyes swept out over the front yard as
he chewed. Then he swallowed and asked, ''You do well?''

Although he wondered where the conversation was headed,
Dean saw no reason not to be honest. ''Well enough, I suppose.''

''Looking for a talented pair of hands to help?''

Dean set down his empty plate and picked up a can of Dr.
Pepper, took a swallow. ''Why? Thinking of giving up your
line of work?''

''Me?'' Ed let out a loud laugh. ''Hell, no. I'd probably
chop my hand off using one of those saws. If not something
more important.'' He ditched his empty plate as well, then
leaned his elbows back on the porch floor, nodding toward a
stocky black teenager standing by himself by the dessert table.
''See that kid over there? Name's Franklin Thomas. His
mother's a widow, valiantly runs a little farm on her own a
few miles up the road.''

Dean squinted, nodded. ''I remember the Thomases.
Gee…that kid must have been all of seven or eight when I last
saw him…''

Ed ignored Dean's reminiscing and pushed on. ''I was out
to the farm not too long ago—their cow's pregnant and Mrs.
Thomas worries a lot—and after I'd checked out the cow, she
invited me inside. Now, you have to understand, these people
aren't exactly flush. But the living room was filled with some
of the prettiest furniture I ever saw. Turns out the boy made
most of it.''

Dean studied the young man, stroking his chin. ''Yeah?''

He paused. He had no way of knowing whether the kid was really as talented as Ed seemed to think he was, after all. If he was self-taught, the construction might be terrible. "I take it you think I should take a look at his stuff?"

"How'd you guess?" Ed replied, then a slight crease brought the heavy brows almost together. "Kid never finished school, though."

"Oh?" Dean said, keeping his expression neutral. "You know why?"

"Only thing his mother said was that he could never seem to keep up with the rest of the class. I gather he can't read very well."

Dean felt an empathetic pull in his gut. "I'll take a look at his work" was all he said, as the first, faint shimmerings of an idea began to form. After a second or two, he added, carefully, "You know if there might be any other furniture makers around?"

"Funny you should ask." Ed took a long swallow of his Coke and stretched out his legs. "Last time I went to one of these local crafts shows, in the fall I guess it was, I was amazed by the number of furniture booths there were. Good ones, too. Not terribly original, maybe, but they could really turn out some solid stuff."

Dean couldn't resist. "How come you know so much about all this?"

Ed laughed and tilted his head back, his Adam's apple undulating as he finished off the Coke. "My mother's an interior designer and my father owns a hotsy-totsy antiques shop out on Long Island." He crushed the empty can, glanced over. "So...you thinking of expanding?"

"Just...toying with a few ideas right now. Nothing definite."

He caught the slow grin creep across the vet's face. "Well, let me know if I can help. A furniture manufacturing plant could be a real blessing for the area—"

"Hey, y'all! Katey told me you were over here."

Startled, Dean looked up at the sound of Sarah's voice as

she came around the side of the house. She actually sounded friendly. She was even smiling.

She was also not alone.

Oh, hell.

"Dean, this is Melanie Kincaid, one of Jen's bridesmaids."

Dean gave a short nod and a half smile.

Violet Eyes practically curtsied.

Sarah flashed Dean a funny look. Didn't last but a second, but he knew right off he didn't like it. It was one thing when she used to play pranks *with* him; quite another when she played them *on* him.

Tugging at the neckline of her T-shirt—pale-blue, like a robin's egg—she zeroed in on Ed. "Hey—the men have a hot game of horseshoes going on behind the house, and they're all betting the Yankee can't throw worth squat."

She stood with her hands on her hips, thumbs forward so her shoulders and elbows thrust out defiantly. A posture Dean remembered well. If Ed knew what was good for him, he wouldn't even *think* about saying "no." Although, Dean thought as his peripheral vision caught sight of the oscillating young woman a few feet away whose perfume was strong enough to be used as a chemical weapon, a part of him—actually, *all* of him—wished Ed would say "no," anyway.

Unfortunately, Ed unfolded his lanky form from the porch steps and stood up, rubbing his hands together. "O-o-ooh," he said. "They'll regret the day they issued *that* challenge. Lead me to 'em, m'dear."

So much for that. Sarah and Ed vanished, leaving Dean with…

"I'm sorry…what was your name?"

"Melanie," she breathed, not in the least offended. "Mind if I sit down?"

"Uh…sure." He wasn't any too keen on having that perfume any closer than it already was, but he didn't know what to do. He made a quick search of the yard. No Katey, no Lance, no Jennifer. Nobody.

Melanie giggled, and Dean decided he'd been consigned to hell.

He tried another smile, wondering what on earth he was supposed to say to this woman. Not surprisingly, she took the initiative.

"Jennifer says you live in Atlanta?" Dark lashes fluttered over eyes the color of irises. She really was quite pretty, he supposed.

He nodded, looked away. "Going back Sunday."

"I know." The blonde squeezed her hands together on top of her knees, the gesture puffing up the pale, smooth tops of her breasts out of her low-cut tank top like rising dough. Dean decided to count the number of cars and trucks in the driveway.

Melanie waved her hand over those breasts. "Whew. Sure is hot, huh? You wanna take a walk or something?"

Or *something* sounded good. But then again, what Melanie meant by *or something* probably made a walk the wiser choice.

"Uh, sure," Dean said, pulling himself off the steps and holding out a hand to help Melanie up. She giggled. Of course. When their hands touched, the only sensation that registered was *clammy*. He quickly released her hands, resisting the impulse to dry his palm on his jeans. "Along the road okay?"

She pouted. Dean wondered for the thousandth time why women thought that was appealing. He, for one, was not interested in liaisons with three-year-olds. "Oh, pooh," she said. "I've walked that road so many times I know every dang ant hole along the way. Let's go over there—" She pointed to a grove of trees backing several pastures. "It's just the prettiest walk."

"Sure," he said, wishing he could put his hands in his pockets, but his jeans were too tight. "That'll be...nice."

Melanie giggled again.

That did it. Sarah's sweet little fanny was now solidly in a sling.

Shadow ribbons snaked across the backyard as Sarah and Vivian gathered up the remains of the feast, foisting off whatever leftovers they still figured were safe on whoever was still hanging around. It was quieter now, and cooler, for which Sarah was immensely grateful. There'd been a mass exodus about twenty minutes ago, including Ed, leaving a few adults to help clean up as well as a small but vociferous gang of kids playing a shrill game of hide-and-seek. As much as she appreciated the adults' help, she wished like the dickens the kids would shut up.

A cool breeze ruffled her hair and teased her sticky skin with a hint of a chill, bringing with it the sultry fragrance from hundreds of feathery, blushing mimosa blossoms choking the enormous tree at the side of the yard. She shut her eyes for a moment and slowly inhaled the sweet, soothing scent. *Relax,* she told herself. *It's almost over.*

At least, her plan for getting rid of Dean seemed to have worked; she hadn't seen him for the last hour. She could only assume Melanie had been keeping him well occupied. To her surprise, an exquisite stab of pain shot through her right temple at the precise moment the thought did.

Sarah crammed the milky lid onto somebody's bowl of potato salad and surveyed the scene in front of her as she wiped off her fingers on the seat of her baggy shorts. There, at least, was something to make her feel better.

Amanda and Percy Jenkins were holding court under the largest of the oak trees in the waning light, their "thrones" two woebegone lawn chairs they'd placed so close together their shoulders were touching. Never had she seen two people so much at peace, Sarah thought with a twinge. Amanda, especially: her dark brown eyes glowed with the special serenity that comes from having discovered the secret to happiness. Sarah wasn't by nature covetous, but just now, she envied the seventy-three-year-old woman with every ounce of her being.

Then there were Lance and Jennifer, about to return to their condo in Opelika to continue unpacking, standing arm in arm in front of the elderly couple, receiving their blessing. She envied them, too.

She turned her back on the scene, fighting to keep the tears under control. It had come so suddenly, this feeling of being…left out, she guessed it was. What was so bizarre was that she'd assumed she was perfectly content. After all, she had her mother and Jennifer and Katey and a good career doing what she loved. How had she missed the fact that she was so incredibly *lonely?*

Yeah, well, living a lie can do that to a body.

"You know, we can't afford to give you much of a wedding present," she heard Amanda say. Banishing the self-pity, Sarah turned back around. Amanda had one hand pressed tightly into her husband's palm, the other methodically stroking the rich coppery fur of the old Irish setter by her side. "But we sure do wish you the kind of love that's seen Percy and me through half a century."

Lance stood behind Jennifer, his arms linked around her waist. He tightened his grip, nearly knocking her off balance and making her laugh. "I think we've got that, Amanda," he said, kissing Jennifer's hair as she grabbed his forearms.

"Yes, honey, I believe you do…oh! Penny…get back here now," she said to the nearly sightless dog, who had sensed someone's approach and wobbled to her feet to greet the newcomer, a trim forty-plus woman with troweled-on makeup and a gold-studded white T-shirt tucked into a pair of shorts obviously borrowed from somebody's Barbie doll.

"Y'all seen Melanie?" Blanche Kincaid asked the group in general, seeming more put out than worried.

"Last time I saw her she was with Dean," Sarah piped up, feeling Jennifer's wide eyes glom onto the side of her face. "Listen—why don't you go on if you're in a hurry? One of us'll give her a ride home."

Blanche's hennaed hair glinted in the shaft of sunlight that had managed to pierce the mimosa branches. "Oh, I'd hate for you to go to all that trouble—"

"It's no trouble. Oh—wait a minute…" Sarah shielded her eyes against the setting sun and pointed to the road. "There they are."

"Melanie!" Blanche beckoned her daughter with one crimson-nailed hand, rattling the collection of gold bangles on her wrist. "Come *on,* honey! You know my program starts at eight!"

Ahead of Dean by a good five feet, the blonde stalked up to her mother's car and wordlessly plopped into the front seat with her arms tightly folded across her bosom, her lips extended into a blue-ribbon-winning pout. Sarah glanced over at Dean.

Uh-oh.

She turned away, feeling the censure from a pair of furious forest-green eyes blaze into her skull. She busied herself with folding tablecloths and stacking them in a neat pile on the picnic table, the oddest conglomeration of thoughts whirling in her head. Again.

Okay, she was glad her plan backfired. She was relieved he'd repelled Melanie's advances—which he obviously had, if Melanie's pique meant anything. But that meant he'd still pester her, which she didn't want.

She stopped, frozen, staring at nothing. Who was she kidding? She wanted him to do a helluva lot more than pester her.

No, no, no, no. She shook her head violently, ignoring her thudding heart, ignoring the heat from Dean's anger and frustration just a few feet away.

Ignoring his heat, period.

She shut her eyes. Oh, Lordy, Lordy, Lordy—she had it *bad.* If he touched her, they'd both ignite. *Whoomph!* Spontaneous combustion, big time. Just like they had nine years ago. Only this time would be worse. Much worse. Or, much better, depending on how you looked at it. This time, she knew what it would feel like, how his mouth, warm and moist and soft, would feel against her lips or pressed in the hollow of her neck, the way his tongue would rasp against her nipples; how he'd caress her breasts so gently, so reverently, as if they were a precious gift; the goose bumps of pleasure his hands would bring as they skimmed her stomach, then lower, to that part of her that no man knew *but* him...

She'd kill for something cold to drink. Or dump over her head.

She tried to steady her breathing, telling herself if it didn't get any worse than this, she could handle it. As long as he didn't touch her, she could get through the week.

She could get through what she had to do.

Someone touched her, and she jumped, ramming her hip into the card table. "What is it, baby?" her mother asked softly. Sarah shook her head, her mouth set, hoping she wasn't blushing, knowing she was. She didn't dare look her mother in the face. "It's okay," her mother said, a queer cast to her voice. "He's talking to the Jenkinses. You wanna go home?"

"Not yet," she said as she exhaled, meeting her mother's knowing, questioning eyes. "I'm not running this time."

Vivian rubbed her back. "Aren't you?"

Sarah's brows dipped sharply. But she didn't reply.

"Hey, you guys...we're leaving."

Grateful for the distraction, Sarah turned to Jennifer, hoping to avoid the inevitable questions in her sister's eyes. So she smiled—far too brightly, she knew—gave Jennifer a big hug, then steered her to the front of the house, her arm around her shoulder. Vivian followed, holding a one-sided conversation with the ancient setter, who'd decided to keep them stiff-legged company.

"You want me to come over tomorrow after work and help you guys with the apartment?" Sarah asked her sister.

"No, we're fine. Lord—I can't believe it. Less than a week." Her hand slipped to her impossibly flat tummy.

The pang of envy made an encore. Sarah swallowed, then said with a wink, "Think you can wait that long?"

A bright, mischievous smile lit up her sister's face. "Guess I'll have to."

"Jen—" Lance stood with the door open, one foot already in the car. "Let's go, honey."

Vivian snorted. "He *already* sounds like a husband, doesn't he?" She shooed Jennifer away. "Well, go on. Might as well let him think he's in charge. At least until the wedding." She gave her daughter a quick one-handed hug, the other hand firmly clamped to the old dog's collar, then said to the setter, "Come on, girl. Let's you and me go back to the house."

"Walk me to the car?" Jennifer asked Sarah after their mother left, squeezing her hand. Sarah suddenly realized how young her sister was, how nervous she must be. Especially about the baby. She nodded, then slipped her arm around Jen's waist and crossed the driveway with her.

On the surface, Dean was making polite conversation with the old couple. What he was really doing was waiting. Waiting until Sarah was alone, until he could have it out with her, and about a dang sight more than just what she thought she was doing by throwing Miss Hot-to-Trot in his path. Sure seemed to him she was going to an awful lot of trouble for someone who no longer cared.

A middle-aged couple—the McCallums, Dean remembered—suddenly appeared, drawing up two more chairs in order to chew the fat with the Jenkinses, giving Dean the opportunity to quietly withdraw.

Maybe he *was* being dense, he considered as he trudged up the back porch steps, thinking Sarah might be inside. Maybe she really couldn't forgive him. Maybe he should accept the fact this was one mistake there was no making up for.

Well, he couldn't.

He ratched open the wood-framed screen door, swollen from the recent rain, then stepped into the house, listening carefully.

Whether it was because he was too stupid or too stubborn, he had no idea, but he wasn't going to give up on at least making peace with her without a fight. Which was just what they were about to have, soon as he found her.

He stopped outside the kitchen door, feeling like a poor man's James Bond. He heard his aunt's voice, then Vivian's, softly chiding. A couple of other voices, female but not immediately recognizable. But not Sarah's. Then, filtering through the muffled conversations and the whirr of several electric fans, he heard his brother from out front, trying to get Jen into the car.

Which, more than likely, is where Sarah was. He tiptoed out before someone asked him to do something.

For several minutes, he stood in the shadows of the porch steps, watching Sarah hang on to Lance's car window, yakking to her sister for what seemed like forever—goodbyes in these parts not being glossed over lightly—then give them a little wave as they drove off. She still had her back to her him, her hands propped on the back of her waist, when Dean snuck up on her. Before she realized he was behind her, he took hold of her wrist, snapped her around. She gasped, then snatched her hand out of his as if she'd been burned.

"What's the idea?"

"That's what I want to know." He kept his voice level, not wishing an audience to materialize. "Why'd you set that she-devil on me?"

Stuffing both hands into her shorts pockets, she started to walk away. "I have no idea what you're talking about."

"Oh, no you don't!" He stepped in front of her to cut off her flight, grabbed her by the shoulders. "We are going to talk this out—"

"Don't touch me!" She wrenched out of his grasp and stepped back, her hands splayed in front of her. "Lay a hand on me again, and I swear to God I'll deck you!"

"What are you staring at so hard, Ethel Parrish?"

Dean's aunt shushed Vivian with a slap at the air, never taking her eyes off the driveway in front of the house. Vivian crimped a sheet of foil around someone's leftover ham and joined the older woman at the kitchen window.

"They're about to have it out, looks like," Ethel said, her mouth tight.

Vivian watched for a moment. "About to, nothing. They are." She glanced at the old woman, then back outside. "He's not going to give up, you know."

"And I can't for the life of me figure out why."

"He's still in love with her, Ethel, whether he realizes it yet or not. Has been since they were kids. I think we both have to just accept that."

"I don't have to accept anything," the old woman retorted. "They're not suited."

"Oh, for the love of…" Vivian shook her head, beads of perspiration trickling down her back underneath her oversize shirt. The emaciated specimen of preserved womanhood in front of her, however, had probably never perspired in her life. "They're all grown up now. What was true then isn't true anymore."

The gray head wagged back and forth slowly. "It just wouldn't be right."

"Ethel. Listen to me." Vivian reached out, clasped Dean's aunt's hand, dry as a withered leaf. "Things have changed. Dean has a successful business, and Sarah's no swelled head. You know that. When you come to think of it, they both work with their hands, as well as their brains and their hearts. One brings beauty, one brings healing. Only difference is Sarah's got a few more pieces of paper than Dean does, mainly because the law says you can't go around mending animals unless you have a degree and a license to do it."

Through the window, she heard the argument they probably thought was a private affair, and her heart twisted at the pain they were both going through. Pain that could have been completely avoided, pain she knew her daughter'd do anything *to* avoid.

"They belonged together, Ethel," Vivian said quietly. "And they'd be together right now—" she took a deep breath "—if it hadn't been for two scared, meddling women who should've kept their damn mouths shut."

"Vivian!"

"Well, it's true. And you know it."

Ethel studied the developing scenario outside and shook her head. "All water under the bridge now, ain't it? From the looks of things, she'll never take him back, anyway. And I can't say as I'm sorry about it."

Vivian was quiet for a moment, then said, "You love that boy, Ethel?"

That merited a sharp glance. "He's kin. Of course I love him." Dean's aunt tilted her head at Vivian, the skin around her eyes crinkling like crepe paper. "What made you ask such a stupid question?"

Well used to the old woman's acerbic tongue, it didn't even occur to Vivian to take offense. "Because I'm trying for the life of me to figure out why you're still so dead set against Sarah and Dean being together."

She could see Ethel's jaw clench, her wrinkled lips pursing as if sucking on a sour candy. Habit. That's all this was, Vivian realized. After so many years of harboring the conviction that Sarah and Dean weren't right for each other, it would take more than a few words to change the old woman's mind.

But then, perhaps that depended on what the few words were.

Vivian sighed, then lowered her voice. "They need to be together. The sooner you accept that, the easier this is all going to be."

The gray head whirled around. "What are you saying, girl? The easier *what's* going to be?"

Unwilling to deal with the scrutiny of those cold blue eyes, Vivian directed her attention outside, praying for guidance. After a long moment, she got her answer. Sarah would undoubtedly have a hissy fit, but Vivian would cross that bridge when she came to it.

Dean didn't doubt for a moment that Sarah would follow through with her threat. Slowly, his own hands rose, mirroring hers, as he took a prudent step backward. "Okay, okay…I won't touch you," he promised, his voice low and controlled, as if talking to a wounded animal. Which he supposed was nearer to the truth than he realized. And his return had only reopened the wounds.

His heart constricted at the agony contorting her features, agony that was *his* fault, *his* doing, and all he could think of was how desperately he wanted, somehow, to make things right between them again.

How desperately he wanted his best friend back.

And that took the edge off the anger. Somewhat, anyway.

"I won't touch you," he repeated. "This time. But no more siccing bimbos on me, you got that?"

Her chin came up, the angles of her face limned in coral from the setting sun. "Melanie's no bimbo!" she retorted with sparking eyes. A woman simply defending another woman, he decided. But at least she lowered her hands. She seemed to teeter for a moment, then abruptly crossed the few feet to the porch. She settled onto the edge of the floor peeking out from under the railing, bracing her hands on either side of her hips. "She's just young, is all."

Dean followed at what he decided was a safe distance. "She's a damn piranha, for God's sake. She tried everything short of chaining me to a tree."

Suddenly she was fighting a smile. Playing a game. Tiny creases danced at the corners of her eyes as she said, "Oh? Too much for you to handle, Dean?"

"Dammit, woman!" His arms flew up in exasperation. "What the Sam Hill is this all about?"

The humor faded. With a half shrug, she said, "It's not about anything. She just wanted to meet you, that's all."

"Right. What, exactly, did you say to her, Sarah?"

Her gaze glanced off his, then she pushed herself away from the porch, aimlessly strolling down the drive. "Nothing much. Except that…" She pivoted her torso, as if trying to decide whether or not to finish her sentence. When she did speak, he caught the tremor in her voice. "Except that there was nothing between us. Anymore." Focused again on the driveway, she crammed her fisted hands into her pockets.

She was lying. Oh, she was doing a damn good job of it, but the words must be burning in her throat, they were such bunk. Her voice always went quavery when she got emotional or was forced to say something she didn't want to. That hadn't changed.

His anger had, however. Completely, this time. Something in her eyes, the shakiness in her voice, had just washed all the fight right out of him.

But he was still curious. "Sarah?"

"What?"

"Did you really think throwing a bosomy blonde in my path would distract me?"

Her shoulders hitched in a little sad shrug. "It was worth a shot."

"After all this time, how could you even think such a thing?"

"I would've thought you'd have at least enough sense to figure that one out on your own." She sounded weary, like a mother who's asked a child to do something a dozen times and still not gotten results.

Frustration flared again, just for a second. "How many times do I have to tell you, I made a mistake?"

Her hand plowed through her hair, stayed there as she shook her head. "Don't you see, Dean? It doesn't matter." Anguish again flooded her features; a cold, sick feeling washed over him that they weren't having the conversation he thought they were having. Her hand fell to her side as she turned, faced him. "It's not just a matter of my forgiving you, if that's what you want. Too much has happened, too much time has passed…"

The look in those honey-brown eyes stabbed him all the way to his soul.

He didn't care what happened now, even if she belted him clear into another zip code. She still cared. A great deal, unless he was way off course.

And, heaven help him, so did he.

He tugged her to him too quickly for her to react, crushing his mouth to hers. The smell of her, the taste of her, the *feel* of her—all sweeter than he remembered. Nine years evaporated into dust the instant his lips made contact, the instant he had her in his arms again. Where she belonged.

One arm easily encircled her slender waist, his other hand

nestling her head, her short, fine hair as silky as a kitten's fur against his rough palm. He could feel her swell against him, trembling and aroused, just like she used to when they were hot and horny teenagers who couldn't do a blessed thing about their grown-up passions. They'd held off so long, so long, until that one night they'd given up and given in—

What the hell was this? Realization pricked his clouded brain: seconds ago, they were swapping skin cells; now she'd gone limp in his arms, her hands at her sides, noncommittal. He reluctantly pulled away from her mouth, daring to search her eyes, only to have his gaze bounce off a pair of identical bronze shields. Impenetrable. Opaque. Cold and hard and unforgiving.

He let her go, then walked back to the house, muttering words he hadn't used in a very, very long time.

The sound of her sneakers pounding against the dirt echoed the hammering inside her chest. Her head buzzed from the blood rushing through her ears; her lips burned, ached, tingled. She tried to touch them, but her fingers were shaking too badly to make contact.

Well, *that* definitely took the prize for the hardest thing she'd ever done, pulling back like that. Dean probably wondered what was wrong with her. Shoot, *she* wondered what was wrong with her.

There was nothing wrong with her, which was the problem. By her count, all systems were go, go, *go*. Too bad she had to abort the flight.

Dammit to hell! How *dare* her body betray her like that! And after one measly little kiss, no less. Sure, she'd kissed a few other men, but only Dean's kisses accomplished so much with so little. He was an efficient son of a gun, she'd give him that. Even if she wasn't giving him anything else. Her hand found its unsteady way to her head, where she smoothed down her hair as if expecting to find it standing straight up on end. Heaven knows, several other things were.

Having reached her car, she fished her keys out of her

pocket, made several unsuccessful attempts to connect key to lock, finally hurled them down into the dust. Her hands flew to her face as she collapsed back against the still-hot door, where she gulped in breath after breath, trying to regain control.

Then her hands fell to her thighs with a loud slap as she let out a rattling sigh. What the hell good was a hyper libido if you couldn't do anything about it?

Mexico called again. Loudly.

But…that wasn't an option, either. Instead, she'd just go for a run until her leg muscles screamed for mercy and her lungs felt as though they'd been turned inside out. After that, she was going to find what was left of that cake and stuff her face until she got sick.

"Hey, Sarah!"

Startled, she twisted around, peering over the roof of her car at the blond teenager climbing into the old pickup parked a few feet away. Dusk had cast a charcoal filter over everything so she didn't recognize him at first. "Hey, Jeff." She frowned. "You leaving without your folks?"

"Mama wants to stay and help clean up for a little while longer, so she told me to go on home, get the animals fed and all that. I'll be back in about an hour."

Sarah nodded and tried a smile. "Sounds like a plan to me." She waved a silent goodbye as he started up the engine.

After Jeff pulled out of the drive, she leaned against the car for another moment or two, still and thoughtless, then decided she was calm enough to safely operate the vehicle. She kicked around in the dirt for a minute or two until she found her keys, but had no sooner picked them up when she heard the screech of tires…immediately followed by the heart-wrenching sound of an animal in pain.

Chapter 6

She grabbed her black bag and battery-powered lamp out of the back of the Bronco and tore off in the direction of the cluster of people gathered at the edge of the front yard. Close by, at a forty-five degree angle to the road, the driver's door ajar, sat the McCallums' truck.

Penny was so quiet and still Sarah at first thought she was already gone. "Hey, girl," she said gently over the knot in her throat, squatting by the dog and setting up the lamp. She placed her fingers at the base of the dog's neck; there was still a faint pulse.

Jeff McCallum was near to hysterics. Barely sixteen, he'd only had his driver's license about a month and had taken such pains to prove to his folks he was a safe driver. And he'd had one of Penny's puppies since he was eight.

"I swear, I didn't see 'er, Sarah. She just come out from behind those bushes. There wasn't nothin' I could do…"

"It's okay, Jeff" came a low, soft voice from over her head. Sarah glanced up to see Dean lay a hand on the boy's shoulder. "It wasn't your fault."

"He's right," Sarah immediately concurred, reaching up and giving the weeping boy's hand a quick squeeze. With a sigh, she pulled her stethoscope out of her bag. "It wasn't anybody's fault."

"Nobody's but mine," Amanda Jenkins said, her voice strangely calm. With some difficulty, she knelt by the dog, took the long graying muzzle into her lap. "I shouldn't've let her loose today, not with all these people around."

Sarah briefly stroked Amanda's arm, then turned back to her patient, who hadn't moved at all. Dean dropped to one knee on the other side of the dog, his veined hand skimming the beautiful fur. "We can't move her, can we?"

"No." She caught the compassion etched on his features in the eerie glow from her lamp, and remembered Dean playing with Penny when she was a pup, all those years ago. "No," she repeated, refocusing on the barely breathing dog. "I don't dare move her until I check her out." With great care, and scant hope, she placed the stethoscope on the dog's abdomen. There was little point to the exam, but she went through the motions because that's what she was supposed to do. Sarah had instantly known the dog was going to die. The only question was, whether she'd do it on her own, or whether Sarah would assist her.

Ever since she was a child, she'd always been able to tell when an animal was ready to let go. She could see it in their eyes. She'd seen animals with near-fatal injuries pull through, and others with less catastrophic problems just give up on her, no matter how adeptly she applied her skill. The old ones, especially, always seemed to know when it was time.

It didn't make things any easier.

Even a cursory exam confirmed her suspicions about the extent of the old dog's injuries. She shut her eyes for a moment, steeling herself. A small hand, smooth and warm, lighted on her wrist.

"She needs to be put down, don't she?"

Sarah opened her eyes, finding her own strength in

Amanda's clear brown gaze. "There's really nothing I can...
I'm so sorry."

Amanda gave Sarah's wrist a slow, reassuring squeeze, then
reached up to take her husband's hand in hers. "Then do it
now. I can't stand to see her suffer no more."

Sarah nodded, then pulled out a vial of Soccumb from her
black bag, quickly filled a hypodermic. "Penny...she'll go to
sleep about fifteen seconds after she receives the injection. She
won't feel anything at all."

Amanda gave her a watery smile. "I know, honey. This ain't
the first time I've been through this, you know."

Sarah tried to smile back. After the slightest hesitation, she
maneuvered the needle into a vein in the dog's forepaw, slowly
injected the thick substance, then waited.

It always hurt. Always. No matter how old or injured or ill-
tempered an animal might be, no matter how much more hu-
mane it might be in theory to put the creature out of its misery,
her heart cracked in two every single time she had to put an
animal to sleep. If her mother had told her once, she'd told her
a hundred times she was such a good vet because she cared so
much, that heartache came with the territory.

Small comfort.

Mercifully, everyone had gone by the time she got back to
her car. Percy said he'd bury Penny out in the pasture the next
morning, where she used to like to sit and watch the cows. He
asked Sarah if maybe she could come around about eleven or
so, he'd like to have a little service, if she didn't think that
sounded silly. Tears stinging her eyes, she'd told him it wasn't
silly at all and that of course she'd be there.

You did what you had to, she told herself. The dog's back
was broken. Even if she'd been a young animal, in perfect
health, what sort of life would she have had paralyzed? *There
hadn't been any choice...*

The driver's side door stood open. She slammed it shut with
all the force she could muster, then leaned her arms on top of
the hood and buried her face in her arms, sobbing like a child.

Seconds later, she found herself cradled instead against a familiar chest, familiar strong arms holding her, rocking her, as gentle fingers caressed the nape of her neck. Not to arouse, but to console.

"Shh, baby…it's okay, it's okay…" Dean's deep voice reverberated softly in her ear as his chin came to rest of the top of her head. She thought maybe he kissed her hair; she was too upset to be sure.

Please, she silently begged, *don't tell me it didn't matter because the dog was old, anyway, or that I did the kindest thing, or that bad things just happen. Please.*

But of course he knew better than that. Instead, he simply held her, his body molded to hers as if they were indeed two halves of a single unit, and it felt good, and right, the way it always had.

Which was exactly what scared her so much.

Her hands had been pressed flat against his chest as he held her; now she sheathed her face in her palms as her sobs grew louder, as she grieved for things that could not be because of decisions made long ago. Physical yearnings, she could walk away from. Walking away from *this* was another matter entirely.

But she did. Somehow.

Somehow she pushed out of that strong, caring embrace and made her way back to her car, leaving Dean standing in the Jenkinses' driveway. Without looking, she knew exactly his expression. His silence told her.

She wished with all her heart it didn't have to be this way. But there was nothing to be done for it.

Dean drove out to the Thomas place the next afternoon, deciding the frown he wore almost constantly these days had become a permanent part of his features. The twenty-minute drive gave him some time to think, for what good it was worth. Which wasn't much. He'd just about decided to stop trying to figure things out, anyway. Seemed like the more he did, the worse things got. But…well, you can't just turn off your brain, you know?

Sarah was naturally at the top of his Things to Worry About list. Talk about blowing hot and cold. Not that her behavior was all that bizarre, he supposed, under the circumstances. Frankly, it was amazing she *hadn't* decked him yet. But he kept seeing something in her eyes he couldn't ignore, couldn't let go of. A combination of things, actually, the signals all mixed up like superimposed radio stations.

Probably the strongest was fear. Of being hurt again, would be his guess. But there was desire, too, laced with the apprehension. Hell, that he could practically feel, it was so strong.

There was something else, though, something he couldn't put a finger on, that had him completely baffled. And trying to figure it out was making him seriously crazy.

Next on the list was Sarah's mother, clearly anxious to see them back together. While there seemed to be little to be gained from pointing out the futility of her goal, her motives still eluded him. And made him more nervous than ever.

But the person who most gave him pause was his aunt. Suddenly, after the potluck, Sarah could do no wrong in the woman's opinion. Smart Sarah, pretty Sarah, nice Sarah. *What a shame the two of you broke up,* she had said, leaving Dean so stunned he couldn't even manage a coherent sentence.

What do you mean, what a shame we broke up? he wanted to shout. *Whose idea was it to leave, anyway? Who called whose third cousin on your Aunt Mildred's side and got me that job in Atlanta?* But he kept his mouth shut, for once, because more and more, the past seemed irrelevant to what was happening now.

Whatever that was.

He pulled the Dakota into a small neat yard choked with hollyhocks and marigolds and petunias and a dozen assorted chickens, and honked, two long beeps and a short. Ed had warned him about the signal. Otherwise, Wilma Thomas was likely to greet him fully armed. A second later, the widow stepped out onto the front porch, nary a weapon in sight, a wide toothy smile fixed on a broad face the color of devil's food cake. Dean supposed her to be somewhere in her early sixties; Franklin had been the "baby," born ten years after what the Thomases had assumed was the last in their series of seven children, who were all long since gone with families of their own.

"Well, look at you, Dean Parrish," she said with a cackle, her hand settled on a wide hip covered in a garish floral duster. "Get yourself in here and have a glass of tea and a piece of pie. And you better hurry before Franklin gets it all. I swear that boy's goin' to grow another six inches this summer."

Minutes later, Dean found himself sitting at a small but painstakingly crafted trestle table, a small lake's worth of iced tea and a good quarter of a rhubarb pie placed in front of him. He promised himself to forget about Sarah and her kin and his kin for the next few minutes and concentrate on matters at hand. And what was at hand was a fine piece of home baking. And an even finer piece of furniture. Dean palmed the top of the piece appreciatively.

"Your son make this?"

Wilma nodded as she went about chopping vegetables for supper on a wooden board set up near the ancient sink, complete with pump. "It's just pine, but he was trying out a new technique, so didn't want to use better wood in case he messed up." Her scrutiny was brief. "You like it?"

"Yes, ma'am. It's very nice. *Very* nice." Addressing the woman's back, he asked, "Where'd he get the tools?"

"Oh, his daddy had accumulated them from time to time, mostly from flea markets and yard sales, you know how it is." She dumped the pile of carrots into an enormous cast-iron kettle on the wood-burning stove, then started peeling potatoes, her gnarled hands wielding the little paring knife with such precision that each peel came off in one long, thin strip. "Then he'd clean and fix 'em up real nice so they worked like new, and all he had to do was buy new blades now and again." She nodded toward the window in front of her, indicating something in the backyard. "There's a separate workshop out back.

With its own generator, before you ask,'' she added, finishing off with another raucous laugh. ''Oh, yeah, that man thought of *everything*.''

''I can see that,'' Dean allowed as he scraped the last of the pie juice from his plate. ''Dr. Stillman said there are other pieces in the living room?''

''Oh, not just in there, honey. All through the house. Just go on and have a look around,'' she said, reducing the denuded spuds into manageable chunks. With a bright smile, she added, ''I trust you.''

Dean chuckled as he rose from the table, wiping his mouth on a pink-and-green flowered napkin. ''I'm sure glad to hear that, Miz Thomas.'' A low whistle floated from Dean's lips the minute he opened the kitchen door.

Another cackle floated from behind him. ''Real nice, ain't they?''

''Yes, ma'am,'' Dean said softly. ''Real nice.'' He walked all the way into the room, the swinging door creaking three or four times behind him before coming to a stop. Ed really did know his stuff. And so did this kid. From tables to chairs to a desk to even a carved headboard in a back bedroom, Franklin Thomas already showed a remarkable talent. The construction was solid and precise, unusual in someone so young. The teenager had truly been given the hands and soul of a master. And of course many of the pieces were two or three years old already, Dean realized in amazement.

Just then, Franklin came in from working out in one of the fields. Shirtless and sweating, his tall, muscular build—ill-concealed underneath the obligatory farmer's overalls—was definitely to be respected. The young man thrust out an enormous hand, accompanied by a smile that somehow managed to be confident and deferential at the same time. ''Dr. Stillman told me you'd be comin' today.'' Coal-black eyes swept the room. ''What do you think?''

Nothing like being forthright. ''Your work shows more than just skill, Franklin. Shows intelligence, too.'' When the dark, thick brows lifted, Dean added, "The way you laid out the wood grains in some of the pieces...brilliant."

Franklin hesitated, then said, running his hand lovingly across the back of a rocker, "I don't recall anybody ever calling me intelligent before. Least, not to my face." He patted the chair, then said, "I didn't even finish high school."

Dean leaned back on the arm of a Mission-style sofa. "Neither did I."

The kid's eyes snapped up to Dean's face. "You pullin' my leg, right?"

"Nope. Just got my GED about five years ago."

Franklin eyed him for a second longer. "How come *you* didn't finish?"

"I didn't know it then, but apparently I had some sort of processing problem. I could read the words okay, but I couldn't interpret what I was reading well enough to make much sense of them. You?"

Recognition, and relief, flickered for a moment in the dark eyes. "Yeah. Sounds about right. So, I decided to make the best use of my hands I could." Franklin held up a pair of mitts big enough to crush a watermelon. "Figured if my brain didn't work, something else would have to."

"Oh, no, Franklin. Your brain works. Just differently. Take it from me. You can't do what you do without thinking about it, choosing the wood and the tools and planning how it all goes together. It's just those damn words that screw us up, you know?"

A gentle laugh rolled from the guy's throat. Crossing massive forearms across his chest, he asked, "So...you got a job for me?"

Now it was Dean's turn to laugh. "Nothing like stating your objective up front, huh?" He took a final turn around the small but pretty living room, then looked at the boy. "As it happens, I'm fixing to expand. Got a contract with Tidewater House to manufacture a whole line of reproduction furniture, and they're beginning to light fires under my butt to get going on it. As soon as I find a suitable place to set up a factory, I'll start production. If you want it, yeah—you've got a job.''

A row of white teeth gleamed in the teak face. ''What's the pay?''

Dean chuckled, then told him a figure that elicited a low, appreciative whistle. ''Man, I could certainly handle that.''

''It would mean moving to Atlanta, of course.'' Dean couldn't promise anything else, not at the moment. Yeah, he knew what he'd like to do, but that didn't mean it was going to happen. Or even that it should.

A cloud passed over Franklin's features. ''Yeah. I know.''

It was harder than Dean thought it would be to drum up much enthusiasm, but he managed. ''Oh, come on, man. Big city. Lots to do, lots of things to see…''

''I don't need to see the big city to know I don't belong there,'' Franklin said quietly. ''But I do need to work. So if that's where the job is, that's where I'll go.''

Dean understood.

''Well…it's official!''

Flat on her tummy on her turned-down bed, Sarah looked up from the book she was reading to see a beaming Jennifer in her doorway. Balthasar chirruped, yawned, then flipped onto his back beside her. ''What is?''

A breeze from the open window flirted with Jennifer's white cotton eyelet baby-doll pajamas as she held up a plastic wand with a little square at one end, bisected with what Sarah thought was a dark blue streak. ''They swear these things are accurate almost all the time,'' she said with a giggle, waving the wand around as if she were about to bestow a knighthood on someone.

Sarah clapped shut her book and sat up, patting the crisp white sheet beside her. ''Well, come here, Miss Preggers,'' she said, tucking underneath her fanny the old Auburn U. T-shirt she slept in, ''and let me give you a hug.''

Jennifer did as she was told, mumbling something into Sarah's shoulder.

"What was that?"

"I *said*—" she bounced onto the edge of the bed, sending the cat looking for other, calmer accommodations "—how funny it is that I'm the one having the first grandbaby. I thought for sure it would've been you."

"Yeah, well," Sarah said with an obligatory smile, slipping a tissue between the pages of her book. "Just goes to show, huh? You never can tell." She tossed the paperback onto her nightstand, then picked up her clock to set the alarm.

Jennifer crashed back on Sarah's bed, her hands pressed to her stomach. "Speaking of 'never can tell,' it's killing me to keep this from Lance."

Sarah glanced over her shoulder as she set the clock back on the nightstand. "So why are you?"

"Because…it's kind of fun to have a secret."

Sarah got up to retrieve a bottle of lotion from her dressing table. "Oh, no, Jen," she said over the little *ping* in her heart. She squirted a dollop in her palm, set the bottle down, briskly massaged it into her hands. "It's not. Having secrets is the pits."

The bed squeaked as Jennifer pulled herself upright. "Hey…what's been eating you, anyway? You've been so weird since…" Sarah heard a little gasp. "You're not still…I mean, you don't still have a thing for Dean, do you?"

She didn't dare answer.

Jennifer moaned. "Oh, Lord…how dumb can a person be? I've been so wrapped up in my own life, with the wedding and the baby and all— I don't know why it never occurred to me you'd still feel something for him after all this time. These past few days must've been horrible for you."

With a tight little smile, Sarah returned to the bed where she sank onto the edge, one foot tucked up under her bottom. "They haven't exactly been easy."

Jennifer again collapsed back onto the mattress. "Leave it to me to marry my sister's ex-boyfriend's brother, huh?"

Sarah joined her, tucking her arm under her head. "Yeah,"

she said on a sigh, contemplating the softly humming ceiling fan. "I've had similar thoughts in the past seventy-two hours."

They lay silently side by side for several seconds before Jennifer gently asked, "Why'd you break up?"

After a moment, Sarah told her, her voice unemotional, almost monotone. *Just the facts, ma'am.*

"Damn." Her sister could be very succinct when she had a mind to be.

"Yeah."

"No wonder Dean looks like he just landed in a pile of horse pucky."

Sarah laughed.

After a long pause, Jennifer asked, obviously picking her words with care, "How close were you two? I mean, did you…?"

"Once," Sarah replied to the fan. "Just…once."

The mattress shifted slightly as her sister rolled her head toward her. "And there hasn't been anyone else?"

"As in dating?"

"As in *anything.*"

"Nope."

She could practically hear Jennifer's brain process this information. "You mean you're twenty-seven and…"

"Only done the deed once?" Sarah finished with a rueful grin. "I don't think that exactly qualifies me for a freak show, honey."

Jennifer twisted around, propping herself up on her elbow. "What would you do if Dean asked you to marry him?"

"And why, may I ask, would he do that?" Sarah said on a startled laugh.

"Just humor me. What would you do?"

Sarah looked back up at the ceiling. "Well, after I picked myself up off the floor, I'd have to say…no."

"That's ridiculous! Hey, I remember Dean, more than you might think. Even when I was a little brat, he was always real nice to me, always treated me like a human being, y'know?

He's a good person, Sarah. And even you said he said he was sorry.''

"Yes, he did."

"So…?"

"So…that's not enough, honey."

"You know what?"

Sarah smiled over at her sister. "What?"

"I think you're completely nuts, that's what."

Once more, the fan got her attention. "I'll take that under advisement."

A foot away, Jennifer let out a groan as if she was about to give birth right there and then.

"I'm coming, I'm coming," Dean growled at the insistently ringing doorbell. He tapped the instant-on lamp on one end table as he shuffled past, wincing when he stubbed his toe on a cast-iron life-size pug dog in his path. "Keep your shirt on," he mumbled, swinging open the door. "Jennifer?"

"You've got to court her, you idiot. You know…flowers and candy and stuff like that."

Dean blinked at Sarah's sister, her arms crossed over her pajamas and robe, turquoise eyes ablaze. One hand stuffed in the pocket of his own robe, Dean jabbed behind him. "Would you like to come in?" he said over a noisy yawn. "And should I get Lance out of bed?"

"Thank you, yes I would, and no, don't bother Lance." She swept past him in a haze of something flowery and a bit too sweet for his taste. "Let him sleep. He won't get much after Saturday."

As things began to come into focus, he had the vague sensation the blue-and-mauve roses in her cotton robe very nearly matched the ones on his aunt's sofa. "Can I get you anyth—?"

"She's in love with you," Jennifer said, continuing her diatribe. "I know, I think it's strange, too, but there you are. And it looks like you're her only chance, too. Either she marries you or she dies an old maid. And I'm here to tell you that is *not* a pleasant prospect.''

Jen paused to snatch a breath, and Dean jumped in. ''This a habit of yours, starting conversations in the middle?''

She'd brushed all the spray out of her hair, he noticed, so it softly swished her shoulders when she shrugged. ''Takes less time that way.''

Which, seeing as it was pushing midnight, was probably a good thing. Dean tightened the belt around his own robe and finger-combed his hair—

His gaze shot to Jen's. ''Hold on—she actually *said* she still loved me?''

''Well, maybe not in so many words. But a sister can tell these things.''

Ah. He was beginning to get the picture. Blissful bride-to-be out to fix up everybody in sight, is what was going on here. His brow puckered. ''Just how much do you know, exactly?''

''Exactly?'' Her shoulders lifted. ''I don't know. Everything, I s'pose.''

''Everything…?''

Jennifer huffed in impatience. ''That after the two of you made love the first time, you up and left with some sorry excuse about not being able to stomach Sweetbranch anymore, making her miss her prom. Which was a *really* jerky thing to do, by the way. Then, Friday night, how you tried to apologize, telling her you'd made a mistake and how, for the *family's* sake, y'all needed to work this out. Which she either doesn't believe, or is afraid to, I can't rightly tell.''

He sagged into a nearby armchair, bracing his much-too-full head in his hand, then peered up at the bearer of glad tidings. ''Jen, honey? Not that I don't appreciate what you're trying to do here, but your sister hates my guts.''

''Oh, she just wants you to think that so you'll stay away from her.''

He almost laughed. Except Jen had crouched down in front of him, grasping his hands in hers. ''Dean Parrish, as God is my witness, I swear my sister's in love with you. She's scared,

and she's hurting, and I'm not saying it's gonna be easy win-
nin' her back 'cause we both know she's stubborn as a blind
mule, but if you want her bad enough…'' She let the sentence
drift off.

He simply stared at her, unable to think. To breathe.

"Jen," he finally said, "my business is in Atlanta."

"Well, that's not exactly the moon, now, is it?" Jennifer
got to her feet, straightening out her robe. "Besides, she can
be a vet there as well as here. So. You want her back or not?"

Dean collapsed back into the chair, his brows tightly drawn.
"I don't know, Jen. Honestly, I don't. We've both changed—"

"So?"

He looked up, willing his heart to break free of the ambivalence choking it. "I'll tell you one thing, though—the part
where I said I was really sorry? That's the God's honest truth."

"Well, *duh*. I wouldn't be here if I didn't think it was. Hey,
for what it's worth? If I were her, I'd forgive you."

"You're very sweet. But you're not your sister."

"Ain't that the truth." Jennifer headed for the door, jiggling
her car keys. "But if I were *you*, I wouldn't let a little ol'
bygone stand between me and my woman. So I'd be danged
sure to get in her way as much as possible."

His woman? Oh, Sarah would love that. Then his brows
lifted. "Get in her way?"

"Yeah, you know…hang around, don't let her forget you
for a moment."

Dean winced. "Was that how you landed my brother?"

"Uh-uh," she said with a grin. "That's how he landed *me*."

After Jennifer left, Dean wandered into the kitchen, poured
himself a glass of milk, sank onto one of the kitchen chairs
and stared into the darkness for a long, long time. And by the
time the milk was gone, he'd come to the conclusion that, even
if courting Sarah wasn't on the docket—sure, he still cared and
all, but, Jennifer's invoking the Almighty notwithstanding,
even he knew a dead horse when he smelled one—there was
still something highly appealing about Sarah's sister's advice.

Just chalk it up to pure, unadulterated cussedness.

* * *

Took Sarah almost ten seconds before she figured out the scraping sound wasn't inside her head. Actually, it slowly penetrated as she lay in bed, her heart thumping unpleasantly in her chest, it seemed to be coming from outside. Right by her bedroom window, in fact.

A bedroom window that was letting in far too much sunlight for seven-thirty in the morning.

She jerked her face toward her clock and discovered to her horror it was nearly ten—she'd apparently slept through her alarm. That revelation momentarily displaced her confusion and curiosity about whatever was going on outside her window, catapulting her out of bed and over to her bedroom door so fast she got dizzy. "Mama!" she shrieked down the stairs, clutching the post on the landing so she wouldn't keel over. "Why didn't you call me?"

"Oh, you're up," Vivian replied mildly as she ambled over to the foot of the stairs. "You get any sleep?"

"I was supposed to be at the clinic at nine! Why are you shaking your head?"

"I called Doc already. Told him you hadn't been sleeping well lately and would he mind if you came in late today, and he said, no, he didn't mind at all and not to worry about it—"

"Why'd you do that?"

Vivian shrugged, unconcerned. "Because I thought it was best."

Through her the-body's-up-but-the-brain's-not haze came a flash of realization. And of determination.

"Mama? I'm all grown up now. So if you don't mind, I'd like to decide what's best for me from now on, okay?"

For several seconds, the two women stared at each other, separated by more than just a flight of stairs. Vivian opened her mouth, shut it again, then walked away.

Sarah didn't know what to make of what had just happened between them. Something had, but she wasn't sure just what. Maybe after a shower and a cup of coffee, it'd make more sense.

Then maybe she'd be gracious enough, she thought as she speared tense fingers through her hair, to thank her mother for gaining her a short reprieve from a world she had to admit she hadn't been ready to deal with at nine o'clock this morning. Not that she'd be much more ready to cope with anything at eleven. But still…

She thudded back to her room, shutting the door behind her. And instantly remembered the other thing that had confused her that morning.

Forgetting all she wore was the baggy T-shirt and a pair of bikini panties, Sarah yanked back the lace curtains and hung out the window.

And came within two feet of Dean's face.

She nearly whacked the top of her head on the window sash.

"Morning, honey," he said, clearly nonplussed at her appearance, as if seeing her eye-to-eye by her bedroom window was perfectly normal. Of course, he was on a ladder, a paintbrush in his hand, the soft rasping of which had replaced the scraping as he methodically stroked the clapboards with it.

She couldn't speak at first. All *Dean* wore was an old pair of low-slung, faded cutoffs and a sheen of sweat. The mid-morning sun mingling with the perspiration made his tanned skin look like—oh, Lord—caramel ice cream topping.

He tilted his head in her direction, laughed that way he did that prickled her skin, then went back to his painting. "Trying to catch some flies there, Sarah Louise?"

She clamped shut her mouth. Then she opened it again, trying for *indignant*. "What are you doing?"

He winked, waving the paintbrush in answer.

"Okay, I'll restate the question. *Why* are you doing this?"

"Because…it needs doing?"

If she'd been closer, she would've belted him. "Okay, smartass—why are *you* doing this?"

"Because your mother asked me if I'd mind and I said no. And because," he added, dipping his brush in the paint bucket precariously suspended from the top of the ladder, "I had high hopes of catching a glimpse of you naked."

The question was, was she close enough to push over the ladder without landing on her head in the azaleas? She considered, decided not.

"Well." She puffed up, realized with a dull thud of disappointment she couldn't think of a scathing rejoinder. "Sorry to disappoint you."

Pausing in his work, Dean regarded her with such heat in those grassy eyes her temperature rose at least five degrees. "Not at all," he said quietly, staring right at her chest. "You know you can see straight through that T-shirt?"

She gasped, then did bump her head in her split to pull back inside. She slammed shut the window, jerked the miniblind cord so the blinds clattered to the sill, then yanked the curtains closed as well.

The room became immediately stifling. No matter, she decided as she gathered up fresh clothes to put on after her shower. She caught a glimpse of herself in the mirror as she passed, checked herself out, decided no, he really hadn't been able to see anything after all. Not much, anyway. Her hand had just lit on the doorknob when she heard tapping on the glass.

She tramped back to the window and raised the blinds, holding the cord taut in her hand. "What?" she said through the glass.

"How 'bout a date?" Dean mouthed.

She lowered the blinds with another rattling crash and went to take her shower.

And refused to believe she'd just had more fun in the past five minutes than she'd had in the past five years of her life.

Chapter 7

Fifteen minutes and one shower later, he was still there. Only now he sat at her kitchen table, enough pancakes to feed the entire congregation of First Baptist piled in front of him. Thankfully, a Braves T-shirt now hid his torso. More or less. Or course, if she'd stopping gawking at him already, there wouldn't be a problem. Even if the damn shirt was snug enough to fit Katey. Speaking of whom…

"Where's the squirt?" she asked her mother, forcing her eyeballs to unhook from those delicious biceps and quadriceps and all those other ceps clinging to his skeleton. Clearly, she'd been looking at one too many cow butts in the last little while.

"Jennifer. Florist," her mother replied, flipping the next batch of pancakes.

"Sorry I can't stay, either," Sarah said with a too-bright smile as she poured herself a cup of coffee. "I'm sure Doc's expecting me—"

"At noon," Vivian interjected. "You have plenty of time for breakfast." She gestured toward the table with a plate of hot pancakes. "Sit."

Subtle.

Gray eyes and brown clashed over Dean's head from opposite sides of the kitchen. Gray won. Sarah sat. So did Vivian. Except, two seconds later, her mother got up to answer the phone in the living room, leaving Sarah to curse her mother's stubbornness about not installing an extension in the kitchen.

"Hey, yourself," she heard her mother say. "No, not busy at all…"

So much for a buffer, Sarah thought with a dispirited sigh, regarding the logger-size breakfast the woman had left in front of her. Actually, her stomach knew the pancakes were there and was growling for them like a starving dog. But first they had to get past her throat, and she wasn't sure she could manage that with any degree of success. Suddenly, her eyes pricked with unforeseen tears. Of anger? Frustration? Fear?

All of the above.

Resentment churned through her at being cornered like this, at being forced to figure out what to do before she was ready, that this had been dumped in her lap when none of it had been her fault to begin with—

Her coffee nearly went flying when Dean's hand landed on her wrist, his thumb gently stroking the top of her hand. "I tried to call you yesterday, but you were never around."

She carefully withdrew her hand and fixed it around her coffee cup, lifting it to her lips. "I was out on farm duty all day," she said simply, the scalding liquid etching a path down her gullet. A pause. "Why'd you call?"

"To see if you were okay. After…what happened at the Jenkinses'."

She allowed a curt nod, curled her other palm around her cup. He was simply being kind. So why did she feel so perilously close to ripping out his entrails? Might have something to do with the fact that between then and now, she sensed that something had shifted between them, something she neither understood nor trusted. "Of course I was okay," she replied in a level voice, refusing to let herself be lured into the depths of those damnably sweet green eyes. "It's my job. It's not the first time I've had to euthanize an animal, after all—"

"Sarah…" His voice washed over her like a gentle spring shower, twisting her gut six ways to Sunday. "You cry every time an animal dies. Always have."

Sarah slammed her not-quite empty cup down on the table, sloshing coffee over her hand. "How the hell would you know what I do? It's not as if you've been around—" She wasn't sure she could control the tears now, and that just irked the living daylights out of her. He'd hurt her, damn it. Ripped her life to shreds. By rights, she should hate him—heck, she wasn't sure she didn't—yet here she was, in spite of everything, wanting him just as much as she always had.

Her own ambivalence infuriated her.

Swiping the coffee off her hand with a napkin, she bit out, "Sunday night was just particularly stressful, that's all. And you happened to catch me when my defenses were down."

"Baby—"

"Don't!" She shook her head sharply, her hand knotted around the soggy napkin. "Just…don't."

The clatter of Dean's fork on his empty plate made her flinch. "Don't *what*, for God's sake? All I wanted was to see how you were doing. Trying to be *nice,* I think it's called. But you gotta go and blow it up out of all proportion. Why are you making this harder than it is?"

Finally, she looked at him, the heat from her eyes battling with his. "Those missing years really don't mean anything, do they? What the hell is this, Dean? You think we can just pick up where we left off, as if nothing happened…?"

Dean pounded the table, making her jump. "Of course I don't think that! But we had something special, once, and I just thought…" He heaved out a sigh. "I've admitted I screwed up, that I've regretted my actions every single day of those nine years you seem to think mean nothing to me. Yet no matter what I do, you take it the wrong way." He grabbed her wrist, his warm, callused fingers pressing into her skin. "What do you *want* from me?"

The one thing she couldn't have, she realized on a jab of pain so sharp, it was a wonder she didn't double right over.

"I want you to leave me alone," she said quietly. *Give me some time to think.* She twisted her hand out from his. "An apology can't erase a third of my life."

"It's a third of my life, too, dammit—"

"Oh, for God's sake, Dean—get a damn clue!" She pushed herself up from the table, the wooden chair scraping across the plank floor. "The only reason you're even in town, the only reason you're sitting here at my kitchen table, is because my sister is marrying your brother. Would you have come back otherwise, Dean? If fate hadn't thrown us together again, would it *ever* have occurred to you to try to fix things between us?"

He glared at her in stony silence for long seconds, then dragged his hand across his jaw. "I don't know," he admitted, startling her. Averting his eyes, he leaned heavily back in the chair, creaking the wood. "Hell. No matter what you do, it just comes back in your face, doesn't it?" Once again, he lifted his eyes to hers. "I'll admit, I haven't exactly thought this through. I just saw an opportunity…damn, that's not coming out right, either." He seemed to hold his breath for a moment, then said, "Maybe I did need fate to give me a push. But what the hell difference does it make how it happens, as long as it does?"

"It just does," she said in a small but steady voice. "To me. It makes a difference to *me.* And because it does, trust me, this isn't fixable, no matter what you do or say or think." She hauled in enough air to fill a party's worth of balloons, let it slowly seep back out, then said, "Maybe we *did* have something special once, Dean. *Past tense.* But a lot happens in nine years, more than you have any idea. I'm not the same dewy-eyed fool who thought the world revolved around you, Dean Parrish. And I never will be again."

Out of the corner of her eye, she saw her mother reenter the kitchen, then felt her hand on her arm. "Sarah Louise…"

"No, Mama." Sarah pulled away from her mother's touch

and crossed her arms, lifting her chin a notch. Or three. "Okay, y'all, listen up— I'm an adult, even have a life of my own. So I'd really appreciate it if everyone would just let me live it, okay? No more conspiracies, no more interferences, no more 'everybody knows better than Sarah what Sarah needs.' Got that?"

Before they could respond, she grabbed her car keys and shoulder bag and headed out the back door, feeling a sense of triumph unlike anything she'd ever felt before. Of course, she knew no one would pay the slightest attention to her. But at least her voice hadn't shook.

Neither Dean nor Vivian said a word until they heard the Bronco leave.

"You should've gone after her," Vivian said, clearing his and Sarah's plates from the table.

"No, I shouldn't've." Dean took a sip of his now-tepid coffee, even as Jen's words meandered around inside his thick skull. A big part of him still wanted to back out. An even bigger part, though, just couldn't. Not yet. "She needs to feel she won this round," he said with a half smile.

Vivian hooted. "Hot damn! So—you are going after her!"

A wry smile tilted his lips. "Now, don't go getting too excited, Vivian. Only thing I'm after right now is to get our friendship back on some sort of footing, okay?"

Sarah's mother gave him a long, assessing look, then said, "Okay. I suppose that's a start. But…you remember that time when you two were little and it'd been raining for a dog's age, and I told you to stay inside because I'd just washed the kitchen floor? But you went outside, anyway, and tracked up the floor, then tried to clean it up using my best towels?"

"Oh, Lord," Dean said on a chuckle. "I'd forgotten about that. Thought you were going to string us up for sure that time. What made you think about that?"

Vivian dumped the dishes in a bowl of soapy water in the sink, then pushed up the sink handle, rinsing off the plates as she continued. "Well," she said over the running water, "I knew Sarah was the instigator. She always was. But she'd rather die than admit she'd done something wrong. And the more guilty she was, the more loudly she protested. Seems to me she screamed something awful that day, even though she was standing there with muddy shoes and a mucked-up towel in her hands.'' Vivian turned off the water and faced Dean, wiping her hands on a dish towel. ''She's never changed. The closer you get to the truth, the louder she's gonna get.''

Dean sighed. But said nothing.

''She's close to breaking, honey,'' Vivian said quietly. ''Nothing in her way now except her damn pride. Hey, you've still got, what? Four days?''

Had making it up to Sarah become a matter of pride for him, too? A mistake was one thing; failure was something else.

Dean crossed his arms over his chest, scowling. He didn't often fail these days. And damned if this was going to be one of those times. Still, he wished he had Vivian's confidence in the situation.

''Hey.'' Vivian poked his shoulder again with one finger, as if reading his thoughts. ''If the good Lord made the entire world and everything in it in seven days, you sure oughta be able to fix things with my daughter in four.''

Yeah, well, somehow Dean figured the Lord got the better end of that deal.

Later, Dean declined Vivian's invitation to supper, using his aunt as a convenient excuse. Actually, he thought she'd probably be having her late-day meal with a neighbor, and so wouldn't even be at home. But, in spite of Jennifer's injunction for him to keep a high profile with her sister, he opted out. Cussedness or no, he wasn't out to wear her down. Exactly.

Lance wasn't home, either, when Dean dumped his truck keys on the hall table about six-thirty. It was dead quiet save for the amazingly loud hum of the unfortunately beer-free refrigerator, from which he extracted a Dr. Pepper with a resigned sigh.

His aunt had made three concessions to modern living; a

color television, a microwave and an answering machine, which she now used to ignore anybody she didn't have a mind to speak to just then. There were five messages this evening, three from Dean's business partner in Atlanta. A couple of years older than Dean and the father of two precocious little girls, Forrest Townsend had been the bookkeeper at that first cabinet shop where Dean had originally worked after leaving Sweetbranch. It had been Forrest who steered Dean toward a remedial program that helped him learn how to compensate for his disability; Forrest who badgered him into getting his GED; Forrest who insisted they go into business together five years ago, Forrest handling the finances, Dean the artistic and product end. No one thought it would work—a dropout from some speck of a town in Alabama and a man with more debts than sense, as Dean's aunt saw it. No one, that is, except Forrest and Dean.

But it had. Better than any of them could have dreamed. And one of the reasons it worked so well was because Forrest was a first-class, card-carrying noodge. The last message, in fact, explained in colorful and explicit detail the fate that awaited parts of Dean's anatomy if he didn't return the call *tonight*. Dean chuckled, imagining his aunt's expression if she'd gotten to the machine first.

He sobered right up, though, when he realized that, somewhere along the way, he'd made a decision—well, sort of one, anyway—that might not go over so well with his partner.

Dean wanted to come home. For good. It made no sense, and he wasn't even sure he could pinpoint exactly when he'd realized it, but this is where he belonged. Always had.

And no, Sarah Whitehouse had nothing to do with his decision.

Forrest launched forth the instant he heard Dean's voice. "Hey, man, Tidewater House has been on my case ever since you left, wanting to know *exactly* when they can expect first delivery."

A frown tightened Dean's forehead. "What are you talking

about? Says right in the contract first delivery's September 10. This is June.''

"Yeah, well, they don't see a factory sprouting up, so I guess they're getting nervous. You got their money, but they don't see anything to show for it.''

"Oh, for the love of Pete—we just got that contract two weeks ago. What's their problem?''

"They know you're out of town, that's their problem.''

"I left for one week for my brother's wedding. It's not against the contract.''

"What can I say? I'm only the messenger, buddy.'' Forrest paused, then said, "Look—you thought that space downtown might be suitable. You want me to go ahead and lease it? We've got the money.''

"No...not yet.'' Dean rubbed the space between his eyebrows with his index finger. "Listen—off the top of your head, you see any reason why the showroom and workshop can't stay right where they are, and the factory be moved out of town?''

"Out of town? Like where?''

"Like...here.''

"*There?* Podunk, Alabama?''

"Hey, hey—Sweetbranch would be a perfect place for a factory. Overhead would be a lot lower out here, for one thing....''

He heard Forrest whistle through his teeth. "I don't know... Where're you gonna get labor?''

"There's quite a bit of local talent, I hear. Maybe some folk's'd relocate. We've got good schools, a great university nearby, culture, sports, recreation—''

"Lord, you sound like a damn chamber of commerce. You found a building?''

"I'm...working on it.''

"Great. No labor that you know of for sure. No building. And a major client breathing down our necks... Oh, hell. It's that woman, isn't it?''

Dean started. "What woman?''

"The one you won't talk about."

"If I don't talk about her, how do you know there's a woman?"

"Because you haven't dated since we started this business, I know you're straight, and because you went practically brain-dead from the moment your brother asked you to be his best man and you knew you were going home. Oh, it's a woman, all right."

"This has nothing to do with—"

"Old girlfriend?"

"How'd you…?"

"And she's still unattached?"

"She's been pretty busy…."

"Aw, man…nobody's that busy." A few seconds ticked by while Dean realized he'd been suckered. "And something tells me she won't leave Sweetleaf—"

"Sweet*branch.*"

"Branch, leaf…some part of a dang tree, who cares? In any case, am I right? That she won't leave?"

Dean dropped onto the arm of the sofa, scrubbing his hand over his face. "Since I can't seem to get past Door Number One, who goes where is moot. I told you, this has nothing to do with her."

"Uh-huh. What the hell you do to her?"

Dean let out a hiss of air, realizing resistance was futile, then explained. Forrest was silent for, oh, maybe two seconds, then said, "Shoot, man, you'll be doing well to even *see* Door Number One, let alone get *through* it. But, hey, I wish you luck."

"Thanks," Dean said dryly.

Another couple of seconds drifted by. "Well…" Dean could imagine Forrest scratching his head. "I *suppose* it could work, having a factory outside the city. Tell you what— I'll call these people tomorrow and tell them we're *negotiatin'* for a place, and they can just damn well keep a lid on it for another couple of weeks. But you don't have a whole lot of time to mess around here, man, you know?"

Yeah. He knew.

After Forrest hung up, Dean just sat, staring at the cast-iron pug, who seemed to giving be him this mocking sneer.

What on earth was he thinking?

"Hey, bro…" Lance came through the front door, jangling car keys in his hand. "Any messages for me?" he asked, dropping his suit jacket over the arm of the sofa.

Dean shook his head. "Where's Jen?"

"We're going out in a while." Lance headed for the kitchen. "She decided she was hot and sticky and wanted a bath—"

"Listen," Dean interrupted. "You know if there's anyplace around that might be suitable to set up a factory?"

Lance poked his head out the kitchen door, popping the top off a Dr. Pepper. "You serious?"

"You think it might work?"

"I think it'd be great," Lance said with a grin, loosening the knot in his tie. "I can give you the names of at least five, six woodworkers off the top of my head who'd give their right arms to have a steady job doing what they love. And, yeah, you should have no trouble finding a place either in Opelika or Auburn."

"Would you be interested in handling the books?"

Lance gave a low laugh as he slid off his tie, undid the top two buttons of his shirt. "I dare you to give the job to anyone else." He tossed the tie on top of the jacket, took a swig of the soda, then asked, his dark eyes twinkling, "What does Sarah think about this?"

Dean glared at the pug. "This has nothing to do with Sarah."

His brother seemed to consider this for several seconds, then said quietly, "You're not sure this is going to work out, are you?"

"The factory?"

"No. Sarah."

"You know," Dean said on a sharp breath, "you're the only person around who doesn't seem to think our getting back together is a done deal.'' He eyed his brother. "I take it you know all the sordid details by now?''

Lance snorted, leaning against the door frame between the living room and the kitchen. "Probably, assuming Jen didn't embellish.''

Folding his hands behind his head, Dean leaned back, propping his stockinged feet up on his aunt's wooden coffee table. "So...what's your take on the situation?''

Lance hesitated, then dropped onto the damask-covered wing chair in front of Dean. "I don't know. Something's going on, though. Something Jen doesn't know about, or I'm sure she would have told me by now. That woman couldn't keep a secret if her life depended on it.''

Frowning, Dean crossed his arms over his chest. "What kind of something?''

Lance threw one hand up in the air, the universal male gesture for "beats me.'' "Sarah's just been...I don't know. Evasive? I mean, she's made no bones that she thinks the two of you have nothing in common anymore, but I don't buy that. I see how she looks at you when she thinks no one's watching—'' A grin hitched up one corner of his mouth. "Sorry, bro—afraid I have to side with Jen on that one. Sarah's...*scared*.''

"Lord. You and Jen aren't even married yet, and you already sound like each other.'' Lance chuckled; Dean massaged the crease between his brows. "I hurt her, Lance. Badly.''

But Lance was shaking his head. "It's not that, I'm sure of it.''

"Then what?''

Lance shrugged. "Got me. I just call 'em. I don't explain 'em. But you know what?'' He wagged his Dr. Pepper can at Dean. "That is one lonely lady.''

"How could she possibly be lonely? She's never alone.''

Lance shook his head. "Not the same thing. Her mother and sisters are no substitute for...'' He paused. Blushed.

A smirk crossed Dean's features. "A toss in the hay?''

"I didn't say that.''

"But that's what you meant.''

"Actually, no. Sarah's worth a helluva lot more than that."

To his surprise, Dean felt his eyes go scratchy. His baby brother was all grown up. Had his own business, was about to be a husband. And more perceptive than most men were at any age.

"Yeah," he agreed. "She is." He sighed. "But, to answer your original question, whatever relationship I might or might not have with Sarah has nothing to do with my decision to put the factory here."

"You sure?"

"I'm sure. It's time I came home." He let his eyes rest on his brother's face. "Been away far too long as it is."

"Even if Sarah isn't part of the package?"

Rising from the chair, Dean walked over to the open window and looked out at the humidity-hazed sky. Robins darted across his aunt's just-watered lawn, stopping occasionally to listen for worms. He could smell earth and petunias and roses and the faint, constant whiff of farm animal that pervaded the countryside. Smells from his childhood, smells from a time when everything made sense. Even though he knew things might look hopeless tomorrow, right now he felt confident and peaceful and downright cocky.

A crazy man, is what he'd become.

He thought of how warm Sarah's hand had felt under his that morning at breakfast. How damn much he'd missed her. How much it would hurt, being here and not feeling comfortable enough with her to kid, to pal around. Not being able to touch her.

"Hell," he said softly. "It's not as if I can force the woman to trust me again. But I'll do anything to prove she can." He turned to his brother. "Anything."

"I'd be careful if I were you." Lance wagged the can at him again. "Never known a woman yet who wouldn't take a man up on an offer like that."

That got a pair of raised brows. "Oh? And how many women might that be, little brother? Two?"

He ducked as Lance's loafer came sailing toward his head.

* * *

She almost missed the roses on the reception desk the next morning.

Despite being up half the night with a foaling mare, she'd left a terse note for her mother telling her not to let her oversleep. So she was up and clean and fed. But not awake. Shoot, she was one step removed from comatose.

Jolene called to her as she passed. "Hey, girl—you blind?"

Sarah backed up and stared blankly at the receptionist. "What?"

"The flowers?" She jabbed a hooked red fingernail in their direction. "They're for you."

"Me?"

"Yeah, you, missy." Jolene cocked her head, one hand on her hip. "You know of another Sarah Whitehouse around here?"

Now Sarah stared at the flowers.

The receptionist had resettled herself at her computer. "You know, it usually is easier to figure out who sent them if you read the card."

As if she didn't already know. But Jolene would give her no peace until she followed her suggestion, so she played along, gritting her teeth. While she was fumbling to get the teensy card out of its envelope, her boss came up behind her. "Mornin', Sarah. Got an admirer, huh?"

"Seems that way." Finally, she just tore the envelope.

I'm not giving up that easily. D.

She wanted to cry. She wanted to scream. She wanted to throw things. "Jolene?" She leaned over the desk, plunked the flowers in front of the startled woman. "Congratulations. You just got yourself two dozen roses."

Enormous dark eyes lit on her face. "You're kiddin'? These are *gorgeous*. Who sent them to you?"

"Never mind. It's not important."

She felt a light touch on her shoulder. Doc. "Come into my office, Sarah."

Like a little girl, she obeyed.

She sat across from Clarence Jefferson, her elbows resting on the arms of her chair, her hands dangling awkwardly at the ends of her wrists. The elderly man settled himself across from her behind his desk and pinned her with walnut brown eyes the same color as his face. His deep voice seemed to originate somewhere around his knees. "I've never seen you like this. You wanna tell me what's up?"

She studied the round face for a second and sighed. "If you're concerned my work is going to suffer…"

"No, Sarah. I'm concerned that *you're* suffering." Large hands tented in front of full lips. "You've been acting strangely all week. Now, this business with the flowers. You looked like the Devil himself sent them to you." His white eyebrows dipped in concern. "Is somebody *scaring* you?"

She brought one hand to her face, then lowered it again. Oh, yeah—somebody was scaring her, all right. But not in the way Doc thought. "No." She let her gaze get caught in his, then sucked in a breath. "Look, something personal's come up that I can't really talk about, but…it's thrown me. That's all." She shrugged, then allowed a small smile. "It's nothing I can't handle." He shot her a look that said he didn't believe her for a minute. "Really. I'm sorry if I've caused any disruption…"

Doc Jefferson held up a hand. "I have no quarrel with your work, Sarah. You're one of the best vets I've ever worked with. I just hate to see you so unhappy."

Her eyes widened. And here she thought she'd been doing such a good job of hiding it. "I'm not unhappy, Doc." She gave a smile bright enough to light up a ride at the state fair. "See?"

The old vet huffed and stood up from his desk. "Coulda fooled me, young lady." He paused. "Take your flowers home, Sarah."

She stood as well, shoving her hands in her pockets. "I already gave them to Jolene…."

"She'll get over it. Take the flowers home. Work out whatever it is about them you have to work out. You got that?"

She lowered her head slightly. "Yes, sir. I got that."

* * *

The flowers had been Vivian's suggestion. Dean hadn't really been sure they were such a good idea. But he didn't know what else to do and he had to do *something*.

There hadn't been much time to worry about it, though, which was just as well, probably. He'd spent most of the morning shuttling his aunt on various errands, including a visit to the mall in Opelika, which had just about done her in. He'd had to laugh to himself, wondering what her reaction would be to one of those megamalls in Atlanta with their two-hundred-plus stores. She'd probably drop her store-bought teeth at the crowds. Not to mention the prices.

"What're you going to do this afternoon?" Aunt Ethel asked, interrupting his thoughts.

The morning had actually been somewhat pleasant. He peered over at her, perched like a sparrow on the end of the truck seat in her crisply ironed cotton dress. "I hadn't thought about it. You still need me for anything?"

"Oh my, Lordy, no. The only thing I'm going to do this afternoon is take a nap." She flapped her left hand at him. "You're on your own."

Dean pondered his freedom for several seconds, his lips pursed. "Fishing," he announced, a wide grin settling across his face. "I haven't been fishing for years. Hey—maybe I'll see if Katey'd like to go with me."

He almost expected an objection, mostly because it was just his aunt's habit to come up with a reason why anything anyone wanted to do was wrong. Instead, she was strangely silent as she watched the road for the occasional critter darting across. At last she said, "That'd be nice. And I'm sure Vivian wouldn't mind at all having an antsy child out from underfoot for an afternoon."

So that's what he did. He wasn't sure who was happier about the outing, Katey or her mother. Apparently, his aunt had been correct, as usual. Vivian had a picnic lunch packed for them within five minutes, tucking a change of clothes for Katey into the old-fashioned wicker hamper.

"In case she falls in. Which she always does," Vivian said with a wink for her baby girl, who was hopping from one foot to the other. With impatience, Dean figured.

Vivian figured otherwise. "You gotta pee?"

Katey nodded once, then dashed to the bathroom.

"You'd think by this age she'd figure out what the pressure meant without being reminded," Vivian said with a chuckle, handing Dean the basket. "So…you send the flowers?"

"Two dozen red roses. Hope that's okay."

"*Okay?*" A low whistle spun from Vivian's lips. "Nothing like going for broke, boy."

He frowned, shifting the heavy basket to his other hand. "You really think it'll make a difference?"

Vivian sighed. "Shoot, honey, I don't know. One thing I learned a long time ago was to never try and second-guess my children.… Hey, baby," she said to Jennifer, just coming in the back door, looking uncharacteristically hot and frazzled in a brightly patterned sundress, her upswept hair coming loose from her topknot. "What're you doing home?"

"Hidin' out," Jen said, sweeping through the kitchen, her arms full of shopping bags. "Do me a favor, y'all—" she dropped a bag as she backed through the swinging door, muttered something unladylike as she contorted herself to pick it up "—and shoot me if I ever decide to get married again."

With a low laugh, Vivian returned to rolling out a piecrust at the counter, the chore Dean interrupted when he'd arrived twenty minutes earlier.

"You don't regret at all having a baby late in life, do you?"

She twisted to him, her eyebrows raised. "Now, where on earth did that question come from?"

With a nervous half laugh, he replied, "I'm not really sure."

Vivian lay down the rolling pin and turned to him, arms crossed, her eyes fixed on his with a steadiness that was almost unnerving. "Katey was a surprise, certainly, but a gift all the same. I've never had one moment's regret about her being here.''

"Wasn't the pregnancy hard on you, though?"

Her mouth twitched at the corners. "At my age, you mean?" Before he could apologize, she resumed her task. "Lots of ladies have babies past forty, Dean. Doesn't mean they have problems.''

Jennifer reappeared, hair subdued, outfit changed to a pair of shorts and a prim little cotton blouse, just as Dean said, "Oh...I didn't mean anything by it. It's just that Lance said you had to go to Montgomery for the last few weeks because there were some complications...?''

"Y'all talking about when Mama had Katey?" Jennifer asked, pouring herself a glass of iced tea. "Shoot, Mama was healthy as a horse the whole time she was carrying Katey." She glanced over at Vivian, who was peeling the piecrust off the floured counter, folding it into quarters. "Weren't you, Mama?" Vivian tossed her a brief smile, then went about unfolding the piecrust over a mountain of peaches. Jen settled back against the counter, the ice tinkling in her glass, addressing Dean again. "But you know about Sarah's having mono, how she'd gone to stay with Aunt Ida over in Montgomery, on account of they didn't want me to get it, for one thing, and, anyway, Daddy didn't think Mama should have to take care of her with the baby coming and all—''

Out in the living room, the phone rang.

"You want me to get that?" Jen asked, but Vivian had already wiped her hands on a towel.

"No, baby," she said, oddly subdued, it seemed to Dean, and went to answer the phone.

Jennifer craned her neck for a minute, to see if the call was for her, presumably, then went on. "See, it was a long, drawn-out affair. Sarah's mono. Most cases are over and done with in six weeks, but Sarah had let herself get run down some, so she kept having these relapses. So Daddy and Mama decided it would be better for her to stay over there while she recuperated. Only, Mama couldn't stand it, being away from her so long, so she asked if Daddy and I wouldn't mind if she went on up for a while." She laughed. "And of course, Katey decided to come while she was there. My nose was bent out of shape for months about that one!"

Vivian returned, immediately returning her attention to crimping the edges of the pie's two joined crusts. He noticed her face was flushed, but then that was hardly surprising in the oven-heated kitchen.

"Who was on the phone?" Jen asked.

"What? Oh, nobody. Wrong number," Vivian said, looking very relieved when Katey came bounding out of the bathroom, ready to go. "Oh, honestly—would you look at yourself?" she said, grabbing her youngest daughter to straighten out her crooked shorts.

"Hey, Jen," Katey said as her mother jostled her this way and that, "you wanna come fishing with me and Dean?"

"In a word—" she bent over, kissed her sister on top of her head "—no."

"Okay, you two." Vivian gave Katey a quick hug, then wagged her finger mockingly at Dean. "You take care of her, young man, you hear?"

"Like she was my own," he replied, and something in Vivian's eyes set off a whole mess of alarms in his head.

Dean hadn't been around kids much since he'd left, except for Forrest's two babies, whom he adored. But even so, he had the distinct feeling Katey was not your average child. To begin with, conversing with her was like talking to a forty-year-old trapped in a little girl's body. Not that she was obnoxious or anything. She just had this *calmness* about her, as if she'd figured out most of the important stuff already, and the rest of it was simply not worth losing sleep over.

Not surprisingly, Sarah quickly became the topic of conversation.

"I told you about her and Dr. Stillman," the child said shortly after they arrived at the creek.

"Excuse me?"

"That there was nothing going on between them."

"Oh, yeah. No, I could see that." He baited Katey's hook, then set up her pole so she wouldn't have to tend to it if she didn't want to.

"So…what're you going to do?"

"Do?"

Her sigh spoke volumes. "About Sarah." She rolled her eyes as if to say "Men are *so* slow."

Part of him wanted to change the subject. Part of him didn't. "What is it you think I should do?"

Katey squatted on the edge of the bank and dangled her fingers in the bubbling water, clearly unconcerned that her actions might keep the fish away. She hitched shoulders that were more bone than substance. "You like her?"

Dean settled on the grass a few feet behind her, leaning against a tree. "Yes, Katey," he admitted. "I like her very much." He paused. "I've known her since I was five. Did you know that?"

She turned to him and nodded, one eye narrowed in the glaring sunlight. "Mama told me, last night. Said you two used to be best friends."

"That's right. We were."

After a moment, during which the child studied him as if he were a new species she'd just discovered, she asked, "What happened?"

"Our lives just…took different paths," he answered simply. "That's all. Grown-ups sometimes lose touch."

Another several seconds' scrutiny, then Katey turned back to the water. "Mama says that her and Daddy were best friends, too."

If there was more to her thought, she didn't elaborate. Instead, she fell into a silence that with any other child would have indicated sullenness or pouting. With Katey, long silences simply meant the child had nothing to say at the moment. He wondered what she was thinking. And he was sure she was, probably a great deal, he'd lay odds. Probably as least as much as he was.

As he approached thirty, the concept of fatherhood—*his* fatherhood—had been occupying his thought with increasing regularity and intensity. Forrest and Nicki's last baby, just now a year old, had a lot to do with it, he supposed. The baby had been born at home, earlier than expected, so Nicki's mother was en route from Greensboro when the baby made her appearance. Dean had drawn baby-sitting duty with two-year-old Leanna while Forrest and Nicki and the midwife brought Leanna's new sibling into the world, which meant Dean saw the baby right after her birth. The little chocolate drop of an infant had opened her black marble eyes and looked up at him, pursing tiny lips and frowning as if to say, "Who the heck are *you?*" and Dean had felt his heart swell with the incredible sweetness of holding this tiny, new person in his arms. And he realized how much he wanted one of his own. Shoot, wanted a whole *passel* of his own.

Now, watching Katey, thinking about Sarah, the regrets began a new song and dance, as he thought about the children that he and Sarah might already have if he hadn't...

This was ridiculous, this constant "if he hadn't" nonsense. The fact was, he *had* left, he *had* broken Sarah's heart, he *had* screwed up. Whether or not he could patch things up was anybody's guess, but there was no point belaboring the past. It wasn't going to change just because he was sorry. No matter how much he wanted it to.

Which was exactly what Sarah had been trying to get through his thick head, wasn't it?

"Oh!" Katey exclaimed, jumping up to her feet. "I think I got a fish!"

Shaken from his reverie, Dean lunged for her pole before the fish dragged it downstream, pulling out a good-size crappie. "That's my girl!" he said, unhooking the fish and putting it in the ice chest. The lovely, excited face that met his when he looked up twisted his heart, bringing up all the "if onlys" all over again.

Chapter 8

At three-thirty, arms overflowing with roses, Sarah nudged open the back screen door with her rear end. "Mama? I'm home," she called, like she'd done every day, just about, since she was old enough to say the words. The kitchen was redolent with thick, golden midafternoon sunlight and the scent of fresh-baked pie. Peach, Sarah thought, her stomach rumbling at the thought. With some difficulty, she hung her shoulder bag on the little wooden hook shaped like a calico cat that Katey had given her for Christmas a couple of years ago, then flopped the fragrant ruby blossoms into the sink.

They really were exquisite, she mused as she plugged the sink, then ran warm water over the cut stems. Hesitantly, she fingered one of the still-closed buds—the air-conditioning in the clinic had kept them tight all day. Here, in the warmth and humidity, they'd probably open pretty fast.

Like her heart ached to open to Dean again.

"Hey, baby," Vivian asked from the doorway. "How come you're home?"

"It was slow, so Doc threw me out. Said he'd call if he needed me."

Her mother sidled up to the sink, brushing back a wisp of hair. "Whoo-ee! Aren't those pretty!"

"Who sent them?" should have been the next question. But it wasn't. Which meant she knew. Sarah's shoulders instantly tightened. "Where's Katey?" she asked offhandedly.

"Down at Sadler's Creek for the afternoon."

Sarah shot her mother a glance. "Alone?"

"No. With a friend. An older friend, too, so she's okay," Vivian said, answering the unsaid concern, while cupping one bloom in her fingers. "Look at how perfect this is. Sure wish I could get my Mr. Lincoln to look this good."

Sarah stretched to open a top cupboard, searching for something classier to put the roses in than the milk jug they'd used at the clinic. "Hey, if you could do that, then *you* could charge eighty bucks a pop for two dozen roses, too." Her hand closed around an old porcelain thing that was stained and chipped, but at least it was big enough. She clunked it onto the counter. "What'd you do...call the florist to see how much they cost?"

Sarah pulled out a large carving knife from a block near the sink and began slicing off an inch from the bottom of each stem. "As a matter of fact, I did."

Vivian let out a resigned chuckle. "I'd ask why, but I don't think I want to know... Oh, you can't put those beautiful flowers in that old thing. Hold on a minute." She stepped out of the kitchen, reappearing almost immediately with a large cutglass vase from the living room. "Here. Use this."

How many times had this vessel actually held flowers? Four, five times tops that Sarah could remember. Without a word, she took the vase from her mother and filled it with water.

"Who sent them, anyway?"

Finally. Calmly arranging the delicate stems, Sarah replied, "As if you didn't know."

Her mother picked up one of the roses and slowly twirled it around in her fingers. "And...how do you feel about that?"

"Other than that Dean Parrish is the biggest fool this side of Texas?"

"Now, come on…" Vivian picked up the full vase and carried it out into the living room, setting it in the center of the oval marble coffee table in front of the sofa. "You have to admit it was a sweet gesture."

Sarah followed, leaning against the door frame, arms crossed. "You put him up to this, didn't you?"

Vivian spun around, her palm pressed to her sternum. "Put him up…? Oh, Sarah," she said on a little choked laugh as she pushed away the comment with a sweep of her hand. She fiddled again with the roses, which apparently weren't sitting just the way she thought they should. "You're talking nonsense."

"Am I?"

No reply.

"Okay," Sarah said on a sigh. "Clearly, all that stuff I said yesterday at breakfast about wanting to be left alone was wasted breath. Not that I'm surprised," she added with a short laugh, then sank into a down-filled armchair opposite the sofa. "What you want…it's not possible, Mama."

Vivian sat on the edge of the coffee table, facing Sarah, the roses framing her shoulders. "Anything's possible if you trust enough. And it's obvious how much he still cares about you.…"

"That's *guilt,* Mama, plain and simple. And the ironic thing is, he's bending over backward to try to make things up to me, thinking *he's* the bad guy in all this." Sarah looked at her mother, her hands spread. "And just how long do you think that 'caring' is going to last when he discovers the truth?"

A fragile thread of silence spun out between them.

"That why you keep pushing him away, honey? Because you're afraid to tell him about Katey?"

Tears flooded Sarah's eyes.

Vivian leaned over and tried to take Sarah's hand in hers, but she pulled it away, pressing her knuckles to her lips. "It's only going to get harder, the longer we wait," Vivian said, her words laced with equal parts sorrow and contrition. "As it is, we should have told Katey long ago—"

"And you know damn well why we couldn't," Sarah shot back, her voice trembling. "As soon as she knew, she'd've let it slip to one of her little friends, and then somehow, Dean would have found out. That would have been disastrous."

But Vivian was shaking her head. "I never said we needed to tell her about Dean. Just that you're her real mother. She needs to know." Vivian sucked in a deep breath. "And you need to hear your own daughter call you 'Mama.'" Sarah's gaze leapt to her mother's. "I know it's eating away at you. Almost as much as Dean's being here is."

Sarah shook her head, her eyes burning. "Not that I'm exactly innocent here, Lord knows, but don't you think it's a little odd that you're so determined to 'fix' things?"

"Oh, honey," Vivian said, her face contorted, "it's like to have killed me, watching you watch her all these years—" Her bottom lip caught in her teeth, she looked away, her brows knit tightly together.

Sarah went on instant alert. "What?"

"I told Ethel."

"You did *what?*"

"It was time." Vivian's timorousness seemed to have vanished; now she met her daughter's horrified gaze without compunction. "Time she knew."

Sarah's stomach plunged; she held her hand to her mouth as she sprang from the chair, paced over to the window seat, back to the center of the room. "We *promised* each other that neither of us would say a single word about this unless we *both* agreed! What's to prevent her from telling Dean…?"

"She won't. Ethel may be a meddlesome nuisance, but she is neither a gossip nor is she malicious. She was shocked, of course, but it was the only way I could get her to understand how important it was to get you two back together—"

"*Meddlesome?* The woman's an amateur compared with you!"

"Sarah!"

"I'm sorry, Mama!" she cried, wiping her cheeks. "But you've gone too far this time." She crossed the room and tore a tissue out of a box next to the phone. "Has it ever occurred to you that maybe I don't *want* to get back with Dean? That maybe I've moved beyond whatever he and I thought we had—"

"Oh, please, Sarah!" her mother huffed, then said, "Has it ever occurred to you that you're just being stubborn? As stubborn as you were nine years ago?"

Sarah stepped back as if she'd been slapped. Her cheeks flaming, she spun around and strode to the window, her arms folded tightly across her aching stomach. She heard Vivian come up behind her, felt her hand on her waist.

"Look, I'll be the first one to admit I made a mistake, honey. A horrible mistake, even if I truly did think it was the best thing at the time. But *you* were the one who refused to let him know you were pregnant. All I did was bail you out."

Tears tracking down her cheeks, Sarah could only shake her head. Not because what her mother said wasn't the truth, but because it was. The look on Dean's face when he told her he was leaving, the way he'd mocked their intimacy... She'd been stunned, and confused, at how he could suddenly turn on her after all their years together. All she knew was that if he really wanted nothing more to do with her, why would he have wanted their child...?

"This is your chance to make things right," her mother was saying. Sarah humphed. "All right, *our* chance. The man obviously still cares about you, he wants to patch things up—"

"And he's going to be devastated when I tell him. Not to mention furious. And what about Katey? How am I supposed to explain this to her?"

"We can't pretend anymore, baby," her mother said simply.

Sarah finally got around to blowing her nose, then managed an approximation of a laugh. "All you kept saying all those years ago was to back off, to be careful, that maybe we weren't right for each other..."

"I was wrong, honey. Dead wrong. Which is something I'll

regret all my days.'' She let out a huge sigh. ''I should have trusted you more. Maybe if I had, you wouldn't have felt the need to sneak off and…'' She stopped.

Sarah was quiet for a long moment, then said quietly, ''And then Katey wouldn't be here.''

Vivian had no answer to that.

Wiping her eyes, Sarah twisted and regarded her mother briefly, then walked back to the sofa, sinking down on it. ''If I live to be a hundred, I'll never believe I managed to get pregnant the first time I had sex.'' Another rueful laugh crawled out of her throat.

Her mother laughed, too, softly, and sat down beside her. They both studied the roses for several seconds, then Sarah said on a shaky sigh, ''Oh, Mama…how did everything get so balled up?''

''I don't know, baby. But seems to me, maybe this is our little window of grace, our chance to finally heal the whole mess.''

With a grimace, Sarah grabbed a little burgundy velvet pillow and hugged it, picking at a nylon thread that had worked its way loose. ''How on earth am I going to get through this?''

Vivian shrugged, with some difficulty, as if her shoulders were too heavy to lift. ''I don't know. But I don't see much way around it.''

Sarah doubled over, cramming the pillow into her stomach as she buried her face in her hands. Her mother's voice seemed to be coming from another state. ''Would you rather *I* told Katey?''

She shook her head, still in her hands, then raised her face to stare at the opposite wall. ''I don't know yet. No. Maybe.'' She blew out a long, shuddering breath. ''I don't know,'' she repeated as she collapsed against the back of the sofa.

''And Dean?''

''Oh, Lord, Mama…give me a minute here, okay?'' She pushed herself off the sofa and once again walked over to the window, as if the enemy lay just outside the walls and she was about to go do battle. ''This isn't like trying to straighten out a problem with the bank, you know?'' She leaned one hand on the window frame, let her head drop forward as she drew in a steadying breath, then lifted it. ''Just…promise you'll be here to pick up the pieces?''

''Oh, honey—'' A second later, she was in her mother's arms. ''Always, sugar. Always.''

Sarah let herself hide in that strong embrace for a full minute, wanting to be a little girl again, for things to be the way they were before all these nasty grown-up responsibilities had trampled her idyllic life. Suddenly, Sadler's Creek sounded like heaven. She'd always gone to the spot as a child, whenever she was upset about something. And Katey was already there, with one of her friends.

Sarah pulled out of her mother's arms, checked her watch. Older friend or no, Katey should have been home by now. She blew her nose, took a final swipe at her cheeks, and announced, ''Think I'll go down and get Katey. The walk will do me good.''

She thought she heard her mother call after her as she barreled down the back steps, but she didn't respond.

Sarah heard his laugh before she heard Katey's. Coming to an abrupt halt, she rested one hand on the sappy bark of a pine tree as she saw the two of them pull in a fishing line with a slapping, wriggling prize on the end of it. Their heads were together, spotted sunlight dancing alternately on honey-gold and maple hair, Dean's rumbling baritone underlying the child's sparkling squeals of delight.

Father and daughter.

Her throat tightened with the sorrow she'd denied for so long. It was one thing to know Dean was her child's father, quite another to be faced with *telling* him he had a child. That *they* had a child. She'd only been putting off the inevitable, the past few days. How was he going to feel when he discovered he'd missed out on the first eight years of his daughter's life?

She could no longer consign Dean to her past…but whether

or not he'd still want to be part of her future was up to him. And suddenly, that mattered. More than she would have thought possible just yesterday.

Sarah leaned closer to the tree, watching as Dean unhooked the hapless bream and tossed it inside the cooler sitting a couple of feet away, absently responding to the giggling child as she waded barefoot into the creek, darting this way and that. Chasing crawfish, Sarah presumed. She smiled, wondered if her mother had packed an extra set of clothes for when Katey inevitably fell in.

A single tear made a run for it down her cheek.

She'd been forced to make the hardest decision of her life when she was the most vulnerable. And what choices had there been? An abortion was out of the question. So was telling Dean. Or raising the child on her own, which would have resulted in the same thing. What would he have done? Come home and insisted on marrying her, probably, in spite of their horrendous last meeting, because everyone would have been on his case to do the "right" thing.

Which would have been the worst thing in the world, given what she thought she knew at the time.

That had left giving the baby up for adoption. With an open adoption, she'd rationalized, at least she'd get to hear how the child was doing from time to time, maybe even see it occasionally.

Her mother had been horrified. Thrilled at finding herself pregnant again at forty, Vivian couldn't imagine ever being able to give up something that had grown inside you for nine months. To tell the truth, Sarah was having none too easy a time coming to terms with the idea herself, but it seemed, for a while, like her only choice. And one that would be good for the baby, she'd told herself.

But Vivian miscarried her baby…and that's when the final plan evolved.

Please, Vivian had begged in tears one day about a week after her loss, *please don't give up the baby, let me raise it as mine instead. No one will know if we handle it just right. That way you'll be around your child almost every day, you know?*

Get to see him or her grow up, know what your baby sounds like, feels like in your arms... We can make this work, you'll see, she had pleaded. *And this way, Dean won't have to know...*

Sarah capitulated, and her mother took on the project with the zeal of an undercover agent, a plan that had only worked because her mother always looked a bit pregnant, anyway, and Sarah didn't show at all until her sixth month, and even then, she'd been able to conceal the pregnancy with baggy sweatshirts.

How perfect it had all seemed. How foolproof.

Until Sarah woke up from the dream her mother had plunged them both into and realized the flaw in the plan. For the birth certificate, of course, listed *Sarah* as Katey's mother, not Vivian.

And Dean as her father.

She could have pretended ignorance, she supposed. Omitted his name, let the record state instead "Father Unknown." But when it came right down to it, when she lay there in the hospital bed, her baby girl cooing in her arms, the only thing she could think of was the miracle that one night of lovemaking had produced, clichéd and corny as the thought may have been. So she put down Dean as the rightful father of that miracle. Even if he never saw her, let the record show whose genes this beautiful child carried.

But her sentimentality had a price. Even though Vivian had home-schooled the child, sooner or later, Katey would need her birth certificate. And then she'd know. And Vivian had a point; the longer they waited, the worse it would be.

Could things possible get more complicated?

"Sarah!"

She jerked at the sound of Katey's voice, thinking she'd been more hidden.

"Come see all the fish me an' Dean caught!" The child seemed to fly over the thirty feet between them and grabbed Sarah's hand, yanking her toward the embankment where Dean was slowly rising to his feet. "Dean says we can cook 'em tonight! And he'll let me help! Oh! And he said he's going to make me a chair just like the one he made for Jennifer and Lance, but small enough so my feet'll touch the floor..."

Sarah barely heard the little girl's ramblings. Dean's moss-green eyes had ensnared hers from the moment Katey started to pull her toward him. As she got closer, the look in them changed from surprise to something soft and smoldering and gentle. She knew she was just projecting her own anxieties, but...it was almost as if he knew.

But of course, he didn't.

Katey dashed back over to the creek and all its treasures, leaving Sarah—confident, cocky, never-at-a-loss-for-words Sarah—unable to think of a single thing to say.

He'd seen her before Katey had, standing by that tree like a cautious doe, so focused on Katey she'd been oblivious to his presence. She'd kept dead still, the breeze teasing her hair, stirring the neckline of the simple white cotton shirt she wore tucked into a pair of baggy shorts, and Dean had been almost afraid to breathe, for fear that, like a doe, she'd start and disappear back into the woods.

Now she was close enough for him to catch a whiff of her hair conditioner every time the wind shifted. He caught her eyes as well, willing them to mesh with his. He saw them widen, almost in alarm, and noticed the red rims.

"Hey, what's this?" He itched to touch her cheek, refrained. "You've been crying?"

She scrubbed her palm into one eye, then the other, jerking her head in denial. Sniffed. "No...it's just...a little reaction to all the dust in the air today."

Right. Sarah wasn't allergic to anything. She could stand out in the middle of a hayfield and not even sniffle.

He wanted to take her in his arms, tuck her head against his chest. Hold her and rock her and plead with her to trust him. Instead, he tucked his thumbs in his jeans pockets, wondering what was different about today. Yesterday she as good as told him to go to hell. Today...today was just different, that's all.

One side of his mouth lifted as something struck him. "Your mother didn't tell you Katey was with me, did she?"

She shook her head, then cleared her throat, lifting that pointed chin to cover up whatever she was really feeling. Apparently, she'd forgotten who she was trying to kid. "I don't suppose that would have served her purpose." Now she made a sound that was half laugh, half sigh. "The woman is incorrigible."

Dean couldn't think of a single reply that wouldn't get him into trouble. Except one. He extended his hand, his head cocked. "Truce?"

After a moment, she nodded again, then slipped her hand into his. "Truce," she agreed, immediately breaking the contact. He wasn't sure, but he thought maybe he saw a faint tinge of pink wash over her cheekbones.

She glanced around her for a moment, toying with the high-school ring she still wore, then walked past him to the cooler. She lifted the lid and gave a short, startled laugh. "How many people you plan on feeding tonight?"

"Katey had a good day."

"More like a good *week*. Y'all leave anything in the creek?" She let the lid slam shut, then made her way to a grassy patch near the water's edge. Shielding her eyes with her right hand, she watched Katey splashing in the water about twenty feet downstream for a moment, then sank cross-legged to the ground.

Cautiously, Dean joined her, close enough to talk, far enough away not to spook her. He leaned back on one elbow, one leg straight out, the other knee bent, tilting his torso just slightly in her direction while keeping his attention directed toward the opposite bank. He heard Sarah pick up something, then send it skipping across the creek.

"The flowers are...really beautiful," she suddenly said. "Thank you."

He almost jumped. "You're welcome." He stole a quick peek at her face, then looked back out over the water. "I was afraid you'd be mad."

"Oh, I was," she replied matter-of-factly. "Madder 'n a cow with a fly up its nose. At first. But..." She shrugged in lieu of finishing the sentence.

"I meant what I said," he ventured. "In the note."

She nodded, squinting in the sun. "I know you did."

He didn't breathe, waiting for the objection. But there didn't

seem to be one. As casually as he could manage, he let his
eyes seek out her face, which she was keeping deliberately
masked. But this was Sarah. *His* Sarah. Her face may have
been still, but he was sure her brain was working overtime.

He wanted to touch her so badly his fingers tingled. A slight
breeze crept across the creek; she shivered, just for a second,
and he saw a little coterie of goose bumps crop up on her
forearms. How soft she was, he remembered, every part of her
silky and smooth, so cool and warm at the same time, balm to
his hands and his soul.

He remembered. And he ached.

He agonized for a full minute, like a kid on his first date
trying to screw up the courage to take the girl's hand in the
movie theater. When he finally decided to just do it—what did
he have to lose?—he felt her fingers tense. But she didn't pull
away, even when he began to gently stroke her knuckles with
his thumb.

"Hey, y'all!" Katey cried. "Look at me!"

Sarah immediately shot to her feet at the sound of Katey's
high-pitched voice streaking over the rasping shrill of a cicada.
Dean could see the little girl hopping from one exposed rock
to another, flapping her thin arms every few seconds or so to
regain her balance.

Sarah picked her way through the bushy growth on the bank.
"Katharine Suzanne—just what the blazes do you think you're
doing?"

Katey froze at the harshness in Sarah's voice, the dark, finely
haired brows pulled tightly together over the bridge of her nose.

"I've done this hundreds of times," she whined, wiggling
a little to adjust her balance. "It's no big deal."

Sarah was quiet for a moment. Dean knew better than to
interfere, to suggest that maybe Katey was just fine. Or worse,
to confess that the child had been performing her balancing act
without mishap for the last hour. Finally, he saw Sarah's shoulders rise, then fall sharply, he assumed from a sigh.

"Just…be careful, okay?"

Katey's face lit up as she nodded with such vigor she nearly
lost her balance again. Sarah walked back up the embankment,

her hands in her pockets, her wide, unlipsticked mouth pulled into more of a grimace than a smile. "So sue me. I worry."

He chuckled. "Isn't that a *mother's* prerogative?"

Sarah had glanced back over her shoulder at Katey as she made her way back; now she whipped her head around, her eyes dark and wide. Then her expression neutralized, and she hunched her shoulders in a half shrug. "I suppose." She flopped back down beside him. "I'm just standing as proxy."

There she sat, her arms loosely clasped together around her knees. Not going anywhere. Not angry or defensive or hostile. Again, the thought came to him that something had changed. And he knew it was more than the roses.

They should talk. *Somebody* should talk. He thought about that for a full minute until he just came out and said, "I've been thinking...about what you said yesterday." He had, too. A lot. "About whether or not I might have ever come back if it hadn't been for Lance and Jennifer getting married."

Sarah slanted him a quick look, then glanced away. "Oh?"

"You're right. I probably wouldn't have."

Her hand found its way to her hair, damp with the increased humidity this close to the water, forking through it as she squinted out over the creek. "That's why I said—"

"No, please..." He touched her arm. It was damp, too. And cool. "Let me finish, okay?"

She folded her hands together again, then nodded, not looking at him.

"You know how you said you thought I'd forgotten about you?"

Her voice was tight. "Yes."

"Well...I figured, after what I'd done, you'd forget *me*." He studied a small section of the creek where bubbles kept coming to surface and popping, idly wondered if a catfish was lying on the bed underneath. "Hell, Sarah...I was scared to death to come home. Figured it just wasn't worth it, you know? I mean, I'd made a new life. And it wasn't as if I had any right to expect you to forgive me..." He shrugged, tossed another stone.

"Then, Lance asked me to do this, and I thought, shoot, I

can't turn down my only brother's request for me to be his best man, can I?'' He looked up at her. "But I was still scared out of my wits. Scared you'd hate me. Or that you'd found someone else.'' His chest heaved in a heavy sigh. "Not that I had any right to think one thing or another about that. I could hardly have blamed you for looking elsewhere. But, still…'' He shook his head.

For a long moment, she just stared straight ahead, twisting that ring around and around her finger. Then she said on a sigh, "Things…can't go back to the way they were, if that's what you're thinking. We're not the same people we were then.''

He laughed softly. "I hope not.''

She turned those liquid amber eyes to him, her mouth set. "No, Dean. You don't understand. Forgiveness is not even the issue here.''

He wasn't sure what she was trying to say, but he was damned if he was going to let her wriggle her way out of it this time. "Then what *is* the issue?''

The grass beside her legs seemed to suddenly consume her interest. Since she didn't answer his question, he assumed there was no answer.

"Hey, you,'' he said softly, stroking the top of her hand, "What I cared about then is still there. People don't change like that. We're both older, maybe a little smarter, but we're still us.''

She swatted at a buzzing something or other, her face betraying nothing of what she might be thinking or feeling. So, on a deep breath, he went on. "If I can find a place, I think I'm going to manufacture that new line of furniture right here.''

Her eyes zipped to his. But still she said nothing.

"I'd still have to be in Atlanta from time to time,'' he said carefully. "But my home would be here.'' He paused. "Where it's supposed to be.''

The gazes tangled for several seconds before she picked up a stone and tossed it out over the water, her mouth pulled down at the corners.

"Would you…rather I didn't come back?'' he asked.

Her sigh blended with the breeze. "I just don't…I don't

want you making any decisions based on what I may or may not do.''

In the long pause that followed, Dean's thoughts threaded with Katey's screeches of glee, the soft whirring of wind-teased willow leaves, the creek's gentle gurgling.

"I know you might find this hard to believe," he said quietly, picking at a piece of long grass in front of him. "But all I really want is to see you happy. After all, we were best friends before we were…'' He took a deep breath, a breath filled with the smell of sweet, clean water and damp earth. And Sarah. "Before things got serious. I sometimes think I miss that most of all.''

He heard a little gulp next to him. Before he could touch her, she scrambled to her feet and started to walk away.

"For God's sake, Sarah—'' Dean jumped up and took off after her. "Stop running!''

"I'm not!'' she tossed over her shoulder as she increased her pace, her arms clamped across her ribs.

"The hell you say!'' He grabbed her as she ducked underneath a low-hanging willow, turning her around so sharply her body slammed into his. "Every time we get into a serious discussion, you're off like a damn greyhound.''

Her mouth was far too close. And not nearly close enough. The old bent willow gently slapped their faces and shoulders with her slender green fingers, as if admonishing them for their foolishness. Sarah opened her eyes wide, those intoxicating whiskey eyes inviting him in whether she wanted to or not…and with a little cry, she looped her arms around his neck.

His hand cupping her jaw, he let his mouth drop to hers, wishing he could somehow convey everything he felt with this one kiss. He stroked her cheek with his thumb, his fingers massaging the little dip in the back of her neck, his only desire, at that moment, to make her understand how much he cherished her.

And always had.

For a few precious seconds, she was his. She melted into him, her tongue meeting his in a slow, tantalizing dance. He kissed her again, and again, his other hand slipping around to the small of her back, gently massaging that sensitive spot at the base of her spine, and she nestled against him with a little moan. Her hands threaded through his hair, the warmth of her through his shirt making him shiver. Her mouth, her body were perfectly aligned with his, and he could feel her temperature rise, her heart rate increase, her breathing almost stop as they savored each other and yearned for more.

Then she pulled away, her eyes so filled with tears he was amazed they weren't streaming down her cheeks.

"This...isn't fair" was all she said, then started back toward the cooler, her hands raised as she shook her head. In the distance, thunder rumbled.

"Sarah—"

"Call Katey, would you?" she said, so coolly that Dean wondered if he'd just dreamed the kiss. "There's a storm coming. We need to get out of here."

All Dean could do was stand there and feel stupid. Something he'd been doing a lot lately. *What* wasn't fair? The kiss? His coming back? *What?*

Then he heard the splash.

A few feet away, Sarah turned around with a resigned sigh. "There she goes. Did my mother pack an extra set of clothes?"

"Uh, yeah..." His brain was definitely split into several noncoordinating pieces. "In the hamper."

"Go fish her out, then. I'll get her changed."

All Dean could do was obey. He trudged downstream to where he expected Katey to be, only to find no sign of her at first. His heartbeat pounded in his ears as he frantically scanned the expanse of water—

"Sarah!" he bellowed. "Get over here!" Panic ripping through his gut, he scrambled down the embankment to where Katey lay in the water.

Which was quickly turning a garish shade of red around her head.

Chapter 9

There was so much blood! Dull, blurred streaks all over Katey's clothes, ghastly red splotches on Dean's, oozing out from underneath Dean's palm, tightly pressed against Katey's forehead—

"She's knocked out, but she's breathing okay," Dean said, trying to assure her, looking as though he could use a stiff drink. "But this is one nasty cut."

Sarah managed a shaky nod as she knelt beside the little girl. Her own heart racing so fast she feared she might faint, she pressed quaking fingers against Katey's neck to feel her pulse, which seemed strong enough.

She'd dealt with much more severe injuries in animals and never panicked. But this was a child. *Her* child. And her child was not only unconscious but bleeding far too much for Sarah's comfort. Cripes—the most Katey'd ever done to herself was scrape the skin off both knees at the same time when she first started riding her bike...

"We need a bandage," Dean said calmly, and she nodded again, willing her brain to work. Her eyes lit on Dean's shirt, a soft chambray, clean and absorbent. Damn…it looked brand new.

"Your shirt?"

Dean immediately handed Katey to Sarah, who replaced his hand with hers over the cut, pressing hard against it, wondering why she couldn't seem to staunch the flow. By the time she looked up, he'd stripped off the shirt and ripped it in two, then into smaller pieces, fashioning one of them into a pad without Sarah's even telling him. Even though his face was gray, his actions were steady and precise.

He gently peeled away Sarah's hand, adjusted the ragged edges of the cut, and pressed the pad over it. "Keep pressure on the wound until I can get it wrapped."

Sarah couldn't help the shaky laugh, even though her stomach muscles felt like gelatin. "Who's the doctor here?"

He clamped his teeth around the edge of the fabric and ripped the shirt again, then offered an anxious grin. "I work in a shop with lots of sharp, nasty tools. And one or two macho types who seem to think they're invincible. Accidents happen, though rarely, thank God. Still, you learn to do bandages." Sarah decided not to dwell on the kinds of wounds sharp, nasty tools might inflict. Dean wrapped a strip around Katey's head, tied it securely so the pad wouldn't shift. "Hey, honey—she's gonna be okay."

Sarah took in a deep breath and tried to smile, even though what she really wanted to do was puke. "I know. It's just…" She swallowed, then said, "There's a pediatric center in Opelika—we need to get her there."

"Not the hospital?"

Adjusting the "bandage," more so she'd feel useful than for any other reason, Sarah shook her head. "No child of…in my care is going to sit around for four or five hours in some ER waiting room if I can help it."

"She's all wet."

"It's ninety degrees. It's okay."

Dean gave her a brief "I suppose you know what you're doing" look, then picked up the limp little girl as if she were a kitten and started toward his truck. But Sarah put a trembling hand on his arm. "Give her back to me. You drive."

She was beginning to feel as though she had gotten caught in an emotional hailstorm. The roses. Her mother. Dean's kiss. Now Katey, unconscious and bleeding in her arms, the poor little banged-up head cradled against her chest. One thing after another—*boom…boom…boom*—no chance to recuperate from one trauma before the next one hit.

Dean steered the truck with precision, even with one hand. His other hand was folded over hers as she held Katey. She was in no position to object; rather, she let herself find comfort in those gentle green eyes when he looked over.

His smile was everything.

"It's okay, baby," he said, like he used to everytime she got upset about some piddly thing or another. But this wasn't piddly. There was a tremor in his voice she'd never heard before, and she found herself fighting tears for at least the tenth time that day.

They drove in silence for several minutes while Sarah desperately tried to master her emotions. She knew it wasn't good for Katey to stay unconscious for long, although she thought maybe the bleeding had finally let up some. Fear for her daughter and fear of telling Dean he *had* a daughter had rendered her dumb.

Just as anxiety threatened to cut off her breathing altogether, she was startled to hear Dean singing. A simple ballad, something they used to sing at church camp when they were kids. He was no Pavarotti, but his voice was soft and warm and kind, soothing a little girl who couldn't even hear him at the moment. A little girl who didn't know he was her father.

Sarah let the tears come. No one would think anything of it, considering the circumstances, not even Dean. No one would know she was crying because she'd made a terrible mistake long ago and wasn't sure if she could fix it. No one would know she was crying because she was in love with a man who she had a pretty good idea was still in love with her and she didn't know what to do about it. No one would know...

"Sarah? What happened?"

She jumped, looked down into scared brown eyes.

"What happened?" Katey repeated. "Where am I?"

"Shh, baby," she said, smiling through her tears. "You just banged your head and got a nasty cut, is all. Dean and I are taking you to see Dr. Williams so he can get you all fixed up."

The eyes widened. "Why are you crying?"

"Oh, honey..." She actually laughed. "Because you scared the bejesus out of me, that's why."

"Hey, bug..." Dean let go of Sarah's hand and squeezed Katey's. "How're you feeling?"

"Awful," the little girl pronounced, snuggling against Sarah. Then she tugged at a dripping braid. "Yuck," she said with a grimace, trying to sit up, immediately collapsing again. "I'm all wet! An' I smell like a crawdad!"

"You know, Dr. Whitehouse, those head wounds bleed something terrible," the plump, middle-aged nurse said with a chuckle as they stood in the examining room. She wrote something on Katey's chart, then glanced at Sarah and grinned. "I'm not sure which one of the three of you looks worse."

Sarah glanced down at her clothes, which were smeared with blood and bits of creek gunk, then at Dean, bare-chested and definitely the worse for wear.

But poor Katey! Her complexion slightly green, she lay cuddled in Dean's arms with her preposterously bandaged head against his chest. She'd finally dried off, but her previously soggy state had proved far more distressing to the child than the stitches she'd had to get for what Sarah called her Super Booboo.

"I think it may be a tie," she at last offered with something akin to a smile.

The nurse gave Katey a short rub on her back, then wagged her finger at the little girl, which was hardly intimidating considering the size of the smile that accompanied it. "Now, don't you be scaring your Mama and Daddy like that anymore, you hear me?''

"Oh, we're not—" Sarah and Dean started simultaneously.

Katey shook her head, then winced. "Sarah's not my mama," she said in a tiny voice. "She's my sister. And Dean's going to be my brother-in-law."

"Your sister! You serious?" the sepia-skinned woman said, brows raised. "Land's sakes, there must be, what? Twenty years between you?"

"Eighteen," Sarah replied politely, wanting nothing more than to go sit down somewhere until her knees felt more secure.

The nurse snickered. "Little surprise package, huh? Same thing happened to my mama. My baby brother's twenty-two years younger than me. But you know what? We all had a *ball* with him when he was a baby. I think he thought he had eight parents instead of two! Okay, sugar," she said, addressing Katey again. "No more hopping around in the creek for a little while, you hear? And don't get mad at your sister if she keeps waking you up every couple of hours or so tonight. We want to make sure you don't have a concussion."

"What's a con...concussion?" Katey asked.

"It's when you jiggle your brain around in your head too much."

Katey's eyes widened and Sarah could see the start of tears. "Oh..."

Sarah stroked her hair and laughed. "They're just being careful, sweetie pie. The doctor says you're just fine."

"Can she have a sucker?"

"Oh, I think she could manage that," Sarah replied, wondering why clinics never gave treats to the parents. Like chocolate chocolate-chip ice cream cones. Brownies. Swigs of brandy.

"Here you go, baby," the nurse said, handing Katey a cherry Tootsie Roll Pop, which brought a bright smile. "So...when you two getting married?"

Sarah nearly choked. "Married? Oh!" she exclaimed, understanding. "His brother's marrying my sister!"

The nurse whipped astute eyes from one to the other. "Oh, I'm sorry. I just could have sworn…"

"We're old friends," Dean supplied, and Sarah breathed a sigh of relief.

The nurse, however, simply looked from one to the other. "Uh-huh. And yesterday, someone mistook me for Madonna."

Sarah said very little on the way home. Not that Dean was surprised, the incident with Katey having unnerved both of them far too much to expect much in the way of idle chatter afterward. And if Sarah's silence had been due to just that, he wouldn't have given it another thought.

But he knew it wasn't. More than likely, it was what was— or wasn't—going on between them that had her plastered against the passenger side door. Elbow propped on the armrest, her chin in her hand, she stared out the window as if Dean wasn't even there.

As if the kiss they'd shared earlier hadn't been…real.

And not just hormonal, either. On either of their parts. The only difference between Sarah's response now and how she used to kiss him back when they were kids was now she kissed like a woman.

Like a woman who cared a lot more than she was letting on.

Early evening now, the west faces of the white farmhouses blazed coral in the low-riding sun. The storm had never materialized, instead leaving clusters of frustrated clouds, puffed up like a bunch of angry Day-Glo cats. Underneath the carnival-colored sky, folks waved to them or yelled "Hey" as they passed, whether they knew them or not, just being neighborly.

It all seemed so normal, so uncomplicated. Which was the way things were supposed to be in the country, after all. Wasn't that why city folks moved to the country, because life was simpler, less stressful?

And just who, Dean wondered, had made up *that* little fairy tale?

For several minutes, he let himself stew, wondering for the thousandth time why Sarah was acting this way, wondering what he could do about it, wondering if he was crazy for even trying. Then he realized all wondering and worrying was laying the groundwork for an ulcer, so he decided to think about something else, anything else but Sarah.

Kids, he decided. He'd think about kids.

So this was what it was like to have a child, huh? Exhilaration one moment, heart-stopping panic the next. And he'd give anything to be able to do it every day of his life. Long as he could share the joy, and the craziness, with Sarah.

Damn—didn't even get a full minute's peace, did he?

All right, all right…he wanted her so much he ached. Okay? Was the world happy now? *He wanted Sarah Whitehouse.* But…not like this. Frightened. Uncommunicative. Withdrawn. Not to mention just plain downright baffling.

They'd come to a crossroads, both literally and figuratively. Dean slowed to a stop, then glanced over his shoulder at Katey, conked out in the back seat.

"She's asleep," he said, concerned. "Isn't she supposed to stay awake?"

Sarah started at his voice, then twisted around and leaned over the seat, placing her hand on Katey's forehead. The little girl stirred but didn't awaken.

"It's okay," she whispered. "She's just dozing. We'll wake her when we get home." She sucked in a breath. "Lord, she looks like she did when she was a baby, that sweet little face. Except for the bandage, of course," she added with a low, wry laugh.

Dean resumed driving, squinting into the setting sun. "You're plumb crazy about her, aren't you?"

He felt her eyes searing the side of his face, then felt the heat abate as she resumed her scrutiny of the road. "What a silly question. Of course I am."

He reached up, adjusted the rearview mirror. "Ever think about having kids of your own?"

She shifted away from him, gnawing on a hangnail. His eyes darted to her face, then back out the windshield. "Criminy, Sarah—wasn't like I accused you of murdering somebody!"

"No…it's not that."

"Then what the hell *is* it?"

She singed him with flashing eyes. "Would you mind keeping your voice down? Or at least your language?"

He held up one hand. "Sorry," he whispered. "But, honestly…the minute things seem to be going okay between us, you clam up or run away. Excuse me, but I'm just a little confused, okay?"

"Excuse *me*," she retorted, "but nobody asked you to come back into my life and confuse *me,* either." Her voice shook; she took a deep breath, then said, "I'd just like some quiet right now, if you don't mind."

"Whatever you want," he managed to say through a tight jaw.

Sarah crossed her arms and fixed her gaze out the window, then shut her eyes. But worry, or something like it, had routed a groove between her brows.

Churning, ticked-off thoughts meandered around Dean's brain before settling down to thinking about fishing, of all things. A long time ago, he remembered his mother telling him there were never any wasted thoughts, that even the strange "where the blazes did this come from?" ones meant something, if you just kept your yap shut and *listened.* So he listened, as best he could, and after several minutes, he smiled.

See, some fish won't bite if the bait is waving in front of them. It's too obviously a trap. No, sir. Some fish, you have to just let the hook lie real still in the water, and then Mr. Fish will come up and not suspect anything and *chomp!*

Trouble was, he'd been trying too hard with Sarah. Using the wrong bait for the wrong fish, as it were. Obviously, the "in your face" approach wasn't working. At least, not well enough. So maybe he should try a different approach.

God, he hated game-playing. But he was desperate.

They'd be back at her house in a few minutes; like as not, half the county'd be there waiting for them. He glanced over at her, saw her eyes were open; she seemed to have calmed down some, though the groove was still there.

"You okay?"

She nodded, then sighed. "Sorry I blew up earlier."

"Forget it." He paused, then they both said at once, "Listen—"

His heart jumped. "What?"

"No," she said, her smile forced. "You first."

He could tell there'd be no changing her mind, so he nodded. "Well…"

Oh, Lord, please let this be the right bait.

"I've been thinking a lot about this forgiveness business," he began. "Expecting you to forgive me for how I treated you and all? So I asked myself what I would do if someone had done something like that to me." He allowed a quick peek at the side of her face. "You know, like lying to me? Making up a story like that?" He shook his head. "And I came to the conclusion that I'd probably feel just like you do."

"Dean—"

"No, hear me out. To be perfectly honest, I don't know if I could forgive anyone who did something like that to me, either. So…I just want you to know that it's okay."

"What's…okay?"

"If you can't forgive me. I understand, I really do. Finally got it through my thick head, I guess. Some things just can't be forgiven, I guess, not something that hurts that badly. I suppose I can't blame you for not trusting me." They'd pulled into her driveway; Dean cut the engine, leaning his arm across the back of the seat, not watching her. "What could I possibly say that would change the way you feel about what I did?"

When she spoke, her words trembled. "So…what are you saying?"

He opened his door but didn't move right away. "That you're off the hook. I'm backing off, leaving you alone, getting out of your life. If that's what you want. After the wedding, I'm gone. And up until then, I promise I won't bug you.''

"I see," she said stiffly. "What about setting up your factory here?"

He shrugged. "It was just a thought, you know? Nothin' definite. All I know is, seems my return has made you one miserable woman. And I can't stand seeing you like this. So, if I can't make you happy by being around, maybe I can make you happy by leaving—"

"They're back! Mama, come on!"

Their eyes met for less than a second before the truck was surrounded by a barrage of relatives and friends and neighbors. Wordlessly, Sarah pushed open her door and lowered herself out of the truck, Dean following suit.

Her expression was branded on his mind, and it wasn't what he'd expected. He'd hoped she'd be surprised. Maybe even worried.

Not *terrified.*

Oh, Lordy, he thought as he pulled Katey out of the back seat, Sarah standing in ominous silence beside him. What had he done now?

Sarah was barely aware of what anyone said to her as she walked up the steps and into the house behind Dean, who held a sleepy Katey securely in his arms. All she heard were Dean's words, playing themselves over and over in her head like Jennifer used to play the same CD until Sarah was ready to throw both the album and her sister out the window.

Some things just can't be forgiven, not something that hurts that badly…

She felt her sister's arm slip around her shoulders.

"Lordy, you look awful," Jen said with a little hug, not even seeming to care about the state of Sarah's clothes. "Everyone's so busy catering to Katey, and I bet you're the one who could use some TLC right now."

"I'd prefer a Harvey Wallbanger."

"Oh, right. This from the woman who gets woozy from white wine."

"Woozy would be good," Sarah said, sighing. "Actually, though, *fed* would be better." She lifted her face like a hound dog. "Fried fish?"

"Enough for half of Opelika," Jennifer said on a laugh. They'd made it as far as the living room, where Sarah sank into the sofa. In front of the roses.

She looked elsewhere.

"Lance retrieved all the stuff from the creek," Jennifer was prattling, "and Mama and Ethel've been frying to beat the band for the past hour. And there's hush puppies and slaw and tomatoes and potato salad and God knows what-all out there."

Sarah tried to laugh, but she was too tired and hungry and upset to manage. "Please, stop tormenting me and just haul me to the food."

Now Jennifer eyed her with one side of her mouth quirked up. "Not in those clothes, I'm not."

Sarah glanced down. "I see your point. Guess I'll change first."

Which she did in record time, into a clean shirt and shorts. When she came down to the kitchen, the large room was crawling with folks like bees around a honeysuckle vine, Katey being the main flower. All the women clucked and oohed and aahed and said "My, isn't she just the *bravest* little thing?" a thousand times, while Vivian clucked the loudest of all. And Katey, who was no fool, immediately seized the moment and said in a small, *small* voice that really, all she felt like was some ice cream, please, and was now reaping the reward of the wounded and shoveling in mouthfuls of Rocky Road like there was no tomorrow.

Jennifer settled Sarah at the kitchen table and told her to stay put and let herself be waited on, for once. So Sarah stayed put, wondering whose full plate that was next to her and if he or she'd mind if she took just one of those hush puppies.

Dean, somehow now respectably outfitted in a deep green

T-shirt, slid down into the seat. She let the hush puppy drop as if it had bitten her.

"Go ahead," he said coolly. "I can get more."

She shook her head and folded her hands in her lap, gripping them to keep from crying. Part of her wanted to plead with him, to tell him it wasn't true, that she could forgive him, that she *had* forgiven him, which she hadn't even realized until just that moment. Another part of her wanted to bolt. For the umpteenth time in six days.

Lord above—what *was* it about this man that tore her in two like this? It was like a little kid's fascination with fire—it'd burn you if you got too close, but oh, it was *so* pretty.

Jennifer placed a mounded plate of food and a glass of iced tea in front of her, then disappeared.

"Try the fish," Dean encouraged, no more personally than a stranger in a restaurant. "It'll melt in your mouth."

Sarah took one look at her supper and suddenly her ravenousness of moments before vanished. She couldn't stand this. The past few days Dean had been variously contrite, pleading, cocky, arrogant, loving, and just plain friendly.

But never distant.

Her eyes stung, and the noise and events of the day had given her a rotten headache. She needed to eat, but that wasn't going to happen next to Dean. She stood up, picking up her glass first, then awkwardly balanced her plate on top of it and wended her way out of the kitchen, seeking solace and solitude on the side porch. A few minutes later, she heard the floorboards groan under her mother's approaching footsteps.

"Katey throw up from all that ice cream yet?" Sarah asked in the gray light, licking her fingers. The food was beginning to make her feel a little better. Sorta.

"You kidding? Since when does a kid get sick when they get what they want?" One hand went to her hip. "Guess you had quite a scare."

"Scare?" Sarah took a swallow of tea and sighed. A soft breeze suddenly pushed through the screen, rearranging her hair. "I thought I was going to lose it. I didn't know such a small head could have that much blood in it."

The peacock-backed wicker rocker creaked as Vivian settled her ample frame into it. "That's pretty much what I thought, that day you took a tumble down the front stairs."

Sarah frowned. "When was that?"

"Oh, goodness—must've been right after we moved into this house. So you were maybe three, four? Anyway, you suddenly decided you were a big girl and didn't need to hold on to the banister anymore. The next thing I knew, you were rolling down the stairs like a rubber ball. Cracked your head open and I thought I'd die." She chuckled. "Screamed so loud Daddy thought *I* was dying, and he came running from his office on the double. I'm here to tell you I never saw a man turn so white in all my days. And him a doctor, no less. It's just so different when it's your own." She crossed one foot over her knee. "Wanna tell me why you're out here and Dean's in the kitchen?"

Sarah had wondered how long it would take. She clattered her empty plate onto a little table beside the chair and drooped back into the chair, one foot up on the rattan footstool in front of her, watching the fronds of a ceiling-high palm swaying overhead. "Oh, you're gonna love this. Seems good old Dean has decided I was right."

"About what?"

"About my not being able to forgive him." She folded her hands in her lap. "He said that, in my shoes, he probably wouldn't be able to forgive me, either. That it would be asking too much. So, out of deference to my feelings, he's going to leave me alone. Back off. Hightail it out of here as soon as the wedding's over." She angled her head toward her mother. "Just like I asked."

"Oh. Hmm."

Sarah laughed, a harsh sound that hurt her throat. "Yeah. *Oh.* Here I was," she said, flinging her hand outward, "trying to figure out how to tell him about Katey, *ready* to tell him about Katey. And now…'' She gestured helplessly, then pressed her hand to her mouth, her eyes swimming.

Vivian reached over, stroked her arm. "Trust, baby. You've got to trust how you feel about each other."

Sarah raised her face, sniffling. God, she hated to sniffle. Angrily swiping at her nose with the back of her hand, she bit out, "Uh-huh. And trusting my feelings worked so well the last time, didn't it?"

"But this isn't then, don't you see that?" Her mother seemed unperturbed either by her daughter's outburst or what had caused it. She stayed quiet for a minute, apparently thinking things through, then said, "I sure don't know, though, what this sudden change in tactic is all about."

Sarah was blowing her nose in her napkin. She stopped in mid-snort and stared at her mother. "Tactic?" The napkin lowered. "What do you mean, *tactic?*"

Vivian ignored her, blankly surveying the darkness on the other side of the screen. "But I *do* know the man's nuts about you." Settling against the back of the chair, she folded her hands across her middle and said, "This time, love's gonna win out. You'll see, baby. You'll see." With a last little pat, Vivian stood up and took Sarah's empty plate, then went back into the house.

Sarah gulped in a breath and let it back out on a sob, wondering how to break it to her mother that she was in serious need of a reality check.

Then, through the open French doors leading to the living room, she heard Katey's laughter. Followed by Dean's. She bit her lip as her heart twisted like a wrung-out washcloth.

In spite of Dean's precipitously changing the rules, the basic game plan hadn't changed: she still had to tell him the truth. So she got up, took in a deep breath and started toward the living room.

Just in time to see Dean walk out the front door.

Chapter 10

Dean winced as he straightened out his abused back, glowering at the burgundy-and-tan floral wallpaper in his parents' bedroom. The stuff must've been put on with superglue, he decided as he wiped his forehead and sweaty chest with an old towel his aunt had given him to use as a rag. He'd spent all day Thursday whacking at it, and now, the next morning, he'd still only managed to strip two walls. He'd hoped the physical activity would relieve some of his tension; instead, he was ready to use a blowtorch on the damn walls and be done with it.

His aunt had reacted with little surprise when he said he wasn't going to sell the house after all, but was instead going to fix it up and live in it. And she'd been downright jubilant about his plan to locate the factory in the area.

''It'll be good to have you home'' was all she'd said, but her eyes had glittered and she'd smiled widely enough for Dean to actually glimpse teeth.

He checked his watch; he had an appointment with a Realtor in Opelika at eleven to look at possible sites, so he had to get cleaned up. Jennifer had called last night, too, requesting an audience. That, he wasn't looking forward to.

He threw the scraper onto the floor with a satisfying clatter, then ran down the stairs, checking to see how Franklin was getting on with stripping the kitchen cabinets. The young man had been extremely relieved to discover he wouldn't have to move to Atlanta, after all. He was also more than happy to get on the payroll early by helping Dean with the house.

"How's it going?" Dean asked, pulling his T-shirt back on over his head.

"Counted twelve coats of paint, so far." The young man lifted an arm to swipe a ribbon of sweat from his face. "Heck—kitchen'll be twice as big when we're done."

Dean took a deep breath, then choked on the paint remover fumes. "You be sure to take off the doors and strip them outside, you hear? I don't want to come back to find you keeled over like a dead bug in the middle of my house."

"Don't you worry, Mr. Parrish," Franklin said on a deep laugh. "It'd take a lot more'n a few fumes to do me in." But he began unscrewing one of the doors, anyway. "Now, you're not coming back to the house today, is that right?"

"Not for a week. After the wedding, I've got to go back to Atlanta, get things squared away there before I can return. But I don't think you'll be hurting for things to do while I'm gone."

"You can say that again."

"Hey—how's that cow?"

"Fat and sassy. If she don't have that calf soon, either she's gonna explode or Mama is. And I don't want to be around in either case, believe you me."

Dean laughed, then left, zipping back to his aunt's to change into khakis and a knit shirt before his appointment. By the time he met Jennifer for lunch at a little diner in town two hours later, he was feeling almost mellow. The agent had shown him several properties, and the rents were downright cheap by Atlanta standards. He could be ready to start production in less than a month if necessary, which should appease his client.

His sense of well-being evaporated, however, the instant he caught Jennifer's expression as he approached her booth. Blazing away in a bright red sleeveless top, she'd already ordered and was stuffing in French fries as if she hadn't eaten in a week.

"Uh-oh?" Dean said as he slid into seat opposite her.

She glared at him. "What the *hell* are you doing to my sister?"

Several patrons turned their heads; Dean lowered his own as he unfolded his paper napkin and spread it across his knees. "Nothing," he whispered.

"Which would be my point," Jennifer parried in typical Jennifer logic. She lugged a hamburger the size of a small planet up to her mouth, chomped into it. "I thought I told you to keep a high profile," she managed to say, quite clearly, from around the bite in her mouth, sounding like a mother scolding a recalcitrant child.

"I tried that, Jen," Dean said, keeping his voice even. "It worked about as well as trying to spread cold butter on fresh bread—"

"What can I get you today, good-lookin'?" interrupted a salmon-haired waitress with a figure that had gone a lot farther south than Alabama.

Dean nodded toward Jennifer's rapidly disappearing lunch. "What she's having."

"And could you bring me another glass of milk?" Jennifer added, watching the woman bumble off to the counter with their order, before renewing her attack. "Look, buster, the last thing I need to be doing today is trying to patch up my sister's sorry excuse for a love life. In case it escaped your attention, I'm getting married tomorrow, and I'd really appreciate it if my maid of honor wasn't blubbering her eyes out during the ceremony—"

"Sarah's been crying...?"

The waitress plunked an oval earthenware plate piled with food in front of Dean, let her gaze linger a little longer than necessary, then merrily trundled over to another table.

"Like Niagara Falls." Jennifer stuffed the last bite of hamburger into her mouth. Clearly, her concern for her sister had not affected her appetite. "You've got to do something."

Dean took a double bite of the overdone hamburger. "And what," he finally said, "do you expect me to do, exactly?"

"Throw her down somewhere and have your way with her, maybe?"

"Oh, *that* would go over well."

Her own fries long since dispatched, Jen was now blatantly snitching his. "Why *haven't* you been around, anyway?"

"I've been too busy," he said around another mouthful, pushing his plate over so she wouldn't have to reach so far. "Jen…listen to me. It's just not up to me anymore, whether or not Sarah and I work this out."

"And how do you figure that—is that chocolate cream pie over in the case, do you think?"

He twisted around and caught the waitress's eye, ordering two pieces of pie when she came over. Since he'd lost out on his fries, the pie wouldn't hurt. "I don't know what else to tell you," he said around the last bite of his burger. "I've tried pleading, groveling, chasing, charming and something damn near to seducing. Nothing's worked."

"Then you have to try harder."

The waitress set down the pie in front of them. Dean picked up his fork, fiddled with it for several seconds, then dared to meet the determined gaze in front of him. "Jen, I've tried as hard as I can. I think we're all agreed that there's something else going on here, but until Sarah or *somebody* gives me a clue as to what that something is—" he guillotined the end of the pie, shoved it into his mouth "—I'm fresh out of ideas, I'm afraid."

Jennifer forked in her pie in uncharacteristic silence.

"Shoot, Jen—are you *that* used to always getting your own way?"

He was surprised to see tears glittering in those turquoise eyes when she looked up. "In case you haven't figured it out, this has nothing to do with me. Well, okay, I'd like to not have my wedding ruined, it's true. But I'm much more concerned that my sister's *life* isn't ruined, you know?''

He handed her a paper napkin, and she loudly blew her nose. ''Not nearly as concerned as I am, Jen,'' he said softly. ''But I can't make her happy unless she lets me. And so far, she just doesn't seem interested in doing that.''

''I just wish I understood *why*,'' Jennifer said on a huff.

''So do I, honey. So do I.'' Still chewing, he picked up the guest check that the waitress had let flutter onto his side of the table, glanced at it, then rose from the table. ''You done?''

''With lunch? Yeah, I guess.'' Jennifer downed the last of her milk, then slid out of her seat, slinging the thin strap of a dainty red purse over her shoulder. She poked his arm as he started toward the cashier. ''With you? Uh-uh.''

As they stepped out into lung-searing midday heat, she asked, leading him toward Lance's office, ''So what are you going to do tonight?''

Tonight. The rehearsal dinner. Dean squinted through a scrim of heat at some kids crossing the street, draggling a half-grown, gangly pup along with them, and his heart cramped at the pure, unbridled joy radiating from the little group. He shifted his gaze back to Jennifer's tight-lipped expression. ''Jen—give it up, okay? If Sarah doesn't meet me halfway, there's not a whole helluva lot I can do.'' He leaned over and planted a kiss on top of her curls, which were beginning to frizz in the humidity. ''See you at the church at four, right?''

''Yeah,'' she said on a rush of air as they reached the renovated Victorian in which Lance rented a little office for his accounting business. ''I guess.'' With a despondent little wave, she disappeared inside the building.

Dean walked back to his truck in slow motion, mulling over the conversation. The more he thought about it, the more frustrated he got. All that revelation about fish and bait was all well and good, but it all still boiled down to the fact, at some point, the fish still had to take the bait.

But maybe that was the problem, he thought as he headed back to his aunt's house. Maybe Sarah'd taken the bait *too* well. Maybe now she was afraid he'd really changed his mind, and she didn't know how to change it back.

Good Lord. This was enough to make him forget he'd ever learned the word *woman*. Now he'd blown it—*again*. Why couldn't he have just left well enough alone? He'd at least been making some progress, and then he had to go get some hare-brained idea about fish and bait.

Think. He had to think. He had one more day.

For twenty minutes, until he pulled into his aunt's driveway, he kept drawing blanks. He'd already tried everything, just like he'd told Jennifer.

When in doubt, his mother had always told him whenever he complained about things getting screwed up, *try praying about it.*

Huh.

But what to pray for? Asking God to deliver Sarah up to him didn't sound quite right. Even he knew you can't pray for something just because you want it, because that's selfish. So, it had to be an unselfish asking.

But how about…just asking God to bring Sarah a sense of peace about whatever it was that was tormenting her so much? And if somehow, Dean could be a part of that, well then, he was willing to do what he could.

Satisfied, and more settled about all of it than he'd been since he'd come home, he went into the house, startled his aunt with a big hug, then called Forrest in Atlanta and told him about his meeting with the Realtor.

"You're going to wear *that?*"

Sarah glanced down at the simple black silk sheath and frowned. "What's wrong with this?"

Jennifer—who was poured into a white linen sundress splashed with red Georgia O'Keeffe-esque poppies—heaved a dramatic sigh as she swept into the room. "Hello? It's *black?*" She flapped her hands at her. "Take it off."

"And replace it with…?"

"You mean, that's *it?*"

"Jen, you've lived with me all your life. You know what I wear."

"Well, I obviously don't expect you to wear stockings and heels to go mucking around in a barn. But you mean, there's really nothing else?"

"Not unless something miraculously self-generated in my closet since the last time I looked, no."

"Then you'll just have to wear something of mine."

"Oooh, no. I'm five inches taller than you are. Your stuff'll come up to my fanny."

"And this is a bad thing?"

"Oh, Jen—get serious."

"Oh, I'm serious. Trust me. Hey—I gave in about your wearing lavender. But there is no *way* you're wearing black to my rehearsal dinner."

"Black's sophisticated."

"Black's *funereal*."

Sarah sank onto the edge of her bed, emitting a particularly loud sigh of her own. "Considering how I feel, I'd say it was entirely appropriate."

Since Jennifer was busy flicking through the paltry selection in her closet, Sarah couldn't hear what she assumed was a snide reply. Suddenly, her sister twirled around with a peach crepe shirtwaist clutched triumphantly in her hands.

"What's wrong with this?"

"I'd look like Aunt Ida."

"Like you don't in *that?*"

She had a point.

"Humor me." Jennifer thrust out the dress. "Try it on."

Sarah had acquired the dress under protest, right after Katey's birth. Aunt Ida had insisted she needed to buy something with a waist in it to make her feel skinny again. To shut the garrulous woman up, she'd bought the first thing her aunt hadn't made a face at, worn it once, then ignored its presence in her closet ever since. It was the last thing she felt like wearing tonight, but, once again to shut someone up, she put it on.

"Now, *this* has promise," Jennifer said. "Look...blouse it

a little, like this…'' She poufed out the bodice over the belt. ''That brings the skirt up a little higher and makes the slit sexier.…''

''I'm not doing sexy, Jen.''

''Yes, you are. Be quiet. Okay, now…'' She undid the top three buttons and hitched up the collar so that it framed the back of Sarah's neck. Jennifer twisted around and looked in the mirror at Sarah's reflection, then pulled her mouth into an appreciative smirk. ''So, what do you think? And negative answers are not acceptable.''

''It's…not bad,'' Sarah admitted, studying her reflection.

''Are you kidding? You *rock.* Oh—hold on…I'll be back in a sec.''

She dashed out, returned with a set of plain oversized pearl earrings.

''I've never seen you wear these,'' Sarah said, clipping them on.

''I bought 'em on impulse about a year ago. But they're too understated.''

True, compared with the two-inch-wide bright red enameled flowers with the rhinestone centers currently positioned on either side of her sister's face. In any case, the pearl earrings worked quite nicely with both Sarah's square jaw and the outfit, which she had to admit was better than the black.

Even if, as she'd said, the black was better suited to her lugubrious mood.

''Jennifer!'' Vivian called up the stairs. ''Lance is here, honey.''

''Be right there,'' Jennifer yelled back, then gave Sarah a hug. ''You look wonderful,'' she said with a giggle. ''Knock 'em dead.'' Then, clearly pleased with her fairy godmother work, Jennifer floated out of the room.

Knock 'em dead? Oh, sure. The way Sarah's stomach felt at the moment, the only one likely to be dead by the end of the evening was she.

Oh, how she dreaded this dinner, having to sit next to Dean, because she didn't know what to do. She was hopeless at man-

woman games, having never had either the need or the incli-
nation to play them. She needed—wanted—to tell him about
Katey, but now was more afraid than ever what his reaction
might be. Of course he'd be shocked. Probably angry. *Probably?*

What if he really *couldn't* forgive her? One hand pressed
into her jittery stomach: it just about killed her to think
that…that—she shut her eyes, admitted to herself the one thing
she'd refused to admit for the past week—that they might be
this close to getting back together.…

Talk about the past catching up with you.

Funny, how they'd both acted from what they thought were
noble motives, like some turn-of-the-century O'Henry story.
He didn't want to trap her; she then didn't want to trap *him.*
And here, all along, they would have both been perfectly happy
being "trapped." Things wouldn't have been easy, God
knows, but they would have worked it out, somehow. Just like
they'd planned to all along.

But they hadn't. And now there was one holy mess to clean
up. And, at the moment, a wedding rehearsal and dinner to get
through.

"Sarah Louise? Come on, honey, or we'll be late."

She sighed so loudly, Balthasar actually looked concerned.

Only Sarah could look that good in that dress.

Criminy—it looked like something his aunt would wear. To
church. On Sarah, however, *church* was the last thing that
came to mind. She looked like a rose. An incredibly *sexy* rose.

A rose he was having an increasingly difficult time ignoring.

He meant what he'd said to Jennifer, that Sarah would have
to be the one to make the next move. And if she really didn't
want to work things out…well, that was that, wasn't it?

But if she did, she'd have to tell him. Plainly, unequivocally,
so there was no doubt. Which meant he'd just have to stay out
of her way a little while longer. A plan that would have been
fine, in theory, had dear, darling Jennifer not insisted they sit
next to each other at dinner. So here he sat next to this fragrant

rose of a woman who made his blood simmer, the tension between them probably causing interference on televisions within a five-mile radius.

Jennifer threw him an occasional nasty look, shifting her eyes in her sister's direction as if to say "What are you waiting for?" And Vivian, too, was doling out her fair share of unspoken censure, although at least *her* annoyance seemed to be equally divided between them.

He couldn't see Sarah's face, of course, but he could tell by her silence—as well as her uncharacteristic lack of appetite—that she was probably fighting for control. She went through the motions for probably a half an hour, then suddenly tucked her napkin underneath her plate and left the table. And, just as suddenly, he didn't give a damn about fish or bait or sisters-in-law or any of it.

He found her outside, on a deck overlooking the lake. He didn't ask, he didn't question, he didn't hesitate. He just swept her into his arms and held on tight, as if they would both die if he let go.

Sarah knew he would follow her. She would have been even more upset if he hadn't. And didn't *that* make a whole lot of sense?

At that moment, she could have no more resisted being drawn into his embrace than she could have gone up two bra sizes. She burst into tears, clinging to the lapels of his sport jacket as hard as he was clinging to her.

"What are we doing here?" he asked softly, stroking her hair.

"D-don't know about you," she hiccuped, "but I'm h-having a damn g-good cry."

He laughed and hugged her more closely for a second, then held her slightly away so he could look into her face. Terrific. Even the dusky light wasn't going to camouflage puffy eyelids and a swollen top lip. Yet he smiled for her as if she were the most beautiful creature he'd ever seen.

He wiped away her tears with his fingertips, those deep

green eyes as soothing as a sauna. And just as hot. "Your call," he whispered, his breath caressing her face. "What do we do now?"

She sniffled, needing to joke. Needing to diffuse the heat that was threatening a serious brain meltdown. "Find me a tissue, that's what."

"That's my girl," Dean said with a lopsided smile—*damn* that lopsided smile!—pulling out a clean handkerchief from his back pocket. "Miss Pragmatic."

Sarah took the soft cloth, trying not to let their fingers touch. She wiped her eyes, blew her nose, wiped her eyes again. Dean led them over to a bench apart from the restaurant where they were relatively alone and settled both of them on it, his arm protectively draped around her shoulders.

It was her move. Her turn. And possibly the only chance she'd have.

"I...understand now why you left me," she said in a small voice.

His fingers tightened around her shoulder. Just slightly. "You do."

She nodded and continued in a rush, "Now, I don't think that was the smartest decision you've ever made, and I don't know, yet, if I can ever fully forgive you. But I know your motives were unselfish." She offered a tremulous smile. "Misguided, maybe, but unselfish."

She saw hope stir in those kind, sweet eyes, and she wanted to cry out. "Is this...something you can live with?" he asked, his voice soft as a baby's kiss.

Her fingers worried her old high school ring for several seconds before she nodded again, sharply. More words, more risk.

The bench creaked slightly as he shifted his weight away from her.

She studied him out of the corner of her eye. His thick lashes were lowered over eyes that weren't seeing anything, she knew, as a vein pulsed in his temple, a puzzled half smile only fractionally relaxing his stiff jaw.

"Okay..." He drew out the word, his brain obviously trying

to churn through this as much as hers was. His fingers left her shoulder, worked their way up her neck. Much more dangerous territory, she decided, feeling her heart thunder in her chest. "Does this mean...we could maybe give this another shot?"

Why couldn't this be a simple answer?

"*That* I don't know about."

That was clearly not the answer he expected. Wanted.

He tucked two fingers under her chin and tilted her face to his. "Then tell me why not."

But she couldn't. She had to, but not now, she realized. Not when her sister—who didn't know about Katey, either—was getting married tomorrow. She lowered her eyes, then looked back into his, knowing hers were blazing with fear. And need. And confusion.

Just like his.

He stroked her cheek, which brought a whimper, then touched his forehead to hers. His scent—so familiar, so arousing—swirled through her senses. "Sarah, honey—you can tell me anything. You know that. Just like you always could."

If only it were that simple.

As long as she stayed mum, she could pretend there was hope. The minute she revealed the truth, however, it would be over. He'd said so himself, that he would never be able to forgive someone who'd lied the way he had to her. And *her* deception was so, so much worse. Would he even understand that her motives, like his, had been well-intentioned, that she simply hadn't wanted to shackle him to something he wasn't ready for?

Shaking her head, she pulled away from him, the tears coming again.

"Sarah—" Frustration viced his words. "What the *hell* are you so afraid of?"

Of losing you...again.

She just shook her head. Again. Then jumped off the bench and ran away.

Again.

* * *

Dean stared after her for several seconds, then went back inside, knowing he wouldn't find Sarah, not at all sure what he'd do or say if he did. He felt like a not-too-bright dog who knows he's buried a bone somewhere in the backyard but can't remember where, so he has to dig up the whole dang place until he finds it.

Of course, the process is just a bit more difficult if the dog's trying to dig up some *other* dog's bone.

He noticed most of the wedding party had dispersed, some dancing, having drifted outside to the deck. Vivian, however, was still at the table, sipping her wine, lost in thought.

Ah. Vivian.

He walked up and tapped her on the shoulder, making her jerk her hand to her chest. "Got a minute?" he said with a smile he'd dredged up from somewhere. "We need to talk."

"Now."

The breeze off the lake toyed with the hem of Vivian's shapeless dark blue dress as she sat on the bench where he and Sarah had just been. Dean stood in front of her, his arms crossed, his temper just barely in check. "I want to know right now what is going on here. Something has Sarah scared out of her wits. Since she won't tell me about it, I figured you probably could."

Vivian darted a glance in his direction, then folded her arms as well. "You figured wrong."

He narrowed his eyes, the muscles at the sides of his head threatening rebellion. "What? That you can't tell me? Or you won't?"

Cornered. That's how she looked. Her mouth was still locked into a stubborn set that would have taken a jackhammer to prise apart, but her eyes told another story entirely. One he'd very much like to hear.

"It's not up to me—" she started.

"I knew it! So there *is* a problem."

Vivian propelled herself up from the bench and walked a few feet away, her low-heeled black patent pumps hammering against the wooden surface of the deck. The hammering stopped, and she just stood still, staring out at the lake. When she finally faced him again, her expression told him nothing. A puff of air lifted a hank of her graying hair and draped it across her broad face; she gave it a cursory swipe back into its chignon. "You love her?"

And there it was, unwrapped and polished and laid out, gleaming and *real,* in front of him. Not guilt, or regret, or even concern, but the one thing, the only thing, he suddenly realized he'd ever felt for Sarah Louise Whitehouse from the time he was old enough to even have an inkling of what the word meant.

"God, Viv—you know I do."

"Then hang on to that," she said with a curt nod, pushing back the hair again. "Hang on to that like you were a drowning man and that was the only inner tube in the whole ever-lovin' ocean."

With that, she headed back to the restaurant.

"That's it?"

She turned back to him, her head cocked, contemplating. Then she shrugged. "You'll just have to wait until Sarah's ready to talk," she said, not unkindly. "Neither you nor I nor anyone else can speed that up." A resigned smile curved her lips slightly upward, turning her cheeks into balloons. "And then..." Her laugh sounded more like a sigh. "I just hope *you're* ready."

Another shrug, then she disappeared inside. Dean stood in the middle of the deck, his face muscles pulled so taut he felt as if his skin didn't fit.

Wait for what? Be ready for what? What could Sarah possibly have to tell him that could possibly alter the way he felt about her?

And when, *when,* would he find out what that was?

Chapter 11

Jennifer could not have asked for a prettier wedding day, Sarah thought, her bedroom curtain tucked in the crook of her fingers. It had rained after midnight, leaving the air cool and dry, the postcard-blue sky dotted here and there with poufs of clouds that looked like cute little lamby-pies.

The bride had already been in and out of Sarah's room ten times that morning, although Sarah couldn't have pinpointed an actual reason for any of the visits. Jennifer had zipped past *exuberant* to *wired* at least two hours ago. Under other circumstances, Sarah would have been buzzing right along with her. As it was, she was doing well to manage *civil*.

Another sleepless night. Lord, she was getting tired of those, tired of flopping around on her bed and untangling herself from the sheets every ten minutes, tired of smearing cover-up goo under her eyes to hide the circles, tired of being tired. If she'd at least reach some sort of conclusion at the end of these nocturnal marathons, the loss of sleep would be worth something. But she never did. Instead, exhaustion just made her even more confused.

So. The question *du jour* was, once again, what was she going to do about Dean? Why did the time never seem right to tell him about Katey?

Nine years ago, there had been choices. She may not have liked any of them, but they'd existed. Now there were none. At least, not in the "what" categories. Only in the "whens" and "hows."

Neither of which could she even begin to figure out.

Her anxiety was sending her to the john more often than her newly pregnant sister. Unfortunately, in this circus tent of a dress, that mundane activity had taken on the logistical proportions of moving a small army.

Sarah looked at herself in the mirror, feeling like the Cotton Candy That Ate Alabama. Her short hair looked preposterous over the voluminous sleeves and skirt, like an eighteenth-century lady missing her periwig. She had tried everything—curling it, moussing it, spraying it. Two inches just didn't give you a whole lot to work with.

Oh, yeah. The perfect finishing touch to her already rotten mood.

No, she thought as she picked up the matching lace-frosted beach umbrella her delirious sister thought was a "hat." *This* was the perfect finishing touch.

She yanked the thing down to her eyebrows, which made her have to lift her head to see where she was going, then swung open her door and stomped out of the room. Ten feet and fewer seconds was not going to change her attitude very much, she knew. But she was her sister's maid of honor, after all. Grumpiness was not an option.

Jennifer was leaning over her vanity, applying probably the third coat of mascara to her already thick lashes, her mouth hanging open in that way it did on women when they put on eye makeup, as if somehow the muscles in the side of the face made the eyelashes stand out more, or something. Sarah never had figured that one out.

In Jen's reflection, Sarah could see scathingly sexy ivory lace underwear peeking out from underneath a ratty old housecoat, Jennifer's "real" lingerie already either packed for her honeymoon or ensconced in the new apartment.

"Oh, no, silly," Jennifer addressed her mirror as Sarah swooshed through her door. Entangled in the bride's hair, a dozen mammoth curlers wobbled like birds on a telephone wire. Snapping the mascara closed, Jen swung herself off her vanity seat and crossed her room to fuss with the hat and Sarah's hair.

Organza rustled as Sarah pretzled her arms across her ribs. "Well, at least I look a damn sight better than you do."

"Shut up and be still," Jennifer said, standing on tiptoe to reach Sarah's head. After a minute or so of tweaking and twitching, Jennifer said "There!" and parked her hands on her hips in triumph. She pointed to her closet mirror. "Go. Look. Admire the work of a master."

"Wouldn't that be *mistress?*"

Jen smirked. Sarah looked, her eyebrows lifting as the corners of her mouth turned down in reluctant admission that Jennifer was good at this. Soft, wispy waves now framed her face, the hat sat at an angle that made her eyes look huge and mysterious. She pivoted her head from side to side, occasionally poking at a strand of hair. "I don't know how you did it," she admitted, "but at least I don't feel like Margaret what's-her-name in *The Wizard of Oz* anymore."

"Hamilton," Jennifer supplied, removing the rollers. At Sarah's puzzled expression, Jennifer repeated, "Margaret Hamilton played the wicked witch in the movie."

"Oh. Yeah. Whoever." Despite feeling as though someone had tied a brick to her heart and was going to throw it in the pond to drown it, she managed a smile. "Who's going to make sure I'm all pretty once you're married and gone?"

"I thought about that," Jennifer replied dryly. "I dread to think what'll happen if you're left on your own." She let the duster slip off her shoulders, then combed out her hair into a cascade of soft waves that caressed her bare shoulders. "Okay..." She rose from the vanity bench and faced her bed, on which lay her wedding gown. "The moment of truth."

Sarah lifted the airy dress off the bed and slipped it over her sister's arms and head, both of them giggling as Jennifer lost her way for a moment and couldn't find one of the sleeves. Finally, all limbs and corresponding openings sorted out and the dress buttoned in back, Sarah pressed her hand to her mouth.

"Oh, Jen…"

Jennifer undulated a little in the gown, letting it settle, then faced her mirror. And grinned.

"Hey…not too shabby, huh?"

If Sarah had felt like the Wicked Witch of the West, her sister was definitely Glinda. The gown was fairly simple, actually, an embroidered organza with a full, fluffy skirt, fitted bodice, and airy puffed sleeves worn off the shoulders. But on Jennifer it was magic. A wand would have been more appropriate than a bouquet.

Vivian opened the door, Jennifer's veil wrapped over her arm, and broke into a broad smile. "Well, if it isn't my little fairy princess," she said, swallowing back tears. The girls looked at each other, and Sarah knew that everyone in the room was thinking the same thing—that it was a shame Eliott Whitehouse wasn't there to walk his daughter down the aisle. As much as Percy Jenkins was thrilled to do the honors, it wasn't the same.

But it was not a day for regrets.

"Gifts before veil," Jennifer said, rustling to her dresser. "Where's Katey?"

"Probably in the bathroom," Vivian said, smoothing the front of her mauve-and-silver shot silk dress. "I'll get her."

While their mother was gone, Jennifer gave Sarah a tiny box wrapped in silver paper. Sarah opened it and gasped. "Jen! How could you afford these?"

"They're not exactly companions to the Hope diamond," she heard her sister say as Sarah removed the tiny gold balls she usually wore in her ears and inserted the glittering diamond studs. "Besides, don't expect anything for your birthday. Or Christmas, either. For the next ten years."

Vivian ushered Katey into the room, a doll in a tiny lavender replica of the other bridesmaids' dresses, wearing a cleverly arranged circlet of flowers that covered her small bandage almost completely. For Vivian, there was a set of pearl earrings, which she, too, promptly donned; for Katey, a tiny heart-shaped locket with pictures of Jennifer and Lance inside.

The two ladies were helping Jennifer with her veil, a froth of floor-length silk illusion set on a headpiece of real orange blossoms, when the doorbell rang.

Vivian crossed to the window. "Limo's here." She turned to the bride. "Ready, baby?"

Jennifer grabbed Sarah's hand. "In a second."

Vivian's eyes drifted to her daughter's entwined hands and nodded. "We'll see you downstairs."

After Vivian and Katey left, Jennifer gave Sarah a cautious hug, each one fluffing out the other's sleeves when they broke apart.

"Nervous?" Sarah asked.

Jennifer's curls grazed her shoulders as she shook her head. She smelled like spring and love and all things wonderful. "Not one little bit." Her nose crinkled when she grinned. "Just very, very happy."

"You should be. Lance is a great guy."

"So's Dean," Jen shot back without a second's hesitation. She wagged her finger at Sarah. "Don't you dare let that man get away, you hear me?"

Sarah simply smiled and put her arm around her sister's waist. "Come on, lady. There's a big fancy car waiting for you in the driveway. Think it's time to get you to your wedding, don't you?"

Jennifer let her eyes wander around her room for all of two seconds, then sucked in her breath. "Oh, my God," she whispered, squeezing Sarah's hand. "I'm getting *married.*"

"Not if you don't get to the church, you're not," Sarah replied with a laugh, pushing her out her bedroom door and shutting it behind them.

* * *

Sarah had never seen so many flowers in her life. True to Jennifer's extravagant nature, the simple white-walled church had been transformed into a heavy-scented floral paradise. Every window, every dark wood pew, every space that could hold an arrangement was engulfed by luscious arches and swags and bouquets in various combinations of deep green boxwood and pittosporum, pink roses and frilly white carnations, violet statice and larkspur and delphinium and waxy white lilies. The air shimmered with white-gold sunlight pouring in through the open frosted glass windows; ladies fanned themselves with wedding programs as lace collars and airy, broad-brimmed hats shivered in the breeze from three oversize ceiling fans spinning in lazy unison over the guests' heads.

A trickle of perspiration snaked down Sarah's back as she stood at the altar, concentrating on the bridal couple, desperately trying to ignore Dean not six feet away, every bit as gorgeous in a tux as she'd thought he would be. It was hot inside the little sanctuary, despite the drier air and the open windows and the valiant fans, made hotter still by Dean's scrutiny; that, along with lack of sleep and the anxieties of the past week, had rendered Sarah woefully weak of limb. Her knees probably shook more than her sister's during the mercifully short ceremony.

She truly wished she could enjoy it more. It was such a pretty wedding, and Jennifer was so happy. But her unresolved predicament sat on her shoulders like an obnoxious monkey, making her feel as if she was merely looking at somebody's wedding pictures, not really involved, not really *there*.

The ceremony over, she and Dean signed the wedding certificate as witnesses. But before she could slip away, Dean snagged her elbow.

"They want us for pictures, outside." His calmness was disconcerting. "Thank God. I'm ready to melt in here." He ushered her out the side door to the adjacent garden, then gave a low whistle.

"Whoo-*ee*. Jennifer has truly outdone herself this time."

She really had. Sunlight trembled through the bobbing leaves of two enormous ashes, underneath which clustered a grove of miniature peach trees already budded with fruit. A half dozen round tables skirted with lace-topped lavender and sage cloths, reminding Sarah of a group of Victorian ladies out for a Sunday stroll, stood in the plush grass around the fruit trees, the breeze teasing the edges of the lace toppers. Each table held an assortment of elegant hors d'oeuvres on gleaming silver trays, or sparkling crystal bowls of pink champagne punch. The three-tiered wedding cake, each layer harboring clusters of pansies and roses and baby's breath and assorted delicate greenery, held the spot of honor in the center of the garden.

It was magic and romantic and it was everything Sarah could do not to burst into tears.

"Hey, y'all!"

Leave it to the bride herself to break the spell.

"Get over here, would you? I want one of the two of you together."

"She would," Sarah muttered, startled to hear Dean's laugh beside her.

"It's okay," he said. "I promise not to do bunny ears over your head."

She had to smile.

They dutifully trooped over to the spot in front of the rose garden that Jennifer had selected and assumed stiff poses next to each other.

The photographer, a bored-looking little man with probably less hair than he would like, shook his head. "I don't think so, folks. Come on, now—a little closer, please."

She felt Dean's hand light on her waist and she sucked in her breath. With a little jerk, he pulled her to him. "Like this?" he drawled to the photographer.

"Much better." Then the man sighed. "And a smile would be nice, honey. You look as if he's standing on your foot." Hooded gray eyes shifted to Dean. "You're not, are you?"

"Scout's honor." He pulled Sarah even closer. "I have to

tell you something," he whispered, his breath quivering the hat brim. Not to mention her.

"W-what?" she said, trying to ignore the heat searing through the dress where his hand was making contact.

"This dress is definitely *not* 'you.'"

She nearly choked, then whispered back, "This dress isn't *anybody*. But at least it's not lavender."

Dean chuckled, then skirted his fingers along her ribs. She thought she'd faint.

"You know that conversation we started last night?" His voice was soft, but his grip wasn't. "I figure it's high time we finished it, don't you?"

There went her heart rate. "Yes."

He seemed to relax. "When?"

"Later." Her eyes darted around the scene. No one seemed to be watching. Or listening.

"After the wedding?"

"Maybe."

"I leave tomorrow." There went those fingers again.

"I know that!"

"Okay, folks. All done," the photographer intoned, his face betraying a mild curiosity about her outburst. With a laconic shift of his head, he addressed the rest of the bridal party, who were chatting among themselves twenty feet away. "Next victims?"

"*When?*" Dean insisted, pulling her into his ribs so their hips and thighs got all tangled up. Oh, *Lordy*.

"I don't know," she shot back, then tried to pull away from him. Like that was going to work.

"Oh, no you don't," he said mildly. "You're staying with me. Got it?"

Her eyebrows shot up so far the hat shifted. "Says you and whose army? Besides—" she frantically searched her brain for something she could use, then smiled "—I promised Jen I'd keep an eye on the caterer. So go mingle." She wriggled out of his grasp, then, scooping up an armful of skirt, managed an approximation of stalking off.

* * *

Dean sank onto a folding chair at a nearby table and dropped his head into his hands, not giving a damn who saw him or what conclusions would be reached about his dejected pose.

"What're you doing out here all by yourself?"

He lifted his head and met his brother's clear brown gaze. "Moping, if you don't mind," he said on a sigh, straightening up. "And before you ask, no, I don't want to talk about it. I'm tired of talking about it. I'm tired of *thinking* about it."

"By 'it,' I take it you mean you and Sarah?"

"Yeah. But—"

"—you don't want to talk about it. Gotcha."

"So," Dean asked, checking behind his brother and not seeing a vision in white, "how come you're solo? Where's Jen?"

Lance sat down hard across the table, draping his arm along the back of an adjacent chair. "In the ladies' room. Again." He squinted up into a nearby ash with a half smile. "I guess that's to be expected, under the circumstances."

"A little nervous, is she?"

Lance gave him the most self-satisfied grin he'd ever seen on anyone's face.

"A little bit pregnant, is more like it." At Dean's stunned expression, the smile broadened. "Yeah, you heard right. You're going to be an uncle, bro."

Dean shook his head, chuckling softly. "How long have you known?"

"About twenty minutes."

At that, Dean let out a loud laugh. "Well, at least no one can say she forced you into marrying her." He raised one eyebrow. "How far along…?"

Lance shrugged. "About three weeks."

He had to ask. "Was this planned?"

"Not exactly."

Dean couldn't keep the amusement out of his voice. "You guys ever hear of birth control?"

Lance's sigh reminded him of Katey when she had to be patient with grown-ups. "Shoot, I've got about six different kinds in my nightstand." He passed his hand over an embarrassed grin. "Just in case, you know. But…" He shook his head, cleared his throat. "Jen and I both want a large family, and we wanted to start right away." The smile became sheepish. "Which we'd figured had meant on our wedding night."

Dean interrupted, unable to resist teasing his baby brother. "In spite of…your little stash. Just in case."

Color shot up Lance's neck. "Uh…yeah. Anyway," he said, exhaling, "about three weeks ago, Vivian took Aunt Ethel into Auburn for the day, and I guess you could say we kind of, uh, took advantage of the situation…and Jen refused to let me use anything." His shoulders hitched. "Who would've thought we'd hit paydirt with the first try?"

"You mean, you did the deed in our aunt's house?" Dean threw back his head and let loose with a roar. "Wait'll she figures that one out!"

"Why would she do that?"

"Oh, trust me, she will. Unless this baby comes late, she'll be counting on all her fingers and all her toes, and she'll put two and two together so fast it'll singe your eyebrows." While Lance frowned, seemingly contemplating this future complication, Dean clasped his hands behind his head. "God—you're only twenty-three. You really ready for this?"

"Yeah. I really am." His brows inched closer together. "I don't know. Maybe it's because I was so young when Mama and Daddy died. I mean, Aunt Ethel meant well and did her best, but…I want a real *family*, you know? I want to rub my wife's belly and talk to our baby and give it baths and help it take its first steps. And then I want to go through it all over again, and again, until we can have loud, crazy Christmases and backyard baseball and…and all that stuff." He allowed a short, self-effacing laugh. "Do I sound crazy?"

"No," Dean replied softly. "You sound like the sanest person I've talked to in a very long time—"

"Land sakes! What on earth are you doing way over here?" Jennifer had come up beside Lance and now stood with her hands braced on her hips, her veil wrapped three times around her wrist. Between matrimony and pregnancy, the woman glowed like a full moon.

Lance snaked one arm around Jennifer's waist and tugged her to him. "Spilling the beans, that's what," he said, settling his palm on her tummy.

"Oh, yeah?" She brushed back a lock of dark hair that had fallen over Lance's forehead. Then she bestowed an appropriately radiant smile on Dean. "And you had no idea when you made that comment about the rocking chair what you were saying."

"Oh…right." Dean chuckled. "No wonder you got such a weird look on your face." He nodded toward her. "Congratulations."

"Thank you," Jennifer replied with a little nod in return. "But I won't be happy until I can congratulate you and my pigheaded sister."

"Jen—" Lance intervened.

"Well, it's true," Jen said with a slight crease in her brow. "You know they belong together. I know it. Shoot, everyone but Sarah seems to know it." She craned her neck over the crowd. "Now…where could she have gotten off to?"

Muttering the sorts of things one really wasn't supposed to mutter in a church, Sarah stood in the church's minuscule ladies' room with a mountain of pink organza over her head, groping for the pager she'd attached to the waistband of her panty hose.

The Thomases. What could it be this time? Ed had said everything seemed perfectly okay when he checked the cow yesterday. And Wilma and Franklin should have been more than capable of seeing the cow through a normal birth. Sarah swatted a million layers of organza back down, more or less, then swished into the tiny church office, smashing herself behind the desk to use the phone.

"Wilma? What's up?"

"Oh, thank goodness, it's you. I don't know what's wrong, but something sure is. Honey's been making a racket all day long, and I can see her muscles movin', but the calf's not comin'.''

"Where's Franklin?"

"He and some friends went to Montgomery for the day. He won't be back before supper."

"Any of the other farmers around?"

There was a pause. Then she said, "I've seen what those fools can do to a cow, trying to get out a calf. I know it'll cost me some to have you come out, but Honey's my only cow. I want to make sure she's gonna be okay…"

"Wilma! Don't you dare let me hear you mention money again! I just asked in case it took me a while to get out there. I'm at my sister's wedding reception."

"Oh, no! I'd completely forgotten all about that!"

"And you're not to worry about it, you hear me? Babies come when they're ready, no matter what their mother is." Sarah paused, then asked carefully, "Honey really seem to be in pain?"

"Let's put it this way. I never heard her make a noise like she's making now. I'm here to tell you, it makes my blood run cold."

"I'll be there as soon as I can."

Wilma was right; this did not sound good. At all.

Damn. She'd come in the limo with Jennifer. The Bronco with all her equipment was at home, in the wrong direction. If she went back and changed and got her car, it'd take her more than an hour to get out to the Thomases. And if the cow had already been in distress for some time…

No. She'd have to leave directly from here, although she was taking a chance, not having any supplies with her. She didn't even know what was wrong, or what she was going to have to do. For the moment, she wasn't even going to let herself think that the calf might be stillborn. If it was, she'd deal with it, but she wasn't going to imagine the worst.

If the calf was backwards, she'd have to turn it. She'd done bare-handed maneuverings before, but they weren't always successful. She might have to tie something to the calf's legs and pull it out, which required two things: a rope, and an extra set of arms.

She knew exactly who could supply both.

Dean almost jumped at Sarah's touch on his arm. He started to smile, but the anxious look on her face stopped the grin halfway. "What's up?"

"You got a rope in your truck?"

"Uh, yeah—"

"Good. I figured you did. Listen—the Thomases' cow isn't bringing to birth properly. I've got to get out there immediately." She paused. "And all my stuff's back at the house."

"You want me to drive you home?"

She shook her head, and Dean began to envision the Thomases' barn as part of his immediate future. "There isn't time, if my hunch is correct. That's why I asked about the rope." She thrust out her hand. "Congratulations. You are now an honorary veterinary assistant. Say your goodbyes and meet me at your truck in five minutes."

"Our clothes…?"

"Believe me," she tossed over her shoulder as she swished off toward his truck, "the cow won't care."

Chapter 12

In spite of her obvious anxiety, Wilma burst out laughing when she saw Dean and Sarah get out of the truck.

"Lordy, lordy—if it ain't Cinderella and her Prince Charming."

"Very funny, Wilma," Sarah called as they trudged to the house through a undulating maze of squawking chickens, her hem already dragging in the driveway mud. Dean saw her gather up several handfuls of skirt, then let it drop again with a shake of her head. "I need a bucket of water," she told the widow when she reached the porch steps, "the mildest soap you've got, and some old towels." She patted the skirt. "And some safety pins, if you have any. Meet you in the shed."

Honey greeted them with a skull-rattling moo as they entered the sweltering lean-to that passed for a barn. The stench made Dean's stomach lurch; the cow had obviously relieved herself more than once since her labor had started. That, and the rank smell of hot, confined cow nearly knocked him over.

"You okay?" Sarah asked him, her brow puckered. He nodded, afraid to open his mouth. "I'm sorry," she said. "It won't seem so bad after a few minutes."

"If I live that long," he said, forcing the words out.

She gave him a smile that momentarily took the edge off the nausea. "You'll live. Trust me."

He still wasn't sure about that when Wilma appeared with the requested supplies.

"Great." Sarah took the full bucket from her, positioning it close to the cow. "Any pins?" Judging from Sarah's grin when Wilma proffered her hand, there were. Sarah scooped them up, then said gently, "You can't stay."

"I figured," the older woman said, her gaze wandering to the cow. "I take it you expect trouble?"

She rubbed Wilma's arm reassuringly. "She would've delivered by now otherwise. You know that. Which is why you called me, remember?"

"Yeah, I reckon. Okay…" Wilma raised her hands. "I'm gittin'." She gave Honey one last glance, then disappeared into the sunlight on the other side of the door.

The instant Wilma left, Sarah went into action. As if such an activity was part of the normal, day-to-day routine for calving, Sarah began to corral the unwieldy dress with the pins, somehow flattening and shortening it at the same time. That done, she twisted her head and scowled at the sleeves.

She thrust out her hand, several pins glinting on her palm. "You'll have to do the honors. I can't manage with one hand."

Dean stepped over to her, taking the pins. He picked at the sheer balloons, his mouth twisted. Funny, he couldn't smell cow anymore. Just Sarah. He closed his eyes and inhaled.

"Dean."

"Yes?"

"I don't give a damn how you do it. Just pin 'em. The object here is to get 'em out of my way."

"Gotcha." So he pinned. And took unfair advantage of the situation.

Sarah squirmed.

"Dean…?"

"Hmm?"

"You're tickling me."

He let his mouth drop closer to that luscious point where neck and shoulder meet. "Like this?" He gently blew on her neck.

"Dean!" She twitched, the tiny diamond earrings in those perfect little lobes throwing shards of light across her cheeks.

"Yes?"

"Stop that!"

He chuckled, savoring the flush of color along that gloriously long neck, the rapid rise and fall of her breasts not six inches from his lips. "Yes, ma'am." He fastened the last pin and stepped away from her. Looked at her. Laughed. "You look absolutely ridiculous."

She snorted, moving closer to the cow, then flashed him a bemused look. "Says the man in the tux standing in the middle of a barn. I didn't bring you along just to pretty up the place, you know." She flapped her hand at him. "Strip to the waist, buster."

"You didn't."

"Just…do as you're told," she shot back. Blushing.

Dean sighed and removed his jacket and shirt, taking them outside and parking them on a bale of hay that seemed to be planted in the middle of the yard for no other purpose. By the time he returned, Sarah's right arm had disappeared into the cow, her brows nearly meeting with determination. She suddenly winced; he saw every muscle tense as she just stood, frozen. "Oh, yeah," she said after a few seconds, "her contractions are just hunky-dory. Okay…the calf seems to be fine. Just contrary."

"Meaning?"

"Backwards," she said, not looking at him. "If I could just…" She closed her eyes, concentrating.

Dean just stood, watching. Wondering what his part was to be in all this.

"I'm trying to turn the calf around so it comes out head

first,'' she explained, then blew out a stream of air. "The operative word here is *trying.*''

"Not working?''

"Not yet.'' He saw her take a deep breath, reach in more deeply, if possible, then issue a series of not very ladylike grunts and groans. She repeated this process several more times, then finally slipped out her arm, immediately sloshing water from the pail all over it. The front of her dress was already stained with things Dean didn't wish to think too hard about, but she seemed unperturbed. About the dress, anyway. The delivery was something else again.

"He's not budging.''

"He?''

"Only a bull would be this recalcitrant.''

Dean cocked his head. "Isn't that a little chauvinistic?''

"Ask me if I care.'' Then she let out a harsh breath, rubbing the cow's sweating flank. "I really don't want to do a C-section, especially without the proper equipment. So-o-o, I guess that means we try to deliver him breech.''

"We?''

The corners of her mouth lifted, but her eyes were worried. "It's why I invited you to the party. Where's that rope?''

He retrieved it from the corner where he'd thrown it when they'd arrived, held it up.

"Can you do slipknots?''

"Ye-e-es,'' he replied. "I'm not a total doofus.''

"Not total, no,'' she conceded. "Okay, two slipknots, one on each end. I'll try to loop them around baby's hooves, then we'll have to pull him out. God willing, Honey's contractions will keep up enough so we can work with them. Now, the problem is, the calf will try to breathe as soon as it hits air, so we have to work quickly. At the same time, we don't want his hips or shoulders to get caught in Mama's pelvis, nor do we want a torn cow. Got that?''

"Oh, sure,'' Dean muttered. "Piece of cake.'' He handed her the slipknotted ends of the rope. "Okay, Doc—go for it.''

After a few minutes of more blind maneuvering, Sarah

flapped the protruding rope at Dean. "Okay. I think we're set. Loop this around your waist, hold the two pieces, and pull slowly and gently when I say." She shut her eyes for a second, splayed a hand across her chest and sucked in a deep breath, then darted him a not-real-confident smile. "You ready?"

He nodded.

The crease between her eyebrows said it all. But he also knew how dedicated and stubborn and good she was at what she did. There she was, filthy and smelly and paying him less mind than if he were a cow plop, and all he could think of was how much he wanted her.

Brother.

"Now. Pull!" she directed, her arm once again inside the cow. She nodded, concentrating. "Good. A little more…stop!" After a few seconds: "Again, pu-u-ull. Slo-o-owly…come on, baby…*Damn!*"

Dean saw sweat dripping into her eyes, automatically grabbed a towel and wiped her face. She offered a grateful smile, then took a deep breath. "He slipped back," she said, unnecessarily. "Ready to try again?"

"I'm just along for the ride," he said gently, repositioning himself. "Maybe you should be talking to the calf, not me."

She managed a choked laugh. "Good point. Okay…"

Several tries and too many minutes later, the calf was still firmly entrenched inside Honey and Sarah was soaked with sweat and cow crud.

And near to tears.

For at least the fourth time, she bent over the bucket, washing up. Not looking at him. The cow bellowed, rolling her eyes, looking as if she might go down. Sarah jerked up her head, wiped her face with the back of her arm. Dean touched her wrist, and her eyes snapped to his, as if she'd forgotten he was there.

"Scared?"

Her eyes widened, then she nodded. Then, a deep breath, hauling in another round of determination. "Frustrated."

Something occurred to him. "You've never done this before, have you?"

Now he could hear the near hysteria in her voice. "How'd you guess?" She hauled in another deep breath, then another, then admitted, "I've always been able to turn 'em around. Or been able to do a section. But, after a half hour of intimate acquaintance with this calf, I can tell you that this is one big sucker. A big sucker in no hurry to be b-born."

"Hey, baby—" He plopped a kiss on top of her damp, disheveled head. "You can do this." He paused. "*We* can do this."

"You think?" she replied with a small, exhausted smile.

"I know." He took hold of the rope. "Now, get your hand back in there, woman, and this time, don't take 'no' for an answer."

The laugh was real this time.

One more deep breath, then she reinserted her hand. "Pull," she commanded softly, then, after a moment, her eyes closed. "Okay…good, good…pull again…yes!" He saw her face relax, the crease begin to fade as her voice rose with excitement. "Yes! Yes! Yes! Pull, Dean, pull!… Okay! Here we go…" He saw her other hand grasp a tiny hoof, gently work it down, followed by the second hoof, then legs and rump…

"Okay…" She was guiding herself now. "Maneuver the head under the pelvic bone…come on, Sarah…come on, little guy…"

Suddenly, in a huge rush of unpleasant-smelling liquid, the calf spilled to the straw-covered floor, its embryonic sac still clinging to its face. Sarah quickly tore the membrane away, then took a towel and started rubbing it. She cupped her hands around the bull's chest, then shook her head. "Oh, no you don't!" she said sharply, making Dean jump. She hauled the calf up by its hind legs and swung it back and forth, then shook it up and down. "*Breathe,* damn you!"

Dean stood there, fascinated. Horrified. Amazed.

At last, the calf coughed up a bunch of junk from his throat; Sarah immediately laid it down and began rubbing it again, then raised her eyebrows at Dean. ''Hey—I could use a little help here!''

He grabbed another towel and joined her. ''Isn't the mother supposed to be doing this?''

''Usually, yes,'' she panted, watching the calf's face as she spoke. ''Sometimes, though, when the birth's been hard, Mama spaces out for a minute. That's why we've got to get Skeezix here up on his feet and start feeding as soon as we can.''

As if he'd heard, the little brown-and-white calf suddenly wobbled to his feet like a hungover cowboy. He bleated in Sarah's face and she kissed him smack on the nose, then turned him around and shoved him underneath his mother's udder. After some encouragement, the little guy figured out what he was supposed to be doing, and both Sarah and Dean laughed at Honey's perplexed expression at having something foreign tugging at her teat. But after a moment, she lowed and nuzzled her baby's rump.

And Sarah burst into tears—gulping, frantic sobs of relief and pent-up adrenaline. Startled, Dean pulled her into his arms. And chuckled, briskly rubbing her back.

She pushed a short laugh through her nose, rubbing her eyes with the heel of her hand. ''Real professional, huh?''

He looked into her face, wiping away the tears with his fingertips.

''Just…real.'' Planting a quick kiss on the tip of her smudged nose, he added, ''Knew you could do it.''

For the first time that week, her smile brought to mind thousands of smiles from years gone by. ''Thank you'' was all she said.

And his heart melted into a puddle at his feet.

They sat in Dean's truck, staring at Sarah's house, for a full minute.

''Well. *That* was fun,'' Dean commented at last.

Sarah was almost too tired to laugh. ''Next time I'll take you lambing. Talk about *fun.*''

Dean was silent for several seconds. Then, so slowly she

almost didn't notice, he skimmed one knuckle down her cheek. "Next time?"

Her hand closed around the door handle. "Just a figure of speech." She pushed down on the handle, intending to open the door, get out of the truck, get away from what was coming.

She wasn't quick enough.

"Sarah." In one motion, Dean slid his hand down her arm, his fingers cuffing her wrist. "Honey, why are you fighting this so hard?"

"This?" To her acute disgust, her voice wobbled. "What 'this' might you be referring to…?"

"This 'this'…" She had no idea how he accomplished it, but the next thing she knew, she was in Dean's arms, his mouth vanquishing hers in a kiss that would surely go down in somebody's record book as a kiss capable of changing the course of history.

It was certainly changing the course of Sarah's history.

This was far more than the melding of lips and tongues, of mingling breaths and shared sighs. She'd joined lips and tongues and breath and sighs with a few other men in her time. However, all those other times, she'd pretty much been able to feel her extremities when it was over.

When Dean finally lifted his mouth from hers, she was no longer shaking. Her muscles were too far gone to shake. He just let her drift in the depths of those calm green eyes, smiling at her as if she were a miracle.

"I stink to high heaven," she said.

"As if I'd notice?"

She laughed softly, but when he started to speak, she put her fingers on his lips and shook her head. Swallowed.

There was no place, no time, left to run.

"I'm going inside," she said. "Then I'm taking a shower, throwing this god-awful dress in the garbage and fixing you some dinner, which is the least I can do for you after what I just put you through."

She saw hope and disbelief war in his eyes, and fought to keep from blushing at the innuendo implicit in her invitation.

Cooking dinner for him was *not* the least she could do for him. Certainly, it wasn't the *most* she could do for him. For either of them.

But he didn't say a word. About that, anyway. What he did was shift so she snuggled against his chest.

"You know…the only part of that that makes me a trifle nervous is the cooking dinner part."

"I don't…oooh, wait a minute." She sat up, frowned at him. "Ed?"

"Mmm. I believe his words were 'don't accept a dinner invitation unless Vivian's doing the cooking.'"

"He never will let me live that evening down." She blew out a stream of air. "*Everything* went wrong that night. The oven screwed up, the roast was a terrible piece of meat, Katey hurt herself right when I was in the middle of making mashed potatoes so they burned. The list goes on. I'm sure the poor man thought I was trying to eliminate the competition."

"Actually, he used the word *poison.*"

She smirked. "All I'm offering is an omelet and toast. Even I can manage that."

"An omelet and toast would be wonderful." He reached up, grazed his lips over her hair, putting every nerve cell right back on red alert. "But, as I'm no less disreputable-looking—or smelling—than you are, I'm going to run on home and shower and change. I'll be back in half an hour?"

Suddenly, a half hour seemed interminable. And not nearly long enough.

"An hour. It's going to take more than a quick shower to undo this damage."

"An hour it is." He kissed her again, far too persuasively for either of their good, then she forced herself out of the truck and up the front porch steps, giving him a little wave as he drove off.

The house's emptiness was practically tangible. The dress swishing incongruously at her feet—she'd given Wilma back her pins—Sarah trooped down the hall and into the kitchen, suffused with pale amber light. A note was tacked to the refrigerator door, scribbled in her mother's untidy hand. They'd taken Aunt Ida back to Montgomery, Ethel was with them, be back tomorrow evening, she hoped the cow was okay.

It occurred to Sarah she couldn't remember the last time she'd been alone in the house. Not overnight, anyway. Feeling a little unsettled, she poured herself a glass of iced tea, pawed disinterestedly through the small pile of mail on the kitchen table, then pushed through the swinging door into the dining room.

Spears of brassy light pierced the dust-mote-laden air in here as well. One shaft picked through a dozen prisms hanging from an antique hurricane lamp on the buffet, splintering into a hundred tiny rainbows across the opposite wall. With a soft giggle, Sarah placed her hand ''over'' the rainbows, as if trying to capture them, a favorite game when she was little. But, of course, as always, the rainbows only danced on the top of her hand, mocking and eternally elusive.

Smelly and filthier than any civilized human being should ever be, Sarah stood smiling at the multicolored reflections. For right now, she thought she just might be able to believe in magic again. Just for the moment. Just for tonight.

And tomorrow?

She tilted back her head and finished off the tea.

Well, what was the point of being a Southern girl if you couldn't have a good ''fiddle-dee-dee'' now and again?

A note in his aunt's precise script lay on the kitchen table, informing him she'd gone to Montgomery with Vivian and Katey to spend the night with Vivian's sister. Dean chuckled to himself; the old girl was turning into a regular gadabout in her golden years. That last shopping trip, she'd even bought herself a pair of *slacks*.

He stripped out of his clothes right there in the kitchen, dumping the shirt, socks and underwear into the washer, putting the tux back in the rental bag. He wondered what the rental place was going to say about the condition of the suit. Well, if it was beyond hope, they had his credit card number. If the tux symbolized what he thought it symbolized, it was a small-enough price to pay.

Never had a shower felt so wonderful. He stood under the pummeling water for twenty minutes, scrubbing every vestige of barn smell off until his skin began to smart. At last, when he could sniff and not smell cow, he emerged, then stood in his briefs in the center of the room, deciding what to wear. Which should have required the minimal expenditure of brain cells. T-shirt and jeans, right?

Somehow, that seemed…inappropriate. After all, this was his last night.

No. Well, yeah, he did have to go back to Atlanta tomorrow, if for no other reason than to prevent his murder at Forrest's hand. But he refused to accept that this was his last evening with Sarah, he declared to himself as he slipped into a pair of dress slacks, a white shirt and a silk sports jacket filched from a small group of clothes in Lance's closet that for some reason hadn't been moved to the new apartment. This was not his last chance. *But,* he thought as he threaded his tie into a Windsor knot, he wasn't *taking* any chances, either.

By this time his stomach was chiding him for not having eaten at the reception, and he was more than willing to take his chances with Sarah's cooking. Just so long as whatever she served didn't talk back to him, that was okay with him. He grabbed his keys off his dresser and headed for the front door, then stopped, his hand over the knob.

Should he…?

Naw, that was being just a little presumptuous.

Wasn't it?

And why would they still be here, anyway? Lance wouldn't have been foolish enough to leave them where his aunt would find them.

Would he?

He swallowed, his hand tensing, releasing around the cool brass.

All that about not taking any chances…

Aw, hell.

Before he could change his mind, he backtracked to his brother's room, and yanked open the nightstand drawer. His brother had indeed been that foolish.

Chuckling at what their aunt's reaction would be when she found the rest, Dean selected a few items, tucking them discreetly into his pants pocket.

Sarah hoped to God there would be no more cows giving birth or sheep with broken legs or any animal with any ailment for the next twenty-four hours. Or at least until Ed got back from Atlanta.

She'd brought a portable radio into the bathroom with her, and a sultry mix of jazz and blues kept her company while she soaked in a bubble-filled tub. Now she understood why Jennifer liked long baths so much—not only were they relaxing, but somehow, Sarah felt...*prettier.* More feminine. Qualities that had never been of overmuch importance to her before.

Before tonight.

This might be her only shot. Her only chance at loving Dean Parrish, in every sense of the word, again. Jen had even left her a box of condoms—which she'd never gotten a chance to try out, she said—so she'd be safe. From disease and pregnancy, at least. From heartbreak...well, nobody'd come up with protection against that, had they? After tonight, after she told Dean about Katey, all bets were off as to the outcome of their relationship. So, tonight, she would pretend that there was no past, no future, no secrets, no guilt. There was only the present, which she intended to make as perfect as possible.

As if in a dream, she pulled herself out of the tub and dried herself off, then padded back to her room, tucking the towel around her breasts.

The dream came to an abrupt halt when she opened her closet door and was faced with the same pathetic choices that had so appalled her sister the night before. And no Jennifer to bail her out, this time.

"Got any ideas, Bali?" she said to the cat sprawled across her bed.

He yawned and flipped onto his back.

Frowning, she tramped into her sister's room, only to re-member that Jennifer—and her clothes—now lived in an apart-ment in Opelika. She'd taken the last of them over last night, after the rehearsal dinner.

That left her mother's closet. Great. Romantic dinner for two and Sarah would be wearing something stylish from Ample Duds. Well, one of her mother's big shirts over a pair of shorts might look…sexy, maybe?

Who was she kidding? She might as well just throw on a flour sack and be done with it… Hold the phone—what was *that?* Deep in the furthermost recesses of her mother's closet, a sliver of bright teal winked at her. Sarah squeezed herself back into the closet, fumbling for what she hoped was the mystery garment. After a couple of tries, she latched onto whatever it was and extrapolated it from its hiding place.

"Oh…!" Sarah sank back onto the edge of her mother's bed, the dress—for that's what it turned out to be—clamped in her hands.

Her mother had saved it. All these years.

Nine years ago, a heartbroken eighteen-year-old had stuffed her just-purchased prom dress, box and all, into the garbage can out by the kitchen, slamming down the lid loud enough to set off all the dogs. Vivian must've retrieved the dress later. The dyed-to-match shoes were even there, hung around the neck of the hanger in a muslin bag, like a lump of garlic to ward off vampires.

Sarah's hand drifted to her cheek as she sat there, staring at the dress and shaking her head. Why? What on earth had pos-sessed her mother to save it?

Slowly, Sarah stood and walked back to the closet, pushing the door closed in order to see herself in the floor-length mirror hanging on the back. She undid the towel and let it fall to the floor, then held up the strapless dress to her breasts.

Nine years and one broken heart later, it was still *some* dress.

She bit her lip, considering, then unzipped the back and stepped into it.

It probably doesn't even fit—

It fit. Better than ever, because she filled it out more in all the places where *more* is good. Looked terrific with the short hair, too, which now showed off more of her neck and shoulders...

He'll probably be wearing jeans and a T-shirt.

She stood, ogling herself in the mirror like a character in one of those cereal commercials.

It's either this or one of Mama's shirts.

She stood for several seconds, contemplating this dilemma, before finally slipping off the dress and laying it on the bed, then shrugging into one of her mother's tents. After all, she couldn't very well *cook* in it, now, could she?

Besides...it needed to be pressed first.

Dean followed the smoke signals out to Sarah's backyard, where he found her valiantly trying to get a fire going in the grill, alternately puffing and swiping at the billowing smoke.

"Omelets on the grill?" Dean queried as he came up behind her and gently clasped her waist, moving her to the side and away from certain disaster.

Sarah folded her arms across what sure looked like one of her mother's shirts. "I found steaks in the fridge. The baked potatoes are just about done. And I made a salad." She shrugged, staring at the now complaisant fire. "I figured that would be safe. Although I didn't figure on starting an infer...no...?"

He caught the unspoken question at the end of that last sentence. Puzzled, he turned to her and realized she was staring at his clothes.

"Am I overdressed?" He regarded her attire in turn with a wry smile as he plopped the steaks onto the hot grill, where they hissed their protests to no avail.

She slowly shook her head, a wide grin suffusing her face. "Not at all. In fact..." He could have sworn she was blushing. "Can you handle things from here while I go change? If the steaks get done before I get back, I've got the table set on the summer porch.''

Not on the picnic table ten feet away? A frisson of anticipation skittered through his chest at the possibilities. But he didn't dare ask what was going on for fear of bursting the bubble.

She was going to *change?* He chuckled as he flipped the steaks, which sizzled enthusiastically for the second time. Even in that whatever-it-was of her mother's, she looked so appealing Dean was having trouble deciding whether to sample the steaks or the woman first.

He finished grilling the steaks in short order, then transported them as directed to the screened-in porch on the side of the house. Sarah used to like to do her homework out here, he remembered, the blatantly Victorian room furnished with rattan and wicker and lined with a lush display of greenery—ficuses, palms, ferns—all waving sporadically in the gentle breeze that occasionally filtered through the protective mesh.

At one end of the room sat an elegantly laid table for two, set with Vivian's best linens and crystal and china. Not a piece of Corelle or stainless steel to be seen. The perfect setting for a seduction, unless he was *way* off base.

"You little devil..." he said under his breath.

A soft rustling in the doorway caught his attention. Smiling, Dean turned around, fully intending to compliment whatever she was wearing.

Only to find his tongue stiff and uncooperative.

"Sarah?" he finally managed to croak out to the vision in front of him, exquisitely displayed in a dress the color of the Mediterranean Sea. A dress that, despite its amazing brevity, still managed to allow its wearer to retain the dignity and grace that had always set her apart from every other female he'd ever known.

Nerve cells he didn't even know he had began screaming *gimme-gimme-gimme*.

The vision laughed, shaking her head slightly so those tiny

diamond studs in her ears—the only jewelry she wore—glittered in the candlelight.

"I'm her evil twin sister Serena," she said, leaning one arm against the door frame, the other hand on her hip, a position that had a decided effect on the already dicey position of her breasts in the strapless garment. The shiny fabric slithered down over her ribs and hips, only to explode in a full skirt that exposed lots and lots and *lots* of leg, ending in a pair of strappy four-inch heels. Tilting her head to regard him from beneath lashes thicker and darker than he remembered them, she added, "I've stuffed Sarah in the fruit cellar until after you leave."

"You don't have a fruit cellar."

"I also don't have a twin sister."

Dean swallowed. "Would you excuse me a moment? I need to push my eyeballs back in my head."

A brilliant smile told him how much his comment pleased her. "While you're doing that, would you like a beer?"

"You have beer?"

"Rarely. But I ran over to the Jenkinses' and bummed a couple off Percy."

"In *that?*"

She laughed again. "No, no. Before I changed."

"Thank God. You'd give poor Percy a heart attack."

Almost afraid she'd disappear if he let her out of his sight, Dean followed her into the kitchen, lit only by a small fluorescent fixture over the stove. Hoping he appeared at least somewhat relaxed, he leaned against the counter as she opened the refrigerator, the sudden harsh illumination starkly outlining every nuance of the front of her body. He couldn't tear his eyes away from her legs as she bent over to pull two cans of beer out of the fridge. Legs like that should be licensed. Legs like that should not spend most of their waking hours stuffed inside baggy blue jeans inside a barn somewhere.

Then again, maybe they should. Otherwise, they'd cause traffic accidents.

Sarah started to hand one of the beers to him, then jerked it back with a sharp shake of her head. "I just can't see chugging beer from a can in this getup. Wait a minute."

She vanished into the dining room, reappearing a second later with two crystal champagne glasses. "Isn't beer called 'poor man's champagne,' anyway?" She delicately poured the beer into the glasses and lifted hers to his in a toast, with a smile that didn't quite reach her eyes.

He'd heard the wobble in her voice, too, even though she clearly tried to hide it. It was more than nervousness, he was sure. Somehow, somewhere during those few seconds she had been out of the room, some doubt or other had resettled in her thought. He lightly touched her arm with his free hand.

"Hey, honey—something wrong?"

Her brows shot up underneath soft, wispy bangs as she sipped her beer. "Wrong? Of course not." Her mouth twitched up a little. "I'm just starving, is all." She set down her glass and snatched an oven mitt off a hook over the stove, then pulled out the baked potatoes, tossing them onto a nearby plate. "Get the salad, would you?" she called over her shoulder, suddenly a model of efficiency. "Let's get this show on the road—"

"Sarah. Put down the potatoes."

She was facing the counter when he spoke, and he could see her muscles tense in her bare back; then she slowly set down the plate.

Dean took her hand and pulled her around to him. "You're not really all *that* hungry, are you?"

Her eyes entwined with his, wide and trusting and scared as hell, as a tiny sound like a whimper fell from her lips. Dean cradled the side of her face in his hand, letting his thumb skate over her cheek.

"What are we doing here?" he asked softly, letting his forehead nearly—but not quite—touch hers.

"Having dinner?" she replied, her voice squeaky, like a baby bird's.

"I don't think so, honey."

She valiantly attempted a smile. "Then what the hell did I cook those steaks for?"

"Hmm. I could have sworn it was me who cooked the steaks." He tugged her into his arms, letting himself savor the feel of her, the soapy, womanly scent of her, letting the ache blossom into sweet, hopeful anticipation.

"Oh. Yeah." After a moment, she melted against him, her hands linked behind his back. He enfolded her completely, one hand stroking her silky bare back, his chin resting on the top of those soft curls.

"I'm plumb crazy about you, Sarah Louise," he said quietly. Carefully. "I always have been, even at my jerkiest. And I always will be, no matter what stupid things I may do in the future."

He could feel her swallow against his chest. "I know."

He waited. And then it came.

"I'm crazy about you, too," she said, her voice so soft he could barely hear her. "No matter what…" At this, her voice caught, and she didn't finish her sentence.

Dean had never yearned so intensely for anybody, for anything, in his life. He wanted her. He wanted her to want *him*. And he was well aware that, still, in spite of how things appeared, this might not work out. He could barely speak over his hammering heart. "So…what do you think we should do now?"

"Have dinner?" she whispered.

She wasn't biting. Not yet, anyway.

"Okay, baby," he said with a soft laugh. "We'll have dinner. Then afterward, I think we should go dancing."

Her face jerked up to his, the expression vintage Sarah Smart-ass. "This is Sweetbranch. Not exactly replete with nightclubs, you know."

He shrugged. "You do have a radio, don't you?" His mouth hitched into a smile as he teased her shoulder with his fingertip. "Even out here in the boonies?"

"Oh, um…" She shivered from his touch. "Yeah." He went rock hard, pressed her closer, figuring there was little point in keeping it a secret. Her gaze zinged to his, her expression a curious, tantalizing mixture of amusement and cautiousness. "A CD player, even," she said after one too many beats had passed.

"Any jazz?"

"There, um, might be one or two pieces that would...fit."

"Then we're set on the...dancing."

Oh, man...they were *so* close. In more ways than one. But he didn't dare take things to the next notch. Not yet. If he did, everything she'd accused him of that first night would seem to be true. And making love was not all he wanted from her.

Not *all* he wanted from her.

He could feel her heart rate increase as he held her, saw her run her tongue over her lower lip, had to bite his own to keep from swooping down on her right then and there.

She studied him for several seconds, then cocked her head to the side. A smile slowly, shyly pulled at her lips. He almost missed the tremor in her voice. "And after the dancing?"

Now his own heart rate went ballistic; she wasn't suggesting they watch TV.

"After that," he finally managed to say, "is up to you."

Chapter 13

Sarah could feel Dean staring at her all through dinner. Except, somehow, she didn't mind so much this time. It was, at least, an appreciative stare. Actually, he looked as though he wanted to devour her.

For some reason, that made her feel...powerful. In charge. Oh, both of them knew what that dosey-do in the kitchen had meant, and she was well aware Dean had taken the "discretion being the better part of valor" route in not being the one to actually suggest they make love. Well—she bit back a smile, remembering—not in so many words, at least. But that's what was going to happen. As soon as she gave the signal. Which, if she weren't careful, she'd unwittingly give before she was really ready.

Not that she *wasn't* ready. Because she was. She just wasn't right-this-minute ready.

She refused to let herself even consider whether or not she was being fair. Which she wasn't, was she? After all, if he knew, would he be quite so hot to take her to bed?

Not a chance she was willing to take. Besides, how else was she going prove she'd forgiven *him?*

Giving. Taking. She wasn't at all sure which she was doing tonight. A little of both, she supposed. But if this did turn out to be her only chance, she was determined to go out in one helluva blaze of glory.

She was amazed she'd eaten, but when she looked down at her plate, it was empty, so she supposed she had. Dean insisted on cleaning up, that she was to sit tight until he got back. What did he expect her to do—make small talk with a palm?

He'd been gone maybe all of three minutes when she carefully pushed open the swinging door to the kitchen, in case Dean might be in its path. The water was running in the sink; already absorbed in his chore, he didn't hear her at first, giving her a moment to savor the picture of how things might have been. What they might have been even still, had circumstances been different.

He'd removed his jacket and tie and rolled up his sleeves, the white shirt almost luminous against his tanned skin in the incandescent light from overhead. Sarah found the effect incredibly sexy—that hint of muscles rippling from underneath the makeshift cuffs, the light dusting of golden hair on his forearms. It made her want to run her fingers up underneath the cuffs, to unbutton the shirt and splay her fingers across his chest.

Silently, she instead pressed her tingling fingers to her own cheeks, thinking how remarkable she'd never, ever wanted to splay her hands across any other man's chest. And that thinking such things about Dean seemed so natural and good and right.

But what she found most alluring about the tableau was the comfortable ease with which he assumed the household chore. He wasn't doing her a favor; he was simply doing something that needed to be done. As if they were a team, like they used to be before life got so damned complicated. And *that* was enough to make her want to grab him by the hand and haul him upstairs to her bedroom right then and there.

And keep him there, forever, safe in a world in which there were no mistakes.

She momentarily lost her balance in the heels, making her bang into the door. Over his shoulder, Dean threw her a smile. "Thought I'd told you to stay."

"I'm not a dog, for crying out loud," she countered good-naturedly, realizing her voice had gone unnaturally high. She cleared her throat and aimed for *sultry*. "Besides, I got lonely."

He seemed to assess her comment for a moment, then said, "Well, if you're that bored—" he threw her a towel "—you can dry."

She stared at the towel for a moment. This was a seduction? Then she smiled. No, this was *them*.

"Uh...okay. But first let me just—" she reached down and pushed the back strap off one heel, then the other, and kicked off the shoes "—return to sea level." Now barefoot, she joined him at the sink, only to be immediately overwhelmed by the tang of his after-shave, the fragrance heightened by the dish-water steam.

She picked up a dinner plate and gave it a cursory swipe with the towel. "You sure smell a lot better than you did a few hours ago."

He laughed, then leaned over, his hands still immersed in suds, and sniffed her neck. "Mmm...so do you."

Certain parts of her body immediately perked up. Especially when he lingered over her shoulder a fraction longer than nec-essary, his breath causing hers to catch in a rush of anticipation. Then, so softly she almost couldn't feel it, he kissed the junc-ture of shoulder and neck, the same spot he'd blown on earlier, in the barn. A sweet promise of what was to come. She let her gaze drift to his, into those eyes she'd avoided letting herself fall into, and fell. Willingly and completely.

He just smiled then, and nodded toward the sink.

She nodded, too, in reply.

They didn't speak for several minutes as they went about this mundane, everyday job. Dean washed, rinsed, handed the dish or glass or bundle of silverware to her, and she would take it from him as if they were performing some ritual of monumental importance. Over the stream of water, she could hear his breathing, steady at first, then becoming just the slightest bit ragged, the change so minute she wouldn't have noticed it at all except she was so achingly aware of his presence. She knew he watched her as he passed over each item, knew he was imagining what the next few hours would bring. Knew it, because she was imagining exactly the same thing. And knew that to wait longer would serve no purpose save to frustrate the life out of both of them.

Finally, Dean rinsed off the last of the dishes and set them in the drainer, after which he took the towel from her and dried off his hands, still watching her. Still waiting for a signal she had no idea how to give.

She looked up at him, swallowed, then swallowed again. And noticed he'd come to a complete standstill, his hands motionless in the towel.

Somehow, she'd given it. The signal.

She couldn't believe how scared she was. And how much she wanted him. And how scared she was of wanting him this much.

Heart hammering, she twisted around to pick up the champagne glasses to put them away; one slipped out of her hand, shattering around her bare feet. Her lips parted, but no sound made it past the lump in her throat.

"Don't move," Dean instructed, disappearing into the pantry. But by the time he got back with a broom and dustpan, she was squatting, gingerly picking up the larger pieces with hands shaking so violently the shards were a blur. He crouched in front of her, placing a steadying hand on her wrist. "Why are you doing that? Just let me get it."

Eyes stinging, she shook her head, even though she had no idea what she was objecting to as she stared at the broken glass sparkling like frost over the floor. She felt fevered, her senses raw, tattered, oversensitized. The rasp of the broom against the floor, the tinkling glass, even the still-lingering scent of the dish liquid, throbbed inside her, around her, until it was all she could do not to clamp her hands to her ears.

Dean tidily swept up the mess, set the full dustpan on the counter, then lifted her up by the elbows to stand in front of him. One finger, then two, touched her cheek, his fingertips burning a trail of heat where they stroked. With a soft cry, she leaned into him, seeking surcease from the onslaught.

And...forgiveness.

"What?" he whispered.

Never had one word, spoken so gently it hardly seemed to be formed by vocal cords at all, said so much, or had so much power.

But she couldn't answer, couldn't admit her own lack of control, whether from fear or pride or whatever balled-up reason, she had no idea.

"Shall we skip the dancing?" he asked, tucking her chin in his fingers.

He, too, she realized, sought forgiveness. Pleaded for it.

Demanded it.

Her nod was barely perceptible.

In one motion, he swept her into his arms and carried her upstairs.

It wouldn't be her old bedroom, with its frilly trappings and white French provincial furniture; that, he knew, had been given over to Katey when she was born. But the instant Dean set Sarah down just inside the doorway of the darkened room, the fragrance of line-dried linens and lilac potpourri and talcum powder told him he was home.

His breath lodged painfully in his throat.

A sense of unfulfilled longing slammed into him when, not surprisingly, she slipped out of his arms, the dress rustling with each step she took to her dresser to click on a small lamp. The sudden light, dim though it was, made him blink as he watched her then cross to her window, closing lace curtains which a sudden breeze almost immediately billowed back into the room. He expected—willed—her to turn, but she remained in front of the window, the curtains rippling at her back like an overdone bridal veil, as her fingers idly skimmed the sash. Deep in his belly, desire and patience clashed.

Damn near shaking with restraint, he came up behind her—slowly, carefully—pushing the curtains aside to thread his arms around her waist. The satiny material of her dress was warm, slick against his hands; her skin cool, smooth, fragrant beneath his lips. He let his mouth graze her shoulder, drift to the base of her neck, enjoying her fluttering sigh, enjoying the sharp bite of arousal even more.

"It's cloudy again, so there's not much moonlight," she said unnecessarily, pinning his arms in place with hers. Her head dropped back against his shoulder, allowing him an unimpeded view of the swell of her breasts over the neckline of the dress. "So I turned on a lamp so we could see."

"And what is it, exactly, you'd like to see?" he whispered, bringing his hand up to tease one breast through the gleaming fabric.

She hesitated, then covered his hand with hers, assenting, encouraging. "What I thought had been taken away from me for good."

A battalion of emotions screaming in his head, he spun her around, fighting to remain calm, the one in control, when in fact his wasn't sure how much longer he could remain standing. He brought his mouth down on hers, hard, nothing held back, his only goal to convey all the sorrow and frustration and regret of those lost years from his mouth to hers. She opened to him, her own kiss just as hard, just as demanding, and giving, and—dared he hope?—accepting, even as her arms snaked around his neck, clinging to him with a rapaciousness only matched by his own.

Blood-curdling panic and heart-swelling joy, both, raced through him, preventing him from relinquishing her mouth, even for a second, for fear in that atom of time she'd change her mind, pull away, run away. He backed her to the windowsill, bracing her against it, almost sobbing in relief when her legs entwined around his waist—

She jerked away, substituting her trembling fingers for her lips against his.

What?

Their off-sync, frantic breathing brutally shattered the peace of the room as Dean's gaze locked hungrily into Sarah's. And through the desire—and no, this time, his imagination wasn't even a player—he thought he saw...

Ah.

He smiled, shakily, smoothing her bottom lip with one trembling finger. "I've got that all taken care of."

She backed up. An inch, maybe. But she clearly understood. "You do?"

"Yes, ma'am."

She studied his face for a second or two, then burst out laughing, shaking her head, the diamonds winking in her earlobes. "Nothing like playing your hunches."

He captured her face in his hands, hell-bent on making her understand. "I really had no idea what, if anything, might happen tonight. But I wasn't about to take any chances. Not like last time." He nuzzled her forehead, needing to shut his eyes against the fierce, almost unbearable wave of tenderness that enveloped him. "We were damn lucky nothing happened."

Everything stilled.

The silence roaring in his ears, he gathered her close, swearing softly. "That probably was not the best subject to bring up right now. Sorry."

Her hair tickled his chin as she shook her head. "It's not that. Exactly."

He waited a few seconds, then said, "You can change your mind, you know—"

"No!" Her head flew up, amber flames flickering in the depths of those bourbon eyes. "I want this as much as you do." The smile that followed was as enigmatic as the Mona Lisa's. "Maybe more."

He searched her face, realizing what her admission meant. Hope, and a foretaste of triumph, surged through him as he kissed her, softly, knuckling her silken cheek. Then he backed away, skimming one hand down her arm until their fingers linked. She smiled for him, and his heart constricted, exploded. He wordlessly led her to the bed, feeling almost drunkenly romantic.

Romantic? Never before had Dean thought of sex in that connotation. Except once, a long time ago. Sex had always been a purely physical endeavor, pleasant and fun and some-times even ego-building. But, while he had been attracted to all of his partners, and infatuated with a couple of them, love had never been a part of the picture.

Except with Sarah.

Dean stumbled over a slight ridge in the rug, sat down hard on the edge of the bed, laughing as he tugged her into his lap. She laughed as well, a sweet, low sound he caught in his mouth as she melted into his kiss, her arms looped around his neck.

Love. There had to be a better, bigger, more all-inclusive word to describe what he felt for the woman in his arms. How could a word with just four letters possibly be adequate to contain the myriad emotions flooding his heart and brain at this moment?

He wanted her. Needed her. And not just in bed, despite how much he ached for her. Funny how he'd chalked up the…magic of that first time to the fact that it *was* the first time. No scale of comparison and all that.

Yeah, well, just goes to show.

As they clumsily, greedily, crawled over each other to the center of her bed, he was nearly overcome with an almost savage desire to protect her from whatever might make her sad or frightened or angry, even though he knew that, one, she would really pop him one if she knew he felt that way, and, two, that he was actually powerless to keep her from ever being hurt. But tough. That's the way he felt.

This was home, *Sarah* was home, and nothing or no one was ever gonna make him leave again.

She let herself drift, as if in a dream, drugged with the joy of a moment she'd thought she'd never have, knew she'd never

have again. Dean's kisses were unhurried, sensuous, excruci-
atingly gentle, his tongue inviting hers to dance with his as she
felt his hands roam over her arms and shoulders, teasing the
top of the zipper, raising goose bumps of anticipation along
her skin. Giggles drowned in gasps when the next kiss upped
the ante, his mouth now possessing hers—possessing *her*—in
a manner that brooked no argument.

Not that arguing was on her agenda.

Desire, sweet and achey and just this side of salacious, exploded in tiny, brilliant starbursts in her heart, her head, in
places so secret and deep, she barely remembered their exis-
tence. Oh, *mama*—she was already so aroused, just from his
kisses, she wanted to scream *Just get on with it, already!* His
leg wrapped around her thighs, trapping her, drawing her closer
with each kiss, clearly showing her he was every bit as ready
as she was. And heaven knew, he could have entered her right
then and there and they both would have been grateful for the
release, she was sure. But she was determined to make it last.

Or die trying.

Her breath coming in short, frenzied pants, she pushed on
his shoulders, shoving him onto his back on the bed, and straddled him, delighting in his startled expression.

"What *are* you doing?"

"What I've been wanting to do for the last week," she replied, unbuttoning his shirt with fingers surprisingly deft, considering both her nervousness and lack of experience at undressing men. She wrenched the shirt free of his pants, shoved
it aside, claimed her territory. Now the heat burned brighter,
hotter at the sensation of chest hair snagging her fingertips, at
the way his breath caught when she skimmed his flat nipples.
At his lazy, crooked, wonderful smile. She leaned over, placing
a leisurely, lazy kiss on a boyhood scar along his collarbone.

"I was right," she whispered against his skin. "You *are*
more developed than you used to be."

A second later, she heard the rasp of a zipper, then sighed
in relief as her breasts tumbled free of the boned bodice. Another breeze found its way into her room, the sensation of the

moist air caressing her exposed flesh absolutely delicious. Almost hesitantly, Dean touched one nipple, which instantly sprang erect and hard and wanting. She sucked in her breath at the piercing sensation, which trickled like a swallow of brandy from the tip of her breast down her belly, settling into a coiled, blazing knot at her core.

"So are you." He smiled back, cupping both breasts in his palms, thumbing her nipples until she couldn't catch her breath.

But it wasn't enough. Not nearly enough. She had no idea her desire could be this great, that she could ever ache for a man's touch this much.

He knew, lowering his hands to her ribs and pulling her forward in one motion to court her with his mouth. His tongue was so soft and warm, so incredibly wonderful. She felt her skin warm, smelled her own scent of perfume and dusting powder and female heat and wanted to be bare before him, completely open to him so that he could perform such magic on other parts of her body. Tonight, she was completely hedonistic. Tonight, she would not withhold anything from the man she loved.

Impatiently, frantically, she leaned back, yanked the dress over her head, then stood in her childhood room—the room whose walls had heard her whispered fantasies as well as her soul-wrenching sobs of betrayal, disappointment, sorrow— naked except for her cotton bikinis, and wordlessly offered solace.

Never let it be said that Dean Parrish was slow on the uptake.

His gaze never leaving her face, his expression an almost frightening mixture of tenderness and craving, Dean quickly shed the rest of his clothes, then pulled himself upright to sit on the edge of the bed, reaching for her.

And with a silent *fiddle-de-dee,* she went.

Incredibly, he still seemed to be in no hurry, taking his sweet time exploring, kissing, stroking every inch of her bare skin, from her arms to her ribs, her thighs…belly…breasts…*oh!*

She cried out at the sensation he managed to stir with the lightest touch, his fingers so gentle, so adept, circling and skimming and dancing... And she thought, on a soft laugh, how there just was no lighting a fire under a Southern boy, now was there? even though he sure enough was lighting *hers.*

Then he knelt before her, his dawdling kisses tracing a southern route from her navel. She heard herself humming, almost keening, as she let herself float beyond reality, her breath leaving her lungs in a rush when she felt his thumbs hook underneath the elastic waistband of the panties and slide them slowly, oh, so slowly down.

She thought her heart might stop.

"You are one gorgeous woman, you know that?" he whispered between kisses, his breath hot now, torturing, promising, as his palms whisked over her hips, her thighs.

She choked down the laugh at the line. "It's a little late for flattery, don't you think?"

"Oh, baby...believe me, this isn't flattery." He stroked her backside, tugged her closer. "This is a revelation." The kisses became softer, if possible, each one a little lower than the last, then lower still...

With a little cry, she threaded her fingers in his hair.

Again, he knew.

And so did she. She momentarily wondered why she felt no embarrassment at the prospect, decided she was having far too much fun to care. And when he finally—finally!—kissed her *there,* all rational thought shattered into a million incoherent shards.

On a startled sigh, her eyes closed, shutting out everything but the exquisite sensation she had thought pure fantasy until this moment. She may have moaned his name as his hands began to massage her buttocks, his attention becoming even more intimate. From someplace else, she heard her breathing become edgy and high, felt him hold her more tightly as her knees began to buckle.

He coaxed her around and lay her back on the bed, deepening his loving, sweet torment. Emotions spun, dipped, leapt, not just inside her, but around her, as if a flock of birds had somehow gotten inside her room. And all the while, heat licked at the insides of her thighs, at her core, spreading upward, ever upward, until, deep, deep inside, pleasure exploded in a series of short, sharp bursts.

"Oooh...!" she cried out in delighted surprise, emotions and sensation blending for one white-hot second before shattering to kingdom come and back again, as she gripped Dean's shoulders, her short nails digging into his skin. She didn't want it to ever end, didn't think she'd survive if it didn't.

But eventually, it did. And seconds after that, still trembling but completely limp, she found herself fiercely, possessively pressed to Dean's chest.

And completely stunned. Somehow, she knew what they'd just shared wasn't the norm, that few lovers could—or would—care enough to bring such euphoric pleasure to their partners, be unselfish enough to put their own needs on hold like that. She shifted, then nestled his head against her breasts and blew out a long, fulfilled sigh.

Never mind the horde of guilt demons who'd just barged on in.

"No complaints, I take it?" Dean gently teased, brushing his lips over the top of her breast.

"Uh-uh." Then she frowned. "Well...maybe just one."

"Oh? And what could that *possibly* be?"

She let her fingers sift through his hair. "I thought this was supposed to be a team sport."

His laugh was as dark and rich as hot fudge. "I think it's safe to say I was more than just a spectator, don't you?"

"Yes, but—"

He pulled back to look into her eyes, the crooked smile at odds with the crease between his brows. "I didn't miss out on anything, if that's what you're thinking. I did exactly what I wanted to do, okay? I had a good time, it sure as heck sounded like *you* had a good time, so I don't want to hear any more about it. Besides, I guarantee I'll catch up. Which reminds me..."

He pulled away and leaned over the side of the bed, retrieving several foil packets from his pants pocket, which he then tossed nonchalantly on the nightstand.

Turning her back on those various and assorted little demons, Sarah propped her head on her hand and watched this procedure with great interest, just as glad she hadn't had to be the one to supply…things. Then she chuckled. "Mmm…just a little optimistic, aren't we?"

The bed squeaked as Dean gathered her in his arms again, and she noticed wryly that everything—in both camps—had perked right up again. Then she caught his eyes twinkling into hers, love shining from them so clearly it almost made her wince. She mentally tossed those damn demons into a jar and screwed the lid on tight. "Just wanted to be prepared, that's all."

"Prepared?" She let out a sharp laugh. "Shoot—if we use all those tonight, we'll make the *Guinness Book of World Records.*"

"If we use all those tonight, they'll have to sandblast the smiles off our faces."

"If we don't kill ourselves in the process." She heard Dean mutter something about not being able to think of a better way to go as she reached over him and picked up one of the packets, inspecting it as if she'd never seen one before. Which, in fact, she hadn't, since she hadn't bothered to open the box Jen had left. For some reason, perhaps due to there being only one purpose for such an item, she found the whole idea a sudden and inexplicable turn-on.

She could feel his eyes on her as she removed the condom from its wrapper, then handed it to him. His brows lifted. "You sure?"

"Why don't you put on your little friend, there, and I'll show you how sure I am, 'kay?"

He leaned back, arms crossed underneath his head, and grinned. "Why don't you?"

She blushed, and she fumbled a bit, but she did it, and then they began to tease each other all over again with merciless abandon. Sometimes with words, the gentle murmurings of best friends who have crossed the line to lovers; then, increasingly, with their bodies, with hands and mouths and limbs, until she ached, again, for release, was mad for it, but, oh, how much she wanted to pretend a little longer...

But not as much as she wanted to take him inside her most secret place, to bind him to her, even if only for a precious few minutes, to prove to him that she trusted him, forgave him.

Loved him with everything she had.

She rolled onto her back, lifting her knees, the time-honored signal from a woman to a man when she's ready.

He positioned himself over her, stroking her hip. "How long has it been?"

Confusion nudged her off track, for a second. He damn well knew how long it had been—

Oh.

"A while," she said noncommittally, and he kissed her, gently opened her, began easing himself inside...

"Oh, Dean," she whispered, arching toward him, gasping at the sweetness of those agonizingly slow, deliberate, loving thrusts. Wonder almost immediately extinguished the momentary discomfort as her muscles stretched to receive him, welcome him...

Well now, y'all just come right on in and make yourself at home, y'hear?

Suffocating her laughter in the salty dampness of his neck, she wrapped her legs around his back, drawing him deeper, still deeper into her, desperate to banish the emptiness, to capture another memory she'd never thought to have. And yet, even filled with him as she was, it still wasn't enough: clamping her hands on either side of his head, she directed his mouth to her breast.

Taking his cue as if they'd been lovers for years, he first circled her nipple with his tongue, then suckled her, timing the exquisite, gentle tugs with his movements, so amazing, so delicious inside her, and yet still not enough, never enough.

And what made you think this would ever *be enough?*

The thought, unbidden, unexpected, knifed through her, slashing her joy to ribbons. She clung to him then, claiming his mouth, hot tears slipping from behind her eyelids to sear her cheeks as anguish, huge and black and opaque, threatened to eclipse the pleasure spiraling through her... No! *No!* she clenched her jaw, scrabbling to preserve the preciousness of the moment as one might grab for a falling child, only to hear, at Dean's final plunge, a cry torn from her throat that was as much from grief as fulfillment.

She floated slowly back to earth with Dean still inside her, savoring a dozen, more, of those hard, sweet kisses even as she began gathering the tattered remnants of the fantasy, tugging them around her so he wouldn't see, wouldn't know. She could barely feel Dean's weight on her body; but the weight of her sorrow nearly suffocated her.

He braced himself on his forearms, smiling into her eyes. "I don't know about you, honey, but I'm thinking nine years is longer than I care to wait for the next time, don't you?"

Even as she laughed, she felt her heart break all over again.

Dean couldn't bring himself to withdraw from her. Not yet. Not when he'd waited so long for this moment.

He wanted her again, already. He wanted her forever. He wanted to make love to her every night, and to wake up every morning to find her beside him in his bed. He wanted to marry her, to make love without a damn condom and make babies and watch her swell with his child inside of her, to see her face on his children. It had been the only thing he'd ever really wanted since he was eighteen, the only desire that had haunted him all these years, even when he'd pushed it so far back in his brain it no longer had a face or a name but had just become a permanent feeling of emptiness in his gut. He had thought he was already as much in love with her as he could possibly be.

He'd been wrong.

He kissed the tip of her nose. "Would you like to breathe?"

Her laugh was soft. "Not particularly." Then she frowned,

and he saw that odd expression flash through her eyes, that something-is-wrong-but-I'm-not-going-to-tell-you-so-don't-bother-asking look. Even so, he started when she grasped the tops of his arms. "Don't let me go."

"Wouldn't dream of it, sweetheart," he said, now concerned. Only Vivian's counsel, to not push, to let her come to him in her own time, kept him from shaking her, demanding she 'fess up about whatever it was that was bugging her so much.

Instead he drew her close, gentling her head to his chest and stroking her hair. He kissed her on the forehead, whispered, "I do love you, you know."

"I kinda figured," she murmured in reply, snuggling closer. "And...yourself?"

She chuckled into his chest. "Fishing, are you?"

"Yep."

Her stillness sent his emotions into a tailspin, until she said, "Always, Dean. Always have, always will. No matter what."

Again, they lay silent. Something new, Dean realized, one of those subtle shifts that happens in a relationship with the passage of time. They'd always talked each other's ears off when they were young, sometimes holding two separate conversations they'd somehow always managed to keep straight, much to the amazement of everyone around them. Some things, however, could be quite readily communicated without words.

Sarah's hand began to explore his torso with gradually increasing pressure and precision, her lips following in its path. Her touch was pure magic, her uninhibitedness thrilling. But there seemed to be something of desperation in her touches, as if...

As if this was her only shot.

He shoved the thought out of his brain and decided to just go with the flow. Which was beginning to pick up speed again.

"Anything in particular you'd like?" he murmured as his hand in turn played up and down her spine.

"Cute. You sound like a waiter."

She'd made her usual comeback, but he couldn't hear the laughter in her voice. He kissed her quickly on the lips, trying to make contact with her eyes. To his dismay, they'd gone blank, as if she'd stepped away from her mental desk. "I…just want to do whatever most pleases you. You know."

She pushed herself up, looked him right in the eye. "No, Dean. I don't know. My entire sexual experience consists of our toss in the pine needles when we were kids and what we just did tonight. Which means I haven't had much opportunity to build up a repertoire. Let alone a wish list. Shoot, I know more about how pigs do it than people."

He stilled, realizing. "There's really been no one else?"

The grandfather clock on the hall landing chimed something-forty-five. Then she said, "It's not something I care to share with just anybody. That's all."

Dean suddenly felt downright tawdry. "I see."

She twisted to face him, amusement flickering in her eyes. "Let me guess. You wouldn't win any celibacy awards, huh?"

"I guess that depends."

"On?"

"On what the statute of limitations are on celibacy. I guess I sowed an oat or two when I first got to Atlanta, but…" He shrugged. "Let's just say it's been a long time for me, too."

She went silent again. Too silent. And he knew whatever it was that kept bothering her was back again.

He saw her give a quick shake of her head, then clear her throat. "Hey," she said, shifting on top of him. "Seems to me we're spending an awful lot of time talking here when we could be doing other things."

He slipped his hands around her bottom, pressing her to him, ignoring the doubts, reminding himself—sternly—she'd declared her love.

In spite of what he'd done.

"Going for that Guinness record, huh?" he managed to say over the knot in his chest.

"Might as well," she said. "Since you brought so much equipment."

* * *

Sarah awoke with a start about 1:00 a.m., momentarily sure she was either having or had just had the most erotic dream in psychological history.

No dream, she realized, yawning. She really had just made love for more than three hours and lived to tell about it. If she *were* to tell about it, she thought, a small smile touching her lips.

But only for a moment.

She'd have to begin pulling away now, if she had any chance at all of getting through this. The longer she let herself believe this was real, the harder it was going to be. Dean loved her now; by dawn, he wouldn't. It was that simple.

She'd had her one night. And whether or not it was enough, it was certainly more than she'd ever thought she'd have, so it would have to do.

Wrapping the unused top sheet around her like a toga, she slipped out of bed and curled up in the large armchair in the corner of the room with Bali on her lap, not bothering to turn off the lamp for fear the click would wake Dean. For a long time, she simply watched him sleep; then, she lay her cheek on the back of the chair and silently cried herself to sleep.

Dean was surprised to see the room already bathed in silvery mauve light when he awoke, even more surprised to find Sarah asleep like a child in the chair across the room. Lord. He'd slept like the dead. Nothing like heaving calves out of cows, then staying up half the night making love, to take it out of a guy.

He sat up, forking his hand through his hair and yawning for a full ten seconds before crossing to the woman responsible for all of it. Squatting down, he studied her for several seconds, smiling slightly. The sheet she "wore" in lieu of a robe had slipped, exposing one creamy breast, delicately tinged with pink from the morning light, the tip the same pale rose as her full, partly open lips. The nipple was soft and relaxed; he yearned to touch it, to put his lips to it, feel it spring taut in arousal. For *him*. It was dumb, and antiquated, and assured him a lifetime membership in Macho Mindset of the Month Club, but it gave him an inordinate rush to know no one else had ever touched her like that.

No one would ever separate them again, boy.

His gaze raked her glowing skin slowly, luxuriously, up to her face, a shade darker than her breast, her lashes resting against the tops of her cheeks. Then he noticed something else, and shifted his weight to get a better look.

Her lashes were spiked, as though she'd been crying.

No more secrets, he thought, almost angrily. Not after everything they'd shared last night.

He stroked the top of her hand. "Hey, sweetheart," he whispered. As if on cue, one of the Jenkinses' roosters squawked a wake-up call. Sarah jumped, clutching the sheet to her breasts.

He laughed softly, encircling her wrist with his fingers. "Morning, baby. Whatcha doin' way over here?"

Her eyes grew wide, before she looked away, shaking her head. "Couldn't sleep," she mumbled, rubbing her hand over her face.

Dean slicked two fingers down her arm. "You should have awakened me."

She wouldn't look at him. He couldn't decide whether he found her behavior worrisome or irritating. Whatever it was, he didn't like the sense of foreboding that had settled in his gut.

"Honey…" His hand swept up to her face, capturing her jaw. "I can tell something's wrong. Why won't you tell…?" Then it dawned on him. He grasped her hands and pressed them to his chest. "You want promises, don't you? Reassurances that last night wasn't just a one-shot deal?"

"No, Dean, it's not that—"

"You want reassurances, I can do that." He kissed her fingers. "Sarah, sweetheart…marry me. How's that?"

Her laugh was sharp. And sad. "In all my born days," she

said in a shaky voice, "I never expected to receive a marriage proposal from a naked man."

"So don't look below my neck. Marry me, honey. Now. While we're on a roll. I mean, we did a pretty good job of putting the past behind us last night, don'tcha think…?"

"Dean. Stop."

He stopped, as the foreboding hiked one notch closer to fear.

She touched his face, and he saw hers crumple into despair. "You don't know what you're saying—"

"I'm awake and sober and I know damn well what I'm saying. I asked you to marry me…what are you doing?"

She'd stood up, letting the sheet fall so she stood naked in front of him. "You didn't notice last night, and I didn't think it was in my best interest to bring it to your attention."

By now he was thoroughly confused, shaking his head as he scanned what certainly appeared to be a perfectly normal, perfectly exquisite body, the satiny surface of her ivory skin marked only by the occasional mole or freckle. She then pointed to either side of her lower abdomen. "Here. Look."

He saw nothing at first. Then, slowly, like one of those 3-D paintings, they came into view—lines of puckered skin tracing her belly, a faint lavender-silver color. He remembered feeling them last night, thinking nothing about them except that they were part of her uniqueness. He reached out to touch them now, but she pushed his hands away.

"They're stretch marks, Dean. From when I was pregnant."

His eyes jerked to hers, as the sense of doom in his belly exploded into realization.

Chapter 14

Dressed now, Dean sat on the edge of the rumpled bed, staring in disbelief at Katey's birth certificate in his shaking hands. Sarah, clothed as well in a particularly unattractive T-shirt and pair of cutoffs, stood at the window, her back to him. Periodically, he noticed her hand drift to her face, presumably wiping away tears. His brain still too tangled to form a coherent question or comment, he'd yet to speak.

Katey was his daughter. His little girl.

Their little girl.

His breath hitched in his throat. "She really doesn't know?"

Sarah shook her head and swiped at her eyes again. "Not yet."

He lifted up the piece of paper. "She would have found out eventually."

A sharp nod was Sarah's only reply.

There had to be anger, but it hadn't worked its way through the shock yet. Eight years, he'd been a father and not known it. Eight years, a wonderful little girl had existed that carried his genes, born of the only woman he'd ever loved, and no one had bothered to tell him.

Instantly, hot tears sprang to his own eyes and he slapped the paper with the back of his hand, nearly tearing it. "Dammit, Sarah!" He leapt to his feet, took three long steps toward her. "What the hell did you think you were doing?"

"Protecting you," she said softly, still staring out the window.

"*Protecting* me! By not telling me I had a kid?"

Underneath the worn cotton, one shoulder hitched. "And if you'd known, what would you have done? Come home and married me?"

"Damn straight that's what I would have done—"

"Which is exactly why I couldn't let you know about Katey."

"Oh, for God's *sake,* Sarah—that doesn't make a lick of sense."

"Then let me replay the scene for you, mister," she said, turning on him with sparking eyes, the heat, the scent from their lovemaking perfuming the room in the early morning humidity. "You told me you would die if you stayed here. You told me you didn't love me. You even told me the very act that conceived your child was worth little more than a good night's sleep to you."

"But I told you, those were all lies!"

"*But I didn't know that!*" Her eyes were searing hot ambers, locked with his; tears streamed down her cheeks. "I didn't know you'd lied, Dean," she repeated, as if he wouldn't understand. "Don't you see? I thought, if I told you about the baby, that either you wouldn't care, or you'd feel *obligated*—" the word exploded like an obscenity from her mouth "—to come back and marry me." Her gaze drifted back out the window while she rubbed her hands up and down her arms. "I wouldn't have dreamed of trapping you—or me—like that for anything. It wouldn't've been fair to either one of us. Or to Katey."

"So instead you made up this elaborate, preposterous story."

''I'm not looking to shift blame,'' she said quietly, ''but that was my mother's doing, mostly. I got caught up in it, and decided I'd rather call Katey my sister and at least get to see her grow up, than call her my daughter and never see her at all.'' After a long moment, she added, ''I was eighteen and heartbroken and scared, Dean. And not left with a whole lot of options. I picked what I thought was the best of a bad lot.''

Finally, his part in this whole screwup began to sink in. ''That's why you never got involved with anyone…else, isn't it?'' he asked at last. ''Because it might've meant leaving Katey?''

When she faced him, he thought he'd never seen sadder eyes. ''Oh, Dean…believe me, Katey never even entered into the equation.'' She fingered the edge of the curtains, her head coming to rest on the window sash. ''Never.''

His head had begun to ache, a dull throb over his left temple. He desperately needed to think, but he couldn't. Not standing in the same room with Sarah, anyway. Part of him wanted to comfort her. But he was too hurt and stunned and angry. He needed space. Time. A rule book with the passage highlighted, telling him exactly what he was supposed to do right now.

''This…this is just too much.'' He stood for another few seconds in the middle of the room, staring helplessly at her back, then strode out of the room.

Sounds. That's all that was left.

Footsteps thundering down the stairs; the front door creaking open, slamming shut; a truck engine revving up like an old man clearing his throat, then tires spitting gravel as Dean hauled out of the driveway. Then, there wasn't even that much.

Sarah crossed to the disheveled bed, picking up the pillow Dean had used, suffused with his scent. Hugging it to her aching chest, she sank onto the edge of the bed and wept.

When Vivian returned about four, Sarah was seated at the kitchen table, gnawing on an overdone brownie. A corner, hard enough to challenge a hippopotamus's teeth. She'd already eaten most of the edible ones. She'd spent the day in a haze of tears, wishing she'd had company, grateful she didn't. She greeted her mother with the same ambivalence. Ambivalence, and overdone brownies.

Vivian walked into the kitchen, hung her bag by the door. "You baked?"

"Yep." Sarah hacked off another piece of brownie with her teeth.

Vivian sank heavily onto the chair beside her. "What happened?"

"Where's Katey?" Sarah countered, wiping crumbs from her fingers.

"At the kennels, checking on the pups. Well?"

"I told him."

"I figured. And?"

"And he left."

"Well, yes. He needed to get back, anyway—"

"Mama, don't."

Vivian crossed her arms over her bosom, speared her with her gaze. "He loves you."

"*Loved,*" Sarah amended, exaggerating the final *d.* "Maybe."

But Vivian was shaking her head. "He's probably hurt. Angry, even. Doesn't mean anything's changed—"

"Mama, please. When are you going to snap out of this fantasy you're in?" A dozen brownies heaved in her stomach. "I kept his child from him for eight years, for God's sake. You should have seen the look on his face—"

"If it's anything like you looked, nine years ago, I've seen it," Vivian parried, unaffected. "It's not fatal. Either to him, or to what he feels for you."

Sarah shot up from her chair. "It's over, Mama. Okay? He's not coming back, we're not getting married, there is no happily-ever-after here—"

"What's this?" came a small, tight voice from the kitchen door.

Both Sarah and Vivian whipped around. Katey stood stock still, her eyes wide with bewilderment. And the first stirrings of anger. "I went into your room to play with Bali," she said, as if needing to justify herself. "And I found this."

She held out a piece of paper. A piece of paper Sarah realized with horror she'd forgotten to put away.

Oh, God…no. It wasn't supposed to happen this way. Not that she'd yet figured out what the right way was, but this wasn't it. She'd changed the linens, disposed of the unused condoms, everything. And left *this.*

"Katey," Sarah began, then fell silent before the blaze in her daughter's eyes. The child was only eight—who would've guessed she'd know how to decipher the information on a birth certificate? But, as Sarah knew all too well, Katey was no ordinary child.

"*You're* my mother?" Katey sounded almost appalled.

A nod was all Sarah could manage over the baseball-size lump lodged in her throat.

Katey's gaze darted to Vivian. "You lied to me?" Back to Sarah. "You both *lied* to me?"

"Honey," Vivian said, rising and going to her. "There were reasons…"

But Katey backed away, shaking her head. Shock had given way to tears, and Sarah knew the little girl was on the brink of hysteria. Sarah understood. Oh, boy, did she understand.

"You lied to me!" Katey shrieked, then thrust the birth certificate at Vivian as if it had caught fire in her hands, spun around and ran out of the kitchen. Before either of the ladies could reach her, she slammed the front door between them, hard enough to rattle the windows.

Sarah started after her; her mother grabbed her arm. "Leave her be. She's gonna have to sort this one through on her own."

"She's only eight years old, for crying out loud!" Sarah retorted, furious with herself, furious with her mother. Even, irrationally, with Katey for wandering into her room without permission. "How the hell is she supposed to sort out something she knows nothing about?'' She jerked her arm out of her mother's grasp and yanked open the front door, hurtling through it before her mother could recoup.

"Sarah—you're making a mistake!"

Already down the steps, she reeled around, rammed her hand through her hair. "No. I made a mistake eight years ago. Now, since I'd very much like to end this day with as few people hating me as possible, I'm going to go find my daughter and beg her forgiveness. I just hope to God I'm not too late."

She found her in the kennels, crouched in a corner of Mariah's pen, cradling a little black furball in the crook of her arm and bawling her heart out.

Her heart in jagged pieces, Sarah curled her fingers around the wire mesh and leaned her head against the gate. "I'm so sorry, baby," she whispered.

Palsied with sobbing, Katey turned a blotched, wet face to her but said nothing.

"Can I come in?"

Tiny shoulders hitched, one jutting up so she could wipe her nose on the sleeve of her blouse.

Sarah slipped inside the pen, slid down beside her daughter and handed her a tissue from her pocket, which the child snatched out of her hands. Sarah scooped up a puppy, too, her heart breaking anew at the sound of her daughter's staccato breathing beside her. That she had been the cause of Katey's anguish nearly ripped her in two. "We screwed up," she said, aching to pull the little girl into her arms, for her own comfort as well as Katey's.

"W-why didn't you tell me the t-truth?"

Sarah rested her head against the wall, waiting for the Perfect Answer to fall out of the sky. When it didn't, she realized she was on her own. "Listen, baby, I don't expect you to understand all this. Heaven knows, I don't understand a lot of it myself. Just remember that grown-ups aren't always perfect, okay? Sometimes we make mistakes." She huffed. "*Big* mistakes. And I guess Mama and I kinda took the prize, considering the size of the one we made.'' Frowning, she peered over at Katey. ''I'm not saying what we did was right, but we did what we thought was the best thing at the time.''

Katey's sobs began to settle down, at least enough for her to finally get out, ''Dean's my real d-daddy?''

Apparently, this part of it had just sunk in.

''Yeah.''

Carefully, Katey set the pup back down, watched it scuttle back to its mother. ''Were...were you m-married?''

Oh, Lord, Sarah thought. Quicksand would be preferable to this.

''No, honey,'' she said on a sigh. ''We weren't.'' She caught Katey's eyes in hers. ''You know how babies are made?''

Katey nodded. A series of rattling hiccups had replaced the sobs. Now alarm registered on an already ravished face. ''You and Dean...?''

''Yes,'' Sarah replied as calmly as she could. ''Dean and I made you.'' She reached out, smoothed a tendril of hair off her baby's forehead. Katey flinched, as did Sarah's battered heart. ''And you happened out of love, honey, in case you're wondering. But...'' She wriggled her back against the wall, scratching it. ''Things got all fouled up, somehow. He went away, and I thought he didn't love me anymore. Turns out that was a mistake, too.''

''Did he know about me?''

Sarah shook her head. ''No.''

''Why didn't you tell 'im?''

The question of the century, she guessed that was. ''Because he said some things that made me think he wouldn't want to know,'' she finally said. ''Which is where I was wrong.''

Those amber eyes weren't going to let go for a second. Behind them, Sarah could practically hear the thoughts shuffling through that steel trap of a brain. ''Does Dean love you now?''

Sarah tried to slip her arm around Katey's shoulders, but the child shied away. Duly chastised, Sarah pulled her knees up, linked her hands around her ankles. Thought about how much to tell her. "Turns out he always did." She snorted. "Between the two of us, we sure got things balled up. A mess we'd just started to straighten out."

Until I told him about you.

"Does he know about me now? Is that why that piece of paper was out?"

Sarah nodded.

"Then why'd he leave? Doesn't he like me?"

"Oh, sweetie…" Sarah swallowed so hard the lump lodged in her chest. "You know he does. But he's real angry with me. He was…just as upset as you are. Maybe even more."

Katey assumed a pose identical to Sarah's. "He couldn't possibly be madder than I am." In spite of feeling like barn muck, Sarah had to smile.

"Yeah. You're probably right. And I don't blame you. If I were you, I probably wouldn't like me very much right now. I *am* me, and I don't like myself very much." She looked over, regarded the top of her daughter's head. And the justified scowl lodged underneath. "But, well…at least you still *had* me. Maybe you thought I was your sister, but I've always been here for you. We've been together just as much as we would've if you'd known I was your mama all along. But Dean never even got to see you before now."

One of the pups had shimmied over to Katey and was nuzzling her sneaker. She gently played with its ears, but Sarah could sense the tension in her jerky movements. "I didn't know about him, either."

"True."

Katey scrambled to her feet then, whacking dirt off the bottom of her romper as she stalked over to the gate. Before Sarah could get up, she turned to her, her eyes once again brimming with tears. "If I never see Dean again, it's all your fault," she hurled at Sarah, then ran out of the kennel, the soles of her sneakers reverberating against the concrete.

That Dean hadn't received a speeding ticket on the way back to Atlanta was a miracle. That he hadn't gotten creamed by a semi was even more miraculous. Like a saloon brawl in an old Western, so many emotions were fighting it out in his head he couldn't even tell them apart. He had no idea what to do. What to think.

He walked into his stifling apartment, threw a week's worth of mail onto the table by the front door, and caught his reflection in the entryway mirror. Seven days, and he'd never noticed. The resemblance. She looked so much like Sarah, he'd just assumed... But now, he could tell. The shape of her forehead, high and broad. Her wide-set eyebrows. The deep eyelids. She'd gotten those from *him*.

The litany from the past several hours started all over again: Katey was his daughter. His...*daughter*. A daughter whose first eight years, because of Sarah's deceit, he knew nothing about.

Damn, he thought as he walked into the kitchen, pulled a beer from the fridge. Eight whole years, gone. How *dare* she...

How dare she what? Do exactly what he'd done to her?

He popped the top and gulped half the contents.

No. This was far worse.

Than what? Making love to a woman without protection and assuming there'd been no consequences? Leading Sarah to believe he'd never loved her when the truth was he'd never loved anyone else?

But she should have told him. Maybe not right away. But before this.

Certainly before she'd made love with him last night.

His eyes stung; his hand worked its way to his mouth. The fear in Sarah's eyes—*this* was what had scared her so much.

He took another long, cold swallow of beer.

Small wonder.

He drifted into his living room, dropped onto the sofa. There was no air in the apartment, having been closed up for a week. He should open windows or turn on the fans or the air-conditioning. Something. Instead, he just sat. Brooding. An activity he kept up the rest of the afternoon.

Until his aunt called.

"What the hell you doing there, boy?" she said the instant he picked up.

This was a woman who never swore. Ever.

"You know I had to come back," he started, but her snort cut him off.

"What I *know* is, Sarah told you Katey's your little girl and you took off like the Devil himself was on your tail."

He froze. "You knew?"

"Only for a few days, so don't go getting your drawers in a knot. Vivian told me." He heard a dry chuckle on the other end. "Which ticked Miss Sarah off right good, from what I hear."

"I imagine so," he said bitterly.

"Oh, get off your high horse, Dean. We're all in this together. Except poor Katey, who's the only innocent one in the whole shebang. But now it's all out in the open...." She paused. "Katey needs you." Another pause. "So does Sarah. They both think you don't want to see them again."

Pain clamped his heart like a vice. "Sarah told you this?"

"No, Vivian did." After a moment, she added quietly, "You know apologies don't come easily to me, guess because I'm just too blamed stubborn to admit when I'm wrong, but I'm apologizin' now. I should never have tried to break you two up when you were teenagers. I'm sorry, Dean. From the bottom of my heart."

Dean leaned forward, cupping his head in his palm. "Thank you," he said softly. "But I know you were only trying to protect me."

Her laugh startled him. "Wasn't just you I was trying to protect, boy."

Dean frowned. "What're you talking about?"

"Not *what. Who.* Shoot, I knew you'd land on your feet, one way or the other. Parrish men always do. No, honey—it was Sarah I was worried about, not you." Before Dean could even react, his aunt continued. "You know your Mama'd won a scholarship to Columbia University when she was eighteen?"

He started. "You're kidding?"

"Nope. I remember overhearing one of her teachers talking down at the Winn Dixie one day, saying Marion was one of the brightest students she'd ever had the privilege of teaching. She was the editor of the school paper, wanted to pursue a career in journalism. Oh, she had big plans, and it looked like she was well on her way to accomplishin' them, too. 'Cept she fell in love with your father. And got pregnant.''

It took a second to register that Dean would have been the result of that pregnancy. He blew a stream of air between his teeth. "So she got married."

"That's what folks did in those days, Dean. And it wasn't like they didn't love each other, don't get me wrong. Johnny adored your mother, and I truly believe she felt the same way about him. But—'' She stopped.

"But?"

"Did you know your father couldn't read, Dean?"

"Not until later, but yeah, I knew. Mama told me he was dyslexic."

"Then you can understand what it must've been like, a man who can't read, falling in love with a woman who read everything she could get her hands on, who wanted to be a *writer,* for heaven's sake. And there they were, married at nineteen, with a baby on the way, and him only able to scrape by with his furniture-making. I don't suppose it mattered to either of them at first, what with being so much in love, and then you came and they were both just tickled pink with you. I don't think it ever even occurred to Marion she was making a sacrifice, giving up that scholarship and her career for love. She was young. They both were. And they figured, long as they had each other, nothing else mattered.

"But Johnny confided in me once, I guess about the time they were expecting Lance, how he'd catch Marion watching the TV news with a wistful look in her eyes sometimes, or that she'd be readin' the newspaper and suddenly start to crying for no reason he could figure. It was about that time she took up with all that craft stuff she got into, stopped reading the newspaper altogether. And Johnny said, he figured it was on account of him she'd given up her dreams, see. That he should've been man enough to let her go do what she needed to do, rather than trapping her the way he did—''

Anger boiled up inside him. ''Mama never felt that way! I never once got the feeling she resented the choice she made.''

''No, of course not, honey. She was devoted to you and Lance. And Johnny. But he loved her enough to hear what she wasn't telling him. And the guilt over his part in keeping her from doing what she wanted nearly ate him alive.''

''And you were afraid the same thing'd happen to Sarah and me.''

The silence throbbed between them. ''Yes. I was.''

Dean leaned forward with a soft groan, then said quietly, ''Except Sarah and I weren't my parents, Aunt Ethel. I would never have let her make that kind of sacrifice for me, baby or no baby.'' He allowed a rueful smile. ''And she never would have let me stand in the way of her goals.''

''I know that,'' his aunt replied. ''Now. But at the time...'' She sighed. ''I grew up in a time when women didn't have the opportunities they have today, you know? It like to broke my heart when I saw Marion give up her dreams. Then when you and Sarah got so serious, so young, and her so promising, academically...I couldn't stand the idea of history repeating itself.''

''It wouldn't have,'' Dean said wearily, ''if anyone had given us half a chance to prove otherwise.''

He heard his aunt sigh. ''Well, we're giving you that chance now. We all created this problem. Now it's time we all fix it.''

He just needs time, her mother said. He'll come around, just be patient.

Yeah, right.

Vivian said the same things about Katey, more than once in the week after the wedding. The child had not magically adjusted to the idea of Sarah being her mother and Vivian her grandmother. She spoke little, ate less and spent most of her time with the puppies. To everyone's shock, Ethel—who ranked shrinks right up there with devil worshippers—suggested maybe they take Katey to see a child psychologist to help her deal with all this.

But Sarah knew what the real problem was. Something no counselor, however well-meaning and experienced and pricey, was going to fix: Katey had no sooner met her real father than she'd lost him. Her heart ached for her daughter, far more than it did for herself.

Then, late Friday afternoon, Wilma Thomas called Sarah at the clinic.

"Hey, Wilma. The calf okay?"

"The calf? Oh, yes, he's just fine," the widow said with a chuckle. "Listen, that's not why I'm calling. I was wondering if you could stop by and give Franklin a message for me on your way home."

Sarah frowned. "Stop by where?"

"Oh, I'm sorry, honey. I just assumed you knew. He's over at the old Parrish house, and there's no phone yet. Dean hired him before he went away."

She was becoming more baffled by the second. "Hired him to do what?"

"Oh, paintin' and strippin' cabinets, stuff like that. Fixin' it up."

"Oh. To sell, I guess."

"Sell? Uh-uh. Didn't you know?"

"Know...what?"

"He's setting up that factory in Opelika, so he's going to live in his old house. Funny...I just figured you knew." She paused, then repeated, now sounding perplexed herself, "I just figured..."

"No," she said. "I didn't know. But I'll be happy to give Franklin the message. What is it?"

She jotted Wilma's instructions on a Post-it on her desk, then tucked it into her jeans, all the while wondering what to think. After all, since Dean hadn't said boo, it was pretty clear—wasn't it?—he wasn't in any split for her to find out he was moving back. For Katey's sake, she hoped Dean was coming home for good. For her sake, however, she wasn't sure she particularly liked the idea. Unless…

Forget it, she told herself. Unlike her mother, she didn't believe in fairy tales and magic and happily-ever-afters anymore.

A couple of last-minute walk-ins prevented her leaving the clinic until after six. She figured Franklin would be long gone, but, since she'd promised to try to get him the message, she went on up to the Parrish house anyway.

Nope. Too late. No truck parked out front, and as she walked up the porch steps, pushing open the unlocked door, she heard nothing resembling construction noises.

"Franklin?" she called, not expecting an answer. She should leave. Franklin wasn't there, so there was no reason for her to be, either.

But she didn't.

She hadn't been near the house since the night Katey was conceived, when she and Dean had given in to each other underneath that stand of pines beside the pond, their bed a thick blanket of pine needles. She knew that Katey had "discovered" the old house some time ago and was particularly enchanted with the pond. Maybe, one day, after several tons of emotional dust had settled, Sarah would tell her. Maybe.

Franklin had been busy, she thought, her eyes scanning the airy living room. Sarah remembered the old house as being on the bleak side near the end of Dean's time there, when his mother had been so ill. In fact, Sarah hadn't liked going to the house much. Too sad, too dark.

No more. All the walls were painted a soft, buttery color; the floors had been refinished and now glowed like topaz. Hesitantly, she pushed open the swinging door to the kitchen and saw that the horrid mustard color was gone, too, replaced with the same ivory as in the rest of the house. The old cabinets had been refinished, the glass panes clear and sparkling like faceted stones. A brand-new side-by-side refrigerator was already in place, as well as a new gas stove.

She waggled her hands as if she'd touched something hot, then quickly walked out of the kitchen, intending to leave.

Something made her turn as she passed the stairs. She paused, listening. There it was, a definite scrape, like a ladder being moved.

"Franklin?" she called, beginning to climb the stairs. "You here?"

She got to the top of the stairs and listened again. There it was—another scrape. From one of the bedrooms.

"Franklin, it's Sarah. Your mother wanted me to give you a message—"

She pushed open the paneled door, then dropped her jaw. It was the most beautiful little girl's room she'd ever seen. The walls were papered in a tiny print of pink roses and hearts entwined with blue ribbons, with a border of larger roses circling the top; rose-patterned chintz curtains were swagged on either side of the two windows. A maple four-poster twin bed with a matching spread, canopied in lace, sat in the middle of the room atop a thick Chinese rug in the same pastels as the rest of the room. There was a dresser, a highboy, and a desk as well.

And in one corner, a child-size rocker just like Jennifer's and Dean's.

"Think she'll like it?"

Sarah screamed and jumped like a spooked cat.

Laughing, Dean caught her in his arms and hugged her to him. "Sorry, sweetheart," he said, maneuvering her around and kissing the top of her head. "I meant to surprise you. Not set you back five years."

Refusing to let hope cheat her—again—she tried to wrestle herself out of his arms, but he wouldn't let go. "What the hell are you doing?"

He grabbed her again, his breath hot on her lips. "Kissing you, if you'll quit wiggling for a second."

Oh, what the heck. She quit wiggling. His mouth was warm and soft and urgent, and she didn't even think about whether or not she should respond. She didn't have a choice. While his muscular arms entwined around her like a python, she wound her fingers through his hair, over his shoulders, down his hard, muscled back, and she opened her mouth, giving, taking, wanting.

They were both panting when they came up for air.

"That...that was very nice," she managed to say, letting herself float in those bottomless green eyes.

"There's more," Dean said, sending her eyebrows skyward.

"As in...?"

Her heart jittering underneath her ribs, she let him guide her to the master bedroom. He pushed open the door, his smile sufficiently wicked to require licensing in several states.

This room was much more simple. Another four-poster, this time a double, covered with a lovely old quilt that was clearly an heirloom. Lace curtains. A large chest of drawers. Couple of lamps.

A collection of foil packets on the nightstand.

And hope settled right in to stay for good. "When did you...?"

"Drove a moving van down this morning. Franklin and Wilma and Ethel and your mother helped me get everything in place."

She whipped around to him. "Franklin and Wilma? My mother? *Ethel?*" Her eyebrows felt as though they were going to fly off her head. "I was set up?"

"You were set up." Another smile.

Sarah raised her fingers to Dean's face, sighed when he grasped her hand and kissed the palm. She thought she might faint from happiness.

"And...what does this mean, exactly?" she finally said through a throat that didn't know whether to laugh or cry.

"Exactly?"

"Point for point," she said, calmly noting he was unbuttoning her shirt.

"Point one—" he nuzzled the space between her breasts as he unbuttoned a second button, then a third "—I'm home to stay."

She moaned, swallowed, wondering if you could get burned from someone's kisses. "And?"

"Point two—" He pulled her shirttail out of her jeans, worked it off her shoulders, began nibbling her neck. "If I put myself in your position, I can understand why you didn't tell me about Katey."

She took his face in her hands and riveted her eyes to his. "Really?"

His expression turned her knees to chocolate sauce. "Really."

Tears pricked her eyes. "Anything else?"

"Oh, baby," he said, unzipping her pants, working them down her legs. "I'm just getting started."

She stepped out of the pants and kicked them to one side, then tugged at the hem of his T-shirt and peeled it over his head. "I believe," she murmured, kissing his chest, feeling him unhook her bra. "You were on point three?"

"Point three…" He snagged her jaw in his palm and met her eyes again. "I love you more than I can possibly explain with words."

The rest of their clothes tumbled to the floor. Then he picked her up and carried her to the bed, laying her on top of the soft, cool quilt. A warm breeze stirred the curtains, giving her goose bumps; she felt her nipples snap to. Dean noticed, tenderly kissed each one in turn. She smiled, stroking his cheek, glowing with expectation. "Is there a point four?"

He laughed, tracing a warm, lazy finger over her shoulder, down her arm, deliberately avoiding her breasts. "What makes you think there's a point four?"

She drew her mouth down. "There isn't?"

Chuckling, he kissed her again; she lifted his hand to her breast, no longer hesitant about letting him know exactly what she wanted. His mouth traveled from hers, down her neck, his lips teasing her nipple just long enough for her to wonder how she thought she could live without him. How she thought she could live without magic and fairy tales and happily-ever-afters.

Then he stopped. And grinned. And placed a small velvet box right on her navel.

She glanced down. "Point four?"

"Yep."

Sarah opened the box, which contained—

"Three rings?"

Dean removed the small, perfect diamond solitaire from its slot and slipped it on her finger. "This is for now." She arched up, grabbed another easily stolen kiss. "Unfortunately, the other two will have to wait. It takes three days for the blood tests, I believe."

Her laugh echoed in the uncarpeted room. "You want to get married in three days?"

That smile. That smile she had loved since she was three years old. "I want to get married *now*. We've wasted far too much time as it is, I think. Besides, I don't want my daughter to be without her daddy any longer than necessary—"

"Oh, my God! Katey!" Sarah tried to sit up. "We have to tell her—"

Gently, Dean pushed her back onto the bed. "I've already seen Katey, honey. We had a long talk, during which she told me a thing or two."

Sarah rasped her knuckles down his cheek. "I just bet she did."

But he smiled. "It's okay. I still have all my appendages, and we agreed to help each other work this out. But right now…is *our* time." He skimmed her jaw with a fingertip, then gave her a long, sweet kiss that sent liquid fire trickling through her veins. Dean—the Dean she fell in love with when she was a little girl—laughed and gathered her into his arms. "I believe there's this Guinness record we need to be working on…?"

Epilogue

Somebody's laryngitic rooster ground out a sorry excuse for a crow, forcing open Dean's eyelids. He slipped down farther underneath the old quilt, feeling Sarah shift on the other side of the bed. Yawning, he let his thoughts shake themselves and settle like a feather pillow as his eyes gradually became accustomed to the slate light in the room. It was cold. And quiet, except for that dad-blasted rooster.

And the baby's snuffling two feet away.

Dean leaned over the side of the bed, peering through the predawn dimness into the cradle. But Eliott Dean Parrish was still sound asleep, his tiny thumb firmly planted in his perfect mouth. It was everything Dean could do not to pull him into bed with them, to cuddle his infant son and drink in his baby sweetness. Instead, he reached out and unnecessarily rearranged his blankets.

"You just leave him be," Sarah murmured, snuggling close, her breath soft on his bare back. "He wakes up, *you* nurse him."

With a chuckle, Dean rolled over, pulling his warm, naked

wife into his arms. He tucked her head under his chin and gently cupped her breast, glossy smooth and firm with his son's milk, a drop of which smeared on his finger when he touched the already erect nipple. "Can't," he whispered into her hair, still smelling of wood smoke from a romantic encounter in front of the fire last night. "You're the only one in the room with these."

"Mmm…" He heard a snicker underneath his chin. "Last night was fun."

He'd had to be in Atlanta for a week this time; they hadn't made love last night as much as they'd *fused.* He hugged her to him, combing his fingers through her silky shoulder-length hair—their compromise, Sarah called it: long enough for him to play with, short enough for her to easily manage. "Yeah," he said, now skimming his hand over her bare bottom, feeling himself instantly respond to the prospect of a repeat performance. "Got plans for today?"

"It's Saturday, remember?" she said, stretching luxuriously against him, heightening his arousal. "I'm all yours. And Katey's and Eli's, of course."

He looked into her eyes, still dewy with sleep. "You really don't miss the farm work?"

"I told you," Sarah said, snaking her long fingers through the hair on his chest. "Regular clinic hours will do just fine as long as I'm nursing. There'll be plenty of time after I'm done having your babies to resume my intimate acquaintance with the cows in the neighborhood."

"Babies?" he said with one eyebrow raised.

"Hey, Eli's about to outgrow the cradle. It deserves to be put to more than one use, don't you think? Besides, I'm sure you wouldn't dream of letting Lance get to number three before you did."

Dean laughed. "You know me too well, lady."

"I always have."

He didn't miss the tinge of melancholy in her voice. It came less and less often now, but occasionally, it still surfaced. For him, too. Just the tiniest regret for the lost years they could have been together, pricking at their happiness like the very end of a splinter you thought was completely gone.

He hugged her tightly, waiting for it to pass.

"I told Mama and Ethel you'd look at their plans for the remodel."

Dean laughed softly. "Where'd that come from?"

Sarah kissed his chest. "I have no idea. Just popped into my head."

"Mmm." He chuckled. "Leave it to those two to decide that a simple bed-and-breakfast wouldn't be enough. Why on earth do they want to run a full-fledged inn?"

"Because they don't have us to look after anymore," she said simply. And, again, a little sadly. He tucked his fingers under her chin and caught her gaze. "Hormones," she said before he could question her. "I swear. In ten minutes I'll be fine."

He shifted so she could feel his readiness. "If I have anything to say about it, it won't even take ten minutes."

She burst into laughter, the shadow dispersed as quickly as it had come. With a demonic grin, she began to caress him with one finger. "You think we have time?"

"The radiators haven't even starting clanking yet. We have time."

But Dean no sooner lowered his mouth to hers when he heard a voice.

"Mama?"

Sarah flipped around to face their daughter standing in the doorway, tugging the old quilt over her shoulders. Dean pulled her against him, threading his hand under her arm and reclaiming her breast; he wondered if Katey could hear the slight catch in her mother's voice. "What are you doing up, baby?"

"Mama Viv called, asked if I'd like to help do breakfast for the guests this morning. So I just wanted to tell you I'm taking my bike up there, if that's okay?"

"Sure, honey," Sarah said, more quickly than she might have in other circumstances. As Dean listened to his daughter's footsteps tromp down the stairs, he buried his face in Sarah's back and started to laugh. She smacked his hand underneath the covers. But she didn't remove it. "You're terrible."

"That's not what you said last night."

She humphed in response, then caught her breath as he began to nibble her earlobe. "So…" he said, in between tastes of her delectable neck. "Your mother will actually let Katey into her kitchen?"

"Uh…yes…she's…become…quite the cook…oh…" She made a sound that was giggle and groan and sigh all mixed together. "That was nice…"

"Mmm," he replied, slipping his hand down over her ribs, over her belly, soft and puckered from childbirth, then down even lower. "Thank God for that. At least *somebody* will be able to cook around here…*ouch!*" He sat up, rubbing his arm where Sarah had plucked out a hair. "Guess I deserved that, huh?"

"Yes, you did."

He looked back over his shoulder at his wife, his beautiful, sassy Sarah, lying on her back with one arm behind her head. The covers were down to her waist, exposing her full, ripe breasts. She reached up to him, smiling—

The baby wailed. Sarah sighed, then laughed.

"Guess that settles that," Dean muttered with a rueful grin, then leaned over and scooped his infant son out of his cozy bed. "Hey, sport," he said softly as he changed the baby's soggy diaper with the efficiency of an English nanny. "Couldn't give us ten more minutes, huh?" Then he laughed at Eli's enormous toothless grin as the baby flailed arms and legs as if trying to swim the Channel. "Here's breakfast," he said, skootching down under the covers and handing the baby to Sarah, who was lying on her side, waiting.

After a couple of frantic seconds, Eli settled down into a bout of contented, noisy nursing, slurping and gulping as if he hadn't eaten in a couple of days. Dean watched in awe, as he did each time he witnessed this basic ritual, as Sarah alternately stroked the blond peach fuzz on the baby's head and kissed it.

Then he noticed the tear that had slipped out of the corner of her eye.

He reached over and wiped the drop away. "What?" he gently asked.

"I never got to do this with Katey, you know," Sarah said. Then she looked up into Dean's eyes, a peaceful half smile tilting up her lips. "Thank you."

"For what?"

"For not giving up on me. On *us*."

"Shoot, baby..." Dean snuggled closer, draping his arm over Sarah's shoulder under the bedclothes. "Giving up wasn't even an option."

The smile his wife gave him was brighter than the Alabama country sunshine just now skirting the windowsill, streaking across an old patchwork quilt.

* * * * *

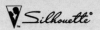

INTIMATE MOMENTS™

presents a riveting 12-book continuity series:

a Year of loving dangerously

Where passion rules and nothing is what it seems...

When dishonor threatens a top-secret agency, the brave men and women of SPEAR are prepared to risk it all as they put their lives—and their hearts—on the line.

Available April 2001:

THE WAY WE WED
by Pat Warren

They had married in secret, two undercover agents with nothing to lose—except maybe the love of a lifetime. For though Jeff Kirby tried to keep Tish Buckner by his side, tragedy tore the newlyweds apart. Now Tish's life hung in the balance, and Jeff was hoping against hope that he and Tish would get a second chance at the life they'd once dreamed of. For this time, the determined M.D. wouldn't let his woman get away!

*Available only from Silhouette Intimate Moments
at your favorite retail outlet.*

Where love comes alive™

Visit Silhouette at www.eHarlequin.com   SIMAYOLD11

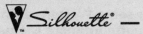

Two powerhouse writers tell compelling tales of love lost—and won.

What happens when you wake up—
and don't know who you are?

These two women
are about to find out in

FORGET ME NOT

Featuring

THE ACCIDENTAL BODYGUARD
by Ann Major

&

MEMORIES OF LAURA
by Marilyn Pappano

Be sure to pick up your copy—
On sale March 2001
in retail stores everywhere!

Silhouette®
Where love comes alive™